WHAT WE DO
WITH THE
WRECKAGE

FLANNERY
O'CONNOR
AWARD
FOR
SHORT
FICTION

What We Do with the Wreckage

KIRSTEN SUNDBERG LUNSTRUM

THE UNIVERSITY OF GEORGIA PRESS
ATHENS

"Wheeling" is reprinted by permission of *The Pinch*,
copyright 2012 by Kirsten Sundberg Lunstrum.

Published by the University of Georgia Press
Athens, Georgia 30602
www.ugapress.org
© 2018 by Kirsten Sundberg Lunstrum
All rights reserved
Designed by Kaelin Chappell Broaddus
Set in 10.75/14 Garamond Premier Pro by
Kaelin Chappell Broaddus
Printed and bound by Thomson-Shore, Inc.
The paper in this book meets the guidelines for
permanence and durability of the Committee on
Production Guidelines for Book Longevity of the
Council on Library Resources.

Most University of Georgia Press titles are
available from popular e-book vendors.

Printed in the United States of America
18 19 20 21 22 P 5 4 3 2 1

Library of Congress Cataloging-in-Publication Data

NAMES: Lunstrum, Kirsten Sundberg, 1979– author.
TITLE: What we do with the wreckage / Kirsten Sundberg Lunstrum.
DESCRIPTION: Athens : University of Georgia Press, [2018]
IDENTIFIERS: LCCN 2018003959| ISBN 9780820353722
(softcover : acid-free paper) | ISBN 9780820353739 (ebook)
CLASSIFICATION: LCC PS3612.U56 A6 2018 | DDC 813/.6—dc23
LC record available at https://lccn.loc.gov/2018003959

This one is for Virginia, girl of my heart
(and the real expert on Tasmanian tigers).

CONTENTS

WHAT WE DO
WITH THE
WRECKAGE

ENDLINGS

Dr. Katya Vidović stands outside the hospital courtyard gate, watching the Reptile Man exercise his pets. He has come to entertain the girls—her patients—who are prone to unnatural behaviors when left unsupervised. They've been known to pull out their own hair by the fistful, to tattoo their inner arms and thighs with the sharp points of safety pins, to slip into the ward's bathroom and quietly vomit the contents of their last meal. Now, however, they sit like angels, their angular bodies arranged just so on the courtyard grass, their spindle-fingered hands folded in their laps as the leashed tortoise lumbers forward before them and the copperhead looks on—languid and apparently bored—from its glass terrarium.

Katya has seen this routine before, but, still, there is something captivating about it. Something fascinatingly grotesque about the bodies of the animals the man brings to display—the vaguely indecent projection of the tortoise's long neck and bulbous head from its shell; the constant, flickering whisper of the copperhead's tongue. Last year the man, who himself is a small and balding curiosity of a person, brought a bearded dragon, its body spined in tiny teeth. Another year, he brought a frilled lizard with a headdress like a mythological monster. These are animals built for other worlds, their bodies armed for hardships that they—in their captivity—will never see.

From her place outside the gate, she looks on as the man tours the tortoise between the rows of girls. Prim-faced Natalie Fletcher, eleven years old, is bold enough to reach out and stroke the knobbly shell. Thirteen-year-old Kristina Berg titters. The animal trundles past them all, indifferent, awkward on the soft turf of the lawn, its front legs bent like inverted knees. As the tortoise moves, the Reptile Man speaks to it in a coo. He does his job with an obvious affection, efficiency, nudging the tortoise back to its crate, where he rewards it with half a watermelon. The fruit glistens, flush red, and the tortoise rips into the rind, its alien face dripping with juice.

To close the show, the man turns to the snake. From beneath a drape, he produces a cage, and from the cage, a live mouse. A ripple of interest stirs the girls, who sit up straighter, crane to see. "In the wild," the man says, "copperheads are incredibly efficient eaters. They require as few as one or two meals per month." He lifts the terrarium lid and drops the white ball of fur inside.

The girls go silent. The snake raises its head.

Katya knows what's coming—a methodical if artificial hunt, a strike, a laborious but bloodless swallow. The girls, however, lap it up. This is hunger as theater, eating as a feat of will.

Scanning them now, she sees the usual responses: Rebekah Silver is covering her eyes; Alina Culbert is hugging her knees to her chest; and near the back, the pair of twins admitted just this morning—nine years old, and the youngest patients Katya's ever had—are sitting side-by-side, grimacing.

Only Simone Hunter seems to look on without revulsion. Simone Hunter—twelve. Admitted last week. Malnourished, amenorrheic, tachycardic. Five-foot-four and eighty-two pounds. Katya thinks over the girl's chart, straining to pull up her mental register of the psychiatrist's notes. She recalls just one word, scrawled in her colleague's soft hand on the page's margin—*Obdurate*. Such an uncharacteristically judgmental assessment. These girls are often perfectionists, narcissists. They are usually anxious or depressed and typically determined in their disordered perceptions of their own bodies and practices. Still, it's a strong word from Dr. Moore, and what the girl could have said in session to warrant it, Katya cannot imagine.

On the lawn, applause erupts—the show is over. The mouse is vanished. The Reptile Man bows, begins to pack up. The girls unfold themselves from their seated positions and stand to file back into the hospital. They will take the elevator up to the ward. Climbing the five flights of stairs is too much physical exertion for them, though surely at least one or two of them will beg for it.

"Come," Katya says, and she opens the gate. She is so accustomed to them, sometimes she forgets how frail they are, but she sees it now as they angle past her—their hollow cheeks still pinked with the excitement of the show, their long arms downed in the fine hair of their starvation, their pronounced scapulas like rigid wings poking up from beneath the fabric of their shirts. An aerie of girls. Or maybe a quiver.

When Simone Hunter passes, Katya stops her. "Did you enjoy it?" she asks. "The show?"

The girl hesitates. She has a broad moon of a face, even as thin as she is, and dark, hooded eyes. She looks Katya up and down, her expression hard. "Who doesn't enjoy a spectacle?" she says. She smiles, then, polite, and Katya dismisses her to follow the rest of the girls inside.

．◆．

Before Katya took this position in Seattle, she was a medical fellow at an American program for girls with disordered eating in Boston; and before that she was completing her medical training in Louisiana; and before that she was a girl herself, living with her grandparents in the top-floor apartment of a house in Zagreb. The house was three floors tall and painted blue. It had a steep-sloped roof, under which Katya's tiny bedroom was tucked. It was a cozy room, except at night, when the shadows of the street below arced up and played on the ceiling's wooden slats. "The owls' puppet show," her grandmother told her, though even as a young child Katya knew that this was an adult's game, an attempt to soften the nightmarish quality of the dark shapes—the fluttered silhouette of a wing and the slithered shadow of a snake—that she was sure she was not mistaken in seeing.

The room—and therefore the angled ceiling and the shadows on it—had once been her mother's. Katya's grandparents had lived in the apartment since their marriage, and they had raised her mother—their only child—there. When Katya's mother died the year Katya was eight, they took her in and gave her the bedroom and everything in it—her mother's old doll with the rag dress, a set of cloth-covered books in a language Katya could not read, a chest full of bridal linens that her mother had never used—and it was as if time inside the apartment retracted, rolled back like a measuring tape snailing into its case. Her grandparents became younger than she'd first believed them to be, and she became an old woman in a little girl's body. This is the paradox of death for the living, Katya learned then: it both stops and accelerates time. It both reanimates the past and fossilizes the future, and everything but the observable present becomes subject to the unreliable whims of sentiment or fear.

In response to this, Katya became a scientist, devoted to the world of the visible and irrefutable. Each day after her classes let out, she walked home through Maksimir Park. In the autumn, she collected specimens of fallen oak leaves to study under the desk lamp in her bedroom. In the winter, she noted what differentiated the snow tracks belonging to squirrels from those belonging to rats. In the spring, she liked to sit in the grass along the bank of the lake, waiting for the dark blots hovering beneath the surface to emerge and prove themselves nothing other than turtles. Once out of the water, the turtles had the amazing ability to arrange themselves—five or six or seven at a time—at near even intervals along the length of a fallen tree branch, their nub feet somehow gripping the slick bark well enough to keep them from falling. *How?* Katya wondered. The world was wide and curious.

At home she would report whatever she had seen to her grandparents over dinner, and they would reply to these benign, physical observations of the natural world with a cheerful encouragement and unwounded interest that seemed impossible for them when Katya's conversation veered toward more personal subjects—where, for instance, her missing father might be, or why he had left before getting to know her, or what correlation might exist between his sudden absence and the slower kind of vanishing her mother had wished for and that her cancer had finally achieved. There were never any answers to these questions, and so—her grandparents made it clear to her when she was bold enough to speak them aloud—it was better not to ask them at all.

She was sixteen when the war began, and whatever she might have asked didn't matter anymore. She was sent to relatives in France for a few weeks, then to a cousin in England, and eventually she made her own way to university in the United States. During Katya's last year of medical school, her grandmother wrote to say that her grandfather had died—a stroke. Katya had exams she couldn't miss, and no money, and so she mailed her grandmother a letter of apology and did not get on a flight home. Time passed. Five years later, another letter arrived, this one from her grandmother's friend, saying that her grandmother, too, was gone—a bad flu, pneumonia, grief. Would Katya come back now?

It was winter when she got this letter, late February of 2008. In Boston, there was snow on the ground—thin, granular, dirty snow. It lay in shrinking circles around the trees and the curbs and the front stoops of the brick houses. It clung in thinning patches to the roofs and sills and the crotches of trees. It made the city hard and tight, black and white. Katya did not love this place as she had loved the blue house and the park and the country of her childhood, but what did that matter, really? She had not been a child for a long time. She had lived half her life elsewhere. And what would be left for her there now? She had seen television footage of the war and its scars—the streets buried in the bones of old buildings, roofs collapsed into the cavities of attics, tanks maneuvering their metal flanks through once quiet neighborhoods. The landscape had changed, and she would be a foreigner there now after so many years away—so many years in the relative comfort of her expatriate life. Her grandparents had sent her away for her own good—her own protection—and she was grateful; but she'd grown too soft to live in the echo of such brutality. She was no longer suited to withstanding hardship or ugliness or pain. She'd be a performance of privilege there at home among the wreckage, the wrecked—her naïveté an obscenity, a shame. She could never return.

To her grandmother's friend, she wrote, "I have adapted to my life here." *Sućut*, she signed her letter. Condolences. She slicked the tip of her tongue along the envelope's bitter edge, sealing it shut.

. •.

Monday morning. Katya is doing her usual rounds. When she enters Simone Hunter's room, she finds the girl on her bed, a spread of books and papers fanned before her on the white cotton blanket. "What's this?" Katya asks, her voice enameled in careful cheer. She remembers the strange stare the girl gave her the other day at the reptile show, the spiked syllables of the word *spectacle* as the girl spoke it. She remembers Dr. Moore's odd note: *Obdurate.* "Are you drawing pictures?" she asks now though, holding her buoyant tone. "I used to like to color too, when I was a girl."

Simone issues a sigh, does not look up. "I'm working," she says. "Do someone else's check up and come back to me."

A flush of heat rushes Katya's face. "Why don't you show me your work?"

"I don't like to be interrupted. The nurse was just here an hour ago. Nothing's changed. I said come back to me."

The girl sits with her knees folded, her back rounded, the scallop of her spine visible beneath the weave of her sweater. She has braided her own hair, and the braid hangs limp over one shoulder, several oily strands coming loose at her face. The room smells faintly of her body odor, of the fermented sweetness of her ketotic breath, of her books—which must be old. She needs a shower, a shampoo, a morning of conversation with the other patients rather than this self-imposed cloistering. Katya makes a quick note of all this on her chart.

"Simone," she says, sterner now, "I have to do my job here."

The girl turns, frowns. "Fine, then. Look if you have to." She nudges some of her papers toward Katya.

The girl's handwriting is neat, exact. These pages, Katya sees, are notes—extensive notes. From one page, she reads.

- *Question: Correlation between rise in materialist culture and extinction of native animal species? * 19th and early 20th c. = U.S. industrialization.*

- *Question: Rise in extinctions during Anthropocene due to environmental change or animal bodies as commodities?*
  (Ex 1: California grizzly hunted as major predator of ranched cattle. Cattle a commodity.
  Ex 2: Western black rhino hunted for medicinal value of its horn. Rhino a commodity.)

From another page, she reads a long list that the girl has titled "North American Extinct Species."

Canis lupus fuscus
(Cascade mountain wolf)
Habitat: British Columbia, Washington, Oregon
Extinct 1940

Cervus canadensis Canadensis
   (Eastern elk)
   Habitat: Southern Canada, eastern and southern
   United States
   Extinct 1880

Ursus arctos californicus
   (California grizzly bear)
   Habitat: Cascade range, northern California
   Extinct 1920s?

On a third sheet, the girl has collaged an even more detailed catalog of individual animals, a black-and-white photocopied image of each cut and pasted above a written description of physical characteristics and habits. *Zalophus japonicus*, a Japanese sea lion; *Ara tricolor*, a Cuban parrot; and at the bottom of the page, a striped creature on all fours, its face depicted in profile so that its wide-open jaw gapes huge and toothy, dangerous, one snap away from swallowing the hole punch in the margin of the page.

"*Thylacinus cynocephalus*, the Tasmanian tiger," Katya reads aloud. "Extinctions."

"These are all extinct?" Katya studies the drawing of the last animal—the tiger, tracing its long body with her forefinger. It's odd looking, disproportionate, not actually a tiger at all but a poor amalgam of several other beasts—tail of a jungle cat, body of a wolf, thick head of a dog bred for fighting.

"Benjamin," Simone says, still without raising her head. She taps the end of her pencil on the striped animal.

"You name them?" Katya asks.

Simone lifts her eyes. "They're not my pets. This is my work."

"Right," Katya says. She examines again the image and the print beneath it, which reads, *Marsupial. Nocturnal. Carnivorous. Last of line, Benjamin, died in captivity, Hobart Zoo, 1936.* "He looks—" She searches for a word. "He looks vicious. That mouth."

The girl snatches the paper from Katya's hands. "You think like everyone else."

The bitterness in her voice takes Katya by surprise. "I'm sorry," she says.

"Just go," the girl tells her.

"Simone," Katya says.

"I said go. I don't want to be bothered now."

In the hallway, Katya opens the girl's chart, writes, *Aggressive, defiant. Not adapting to hospital routines. Refusal to comply.*

At the nurses' station, she directs the nurse on duty to take Simone's vitals in ten minutes. "No longer than ten minutes," she says. "Don't let her put you out."

The nurse nods. "Is everything okay, Dr. Vidović?"

"Everything is fine," she says, and she walks at a clip down the hallway to the next patient's room, her pulse like a wing caught in her throat.

That evening Katya is late leaving the hospital. There's traffic and rain, the freeway a black slick studded by a never-ending train of taillights. Only when she pulls to a stop on the street in front of her apartment building does she remember that Jen has invited guests for dinner—a new neighbor couple from down the hall, Chris and Meg; as well as Tom from school and his most recent girlfriend. The thought of the apartment filled with so many people at the end of the day is exhausting. Who plans a dinner party for a Monday night? Katya lets herself into the building, shakes the rain from her hair like a dog, and takes the stairs up.

Inside, the apartment is lit up like a holiday. Jen has music playing in the sitting room—something international, chipper and taut with the beat of hand drums and maracas. The air is heavy with the smell of curry.

"Home," Katya says from the door, and there's a ring of welcome calls before Jen appears, red hair and pink face beaming with the warmth and light of the evening, to kiss Katya hello. Her mouth tastes of onions.

"You're late," Jen says. "We started eating without you."

"That's fine."

"Not really," Jen says, "but I couldn't keep everyone waiting any longer."

Katya follows her through the warm kitchen and into the sitting room, where their guests are seated cross-legged on pillows around the wide coffee table. Jen makes introductions and Katya nods. "Good evening," she says. "I'm glad you've made yourselves at home."

"Sit," Jen says, her hand at Katya's back, a little shove toward the table. "I'll make you a plate."

Katya would like to beg off, slip away into the bedroom and lie down for a few moments, but she takes the empty pillow and lets Jen bring her a plate heaped with rice and saag and a red lentil something that sears the roof of her mouth as soon as she takes her first bite. There are three bottles of wine on the table, a blown glass jug of water, small ceramic bowls of chutney and yogurt and cilantro— all Jen's touch. When she moved into the apartment two years ago, Jen brought with her this skill for the domestic, and it seemed a revelation to Katya, who had learned to live like a visitor wherever she went, never certain she'd stay long enough to belong to any one place again. Jen filled the apartment with the makings of a home, however—soft blankets and deep cushioned chairs, bright artwork on the walls, flowers in the clay vase on the coffee table, the scent of good coffee issuing from the kitchen like a love note every morning. "This is a treasure," Katya had told her then, "your homeliness." But it hadn't translated, the word *homeliness*. They had their first domestic quibble over the confusion before Katya was able to make clear her intended meaning: "You know how to make a home, and I don't. That's all. No joking. I need this. I need you." She had meant it then, even if now, tonight, she's finding the artifice of it all so wearing.

Over their wineglasses, the others make small talk. The old lady who lives up in 4B has hired a cleaning woman; the new grocery around the corner has an olive bar that's to die for; someone's sister has had a baby. The conversation twines with the music, and Katya allows the two to become one thread of noise, constant and indeterminate. Behind her eyes, she sees the yellow aura of a headache just forming. She tunes in again just as Jen lays her hand on Tom's arm, says, "You're so bad."

Tom shrugs. "I think the name's Arabic for *lofty*, if you can believe that. I looked it up at the start of the year. She's Syrian. Well, her parents are."

"What are we discussing?" Katya asks, and for an instant the others stare at her.

"Kat," Jen says. A sigh.

"I'm sorry," Katya apologizes. "I've had a very long day. Please just go on with your story," she says to Tom.

Tom smiles—broad, benevolent, showy. He strikes Katya as the kind of man who is never sorry to hold the room's attention.

Tom says, "I was just telling everyone about this student I have. Little girl. She's difficult. Stubborn—but I can't say that at school." He winks at Jen. "We're supposed to say 'independent' and 'a girl who knows her own mind.'"

"Ha," Jen says.

"It's all bullshit to make the parents feel better," Tom explains.

"Because really it's their fault, right?" Tom's girlfriend says. "Doesn't everybody know the kid is always the parents' fault?" She's been silent up until now. She's young—younger than the rest of them, anyhow—and has the glassy-eyed look of having had one too many glasses of wine. Katya can't remember her name from the introductions, but she looks strikingly like Tom's last girlfriend, so she'd likely confuse the name even if she could come up with it.

"Of course it's the parents' fault," Jen says, lifting an eyebrow, smiling. "But the teacher can never say that."

The music quiets for an instant and starts up again, this time with the calypso tin notes of a steel drum. The room throbs at its hard lines—the edge of the coffee table, the square outline of the darkened window. Katya touches a damp fingertip to her temple where the seam of the headache is now stitching itself tightly to her skull.

Finally, Katya says: "Maybe your girl is just surviving."

"What's that?" Tom asks.

"Your terror student," Katya says. "The one you mentioned. Her parents are Syrian, you said? Immigrants? Refugees? It's hard to be the only one of your sort among strangers. Maybe she's just surviving. Maybe she requires more empathy than you're accustomed to showing."

For a moment no one speaks, then Jen stands. "I have dessert. Let me clear away these plates."

Meg leans forward. "You're an immigrant also?" It's a statement, but she inflects it like a question, an American habit Katya finds grating. *Say what you mean and mean what you say*, her grandmother used to tell her.

"I heard your accent when we first met and thought maybe Russia," Chris says.

"Christ," Jen says from the kitchen. "Don't say that."

"I was born in Zagreb. I've been here for years."

"Where is Zagreb?" the girlfriend asks. "Is that Poland?"

Tom says, "And you feel like you needed to *survive*? That's the word you used, and I'm curious."

"Tom," Jen calls from the kitchen. "Could you come carry bowls for me?"

He continues, though. "I'm just interested. Because I am empathetic. I am empathetic to my kids, you know."

"You don't have to defend yourself to me," Katya says, shrugging. She wants to slip away to the bedroom, close the door, vanish.

Tom smiles, tight. "We're misunderstanding each other, I think, Kat. It's just interesting, your perspective. You have a unique perspective."

Kat, she thinks, taste of bile at the back of her tongue. "Of course," she says. "Of course we are misunderstanding each other. You're right." She presses a thumb to each temple, circles them once, twice. The calypso song seems to be doing laps around the room. "Does this song never end?" she asks. An uncomfortable laugh from across the table.

Meg turns to her. "We've talked about visiting Croatia, Chris and I. There are those waterfalls. *Plitvice*. Is that how you'd say it? The park. It looks beautiful. But we've thought maybe best to give it a few more years."

"I'm sure that park is beautiful," Katya says. "I've never been."

"Never been?"

Katya shakes her head. "Have you been to every park in America?"

"Do you go home often?" Chris asks.

"I was a child when I left, and there was a war. I haven't been back."

"Your family's here too, then?"

"There is no one left," Katya says. Her impatience throbs in her head. She looks to Tom. "I'm sure I was as beastly as your Syrian just after I left Zagreb. War doesn't allow for homesickness. What is there to miss when there's nothing recognizable left?"

"They've rebuilt, though," Meg says, chipper. "I've seen photographs of the region, and it's mostly restored."

I have not been rebuilt, Katya thinks, but she restrains herself from speaking.

For a long minute, no one says anything, and then Jen returns, a tub of ice cream in one arm and a stack of bowls in the other. "Who has room?" she asks.

Katya stands. "I'm sorry. If you'll all excuse me." She shuts off the music on her way out of the room.

For the rest of the evening, she waits in the bedroom, her head on her pillow and a cool washcloth on her face. She is there when Jen finally comes in, the last of the guests gone.

"That was rude," Jen says. "They meant well."

Katya rolls to her side and takes the cloth from her eyes. "People always mean well. I have a headache."

"Of course you do."

"I worked today. I'm tired. We shouldn't have parties on week-nights anymore."

"You had no obligation but to show up on time and eat. That's it."

"Come lie with me."

"I smell like the kitchen. I need a shower."

Katya watches Jen take off her clothes, walk to the bathroom nude. Jen has fair reddish hair and skin the pale pink of—*Of what?* Katya thinks. Of a sea rose, of a scallop's flesh. *Jakovska kapica.* Flavor of salt and brine, slick mound of meat like a pale pink tongue on the spoon of its shell. Katya made herself sick on such scallops one Christmas when she was small—their taste was so good. Her mother was still living then, and she had chided Katya about gluttony, about know-ing when you've had enough, about self-control. "*Pohlepna djëvojka! Good girls take less than they need.*" Katya's never understood what that was supposed to mean, virtue tied so senselessly to the absence of need. Only humans would entwine the two. Biologically, need is sur-vival. Those who crave and seek and satisfy—they survive.

She gets up and removes her own clothes, opens the bathroom door to a billow of steam. Behind the glass shower door, Jen has her face dipped beneath the water's stream. "Why do you have to be so difficult?" Jen asks. "Why can't you just be normal, you know? Blend in? They're nice people, Kat. Really they are."

"I try."

"No you don't," Jen says. She has not lifted her face from beneath the water. "I need more from you."

"Look at me," Katya says, and Jen shifts, raises her head. "Your friends have made me lonely."

She waits, still, letting the splatters of water hit her feet while Jen's eyes decide.

"Please," Katya says.

"I'm angry."

"Please."

Jen sighs, and Katya steps into her arms.

Two weeks pass. When Katya arrives at the hospital for her Wednesday morning rounds, Dr. Moore is waiting at the nurses' station, frustration on her face. "What is it?" Katya asks, and they step into the small conference room and close the door.

At the table, Simone Hunter and her parents are already seated. The parents are exactly what Katya would have expected—slim and well dressed and the farther side of middle-aged. The father is spectacled, silver haired, wearing a suit. He'll be on his way to a bank or a law office or the boardroom of a tech company the moment this meeting is over. The mother is Simone plus forty pounds and forty years. Simone herself sits between them—sallow, skeletal—and every few seconds one of her parents looks at her with an expression of blinking fear, as if she is all their shared shame and anxiety caged behind bones and skin.

Dr. Moore begins. "Simone, as you'll remember, we agreed that you would gain at least two pounds per week." The doctor slides a sheet of paper from a manila folder on the tabletop—a copy of the contract all new patients sign at admission, agreeing to the nutritional and behavioral plans the program draws up for them. At the bottom of the contract, Simone's tight SH are faint on the signature line.

"That's not a contract; it's a punishment," Simone says.

"Simone," her mother starts. "We love you. Please."

Simone sits rigidly in her chair and does not turn her face to her mother. "You love me when I do what you want," she says.

Her mother looks to Dr. Moore, to Katya. "I'm so tired of everything becoming a battle. This is ridiculous. We're not her enemies." To her daughter, she says again, "We're not your enemies, Simone."

Simone's face is a stone. "And I'm not your lapdog."

A muscle flickers at her mother's temple and jaw. "I can't do this," she says. "I can't do this game of yours anymore."

Dr. Moore raises a hand, and they both go quiet. "Simone, I understand," the doctor says, "that you do not feel you have the control you'd like over your diet right now, but you do know that we are your team—all of us here—and we are not going to force you into anything unhealthy."

"Do you hear Dr. Moore, Simone?" her father asks. He leans toward his daughter but does not look at her—cannot, it seems to Katya, bear to look at her. When he straightens in his seat again, he is weeping silently, this tall man in his suit. He withdraws a square handkerchief from inside his suit jacket and wipes his eyes.

Dr. Moore turns to Katya. "Dr. Vidović, please explain to Miss Hunter the next step in her treatment if she is unable to gain the necessary two pounds per week."

Katya swifts a strand of hair from her face, puts her elbows on the table. "It is simple, but—I will not lie to you, Simone—it is unpleasant. Do you know what a nasogastric tube is?"

"This isn't fair," the girl says. "This is not fucking fair." At her sides, her parents wince as if she's slapped them. "I'm not having a feeding tube."

Katya shakes her head. "It will not be for you to say."

Dr. Moore raises a hand again, stopping Katya. "Simone," she says, "you do have a choice now."

"You're liars," the girl says. The skin of her face has gone as hard as wax after the candle has been snuffed out. She narrows her gaze at Katya. "You will not touch me. Do you hear me? You will not touch me."

Katya meets her stare. "My job is to keep you alive," she says. "I will do my job."

"I think we can take it from here, Dr. Vidović," Dr. Moore says. "Thank you for making time in your morning to join us."

Katya leaves, closing the door behind her, and tells the nurse on duty at the desk that she needs a moment before continuing her rounds. She takes the elevator to the cafeteria, gets in line for a yogurt and a cup of coffee, finds a table in the corner where no one else is sitting. She's not hungry, but she peels the lid from the yogurt container and eats. The yogurt is thick and cold, the goo of fruit preserves at the bottom of the cup so sweet it makes the salivary glands at the back of her mouth ache.

One of the few things her mother would still eat even at her worst was jam—apricot jam spread on a wafer cracker; strawberry preserves taken a half-a-teaspoon at a time, like medicine; plum jam made from the fruit of the tree behind their house. Because of this, Katya's grandmother kept the cupboard stocked with jars—beautiful jars that glowed red and purple and translucent orange, jewels on the papered shelf above the breadbox. On Saturday afternoons, she and her grandmother often bought a flat of whatever fruit was at the market, brought it home, and stood at the stove boiling it down. *For your mama*, her grandmother would say. *For your mama's good health.*

Then later, in her mother's room, which stank with the florid, fermented smell of illness, Katya would lift a baby spoon from the jar to her mother's mouth, feeding her the preserves. *Please, Mama*, she'd beg again and again. *I need you to try*. And when it opened, she'd see against her will her mother's mouth, raw with sores, as pink and pulpy as a peeled blood orange, the tongue like a raspberry. *Click*, the spoon would sound against her mother's yellowed teeth. *Click*. A horrible sound, but it was necessary. For her mother's survival, Katya had to keep lifting the spoon, waiting for the swallow.

In the end none of it mattered, though. It was not enough. In the end, her mother needed nothing, was hungry for nothing, would eat nothing. She drank water that ran through her and came out in the bedpan as clear as it had gone in. "You see?" she'd said one day as Katya took the pan from beneath her. "There is nothing left of me. I'm gone. I've become a sieve. Nothing can hurt me, *moj mačić*. It all just passes through. Nothing can hurt me anymore." Katya had bent to kiss her mother's cheek and the skin was like wax paper under her lips.

In the cafeteria, Katya wads her napkin into a ball and gets up. "Get back to work." She says it aloud without intending to, then looks around, embarrassed, but there's no one near enough to have heard her.

In the corridor, she's waiting for the elevator up when the doors open and the Hunters step out.

"Dr. Vidović," Simone's mother says.

"My morning's quite full," Katya says. She reaches out to hold the elevator door.

"Just one minute of your time," the father says. His face is drawn, his pallor gray, his eyes still red rimmed from the crying.

"Okay," Katya says. A sigh. She lets the door close. "But I have just one moment."

"They've signed another contract," the mother says, outrage edging her voice. "The doctor—that psychiatrist—she's let Simone manipulate her. I love my daughter, but she lies, doctor. She's lying to you all. And she's stubborn. She's not going to eat now if she hasn't already. She won't change, and how long can we let this go on? Do you see what I'm saying? She's a danger to herself. That's why we brought her here. At some point, Simone simply has to be fed, whether she wants that or not." The mother steps close to Katya, grips her wrist with a cold hand. "You see what I'm saying here, doctor? She's a minor. I'm not even sure why we're letting her think she has a choice about this anymore."

Katya withdraws her arm, holds it behind her back. "I understand your concern, Mrs. Hunter."

"Do you?" the father asks. "Because it doesn't seem like that. It doesn't seem like anyone here is really doing anything productive."

The elevator dings.

"Take away her animals," the mother says. Her eyes are wide now and frantic. "Those drawings she does—her horrible books—they're morbid. They encourage her. Take them away until she agrees to eat."

Katya frowns. "I am not a schoolteacher, Mrs. Hunter. You should speak to Dr. Moore about your disciplinary concerns."

"You're not listening," the father says.

"I am listening. I understand your worry." Katya steps toward the elevator.

"You're leaving?" the mother asks. "You're just going to leave?"

"I understand your concern," Katya tells her. There's the golden shush of the doors opening, Katya gets in, pushes the button for the fifth floor.

"That's not good enough. You need to do something," the father says. "We came here so you people could treat her. Why aren't you doing your damn job?"

"It is not that simple, Mr. Hunter," Katya says. There's heat behind her eyes, heat like shame prickling her cheeks.

"You're the doctor," the father says. "We trusted you."

"Yes," Katya says. She pushes the button once more. "You're right to trust the staff."

"Our daughter is killing herself." The father is near tears again, his voice pleading. To his wife he says, "Can nobody hear us?"

"I hear you," Katya says, and the doors close.

She presses her back against the wall, clutches the handrail. *Move*, she thinks, willing the elevator doors not to open on the parents again. *Move*. It takes what seems like several seconds before she feels the movement of ascension, the stomach-swirl of gravity's tug inside

her body, and she can relax. "God," she says. Her heart is still racing.
She tips her head back and catches an image on the ceiling. What is
it? She's disoriented until she realizes she's looking at a mirror, seeing
herself reflected—white wings of her coat, white round of her face.
She lifts her arms to be sure, and the reflection follows her. Flap. Flap.
It is her, after all. *A little bird*, she thinks. *A little bird trapped in a cage
of its own making.*

∴●

That night, home late again, Katya finds a note from Jen on the
kitchen counter: *Out to the movies with Tom. Plate for you in the fridge.
Back late. Don't wait up. XOXO.* She takes the plate to the desk in the
bedroom, opens the laptop, eats the ham sandwich while reading the
day's news. Political unrest in the UK. A black man beaten and left
bleeding for an hour on a dark street in St. Louis. A new mosquito-
borne virus in South America. She remembers Simone's tiger then—
what a horrible world, full of dangers, monsters. She wants to see how
much liberty Simone took with her drawings, and so she Googles Tiger + Benjamin + Australia. Immediately, a strip of black-and-white
images materializes on her screen. *Benjamin, the last known Tasmanian tiger. Captured 1933, died 1936.*

The animal is just as odd as she has remembered, just as the girl
rendered it—long caninelike head and pointed ears; muscular, striped
body; tail of a jungle cat. She clicks a YouTube link and watches BBC
footage of the animal in its enclosure at the Hobart Zoo. It stalks
back and forth across her screen. The enclosure appears to be small,
nothing but a cement paddock, fenced on all sides. For an instant, the
animal pauses in its pacing and looks into the camera, its eyes fixed,
alert, undeniably frantic. It opens its massive jaw in—what? A growl?
A yawn? A cry? There is no sound to this old film. The screen goes
black.

Katya pushes refresh and watches the clip again and again and again. It is compelling, but why? And why, in particular, for Simone? What does the girl get out of all her note-taking and categorizing? Anorexics long for control—she knows this. And there must be some measure of satisfying control for Simone in the keeping of data. Katya remembers her own observations of the turtles and fish and foliage at the park as a girl, the safe certainty and constancy of fact against the frightening helplessness of her life in those years after her mother's death. Perhaps it is just this for the girl, too—control in order, self-protection in control.

She scrolls, lands on a nature documentary about Australians who believe they've seen Tasmanian tigers recently, living examples still eluding human capture out in the woods. "They're a menace," a pink-scalped man in a rain poncho says into the camera. "They're predators. They'd kill a child if they felt threatened or hungry. They'd terrorize our national parks." A voiceover contradicts the man, citing evidence of the tiger's weak jaws, incapable, even, of killing a sheep.

Katya chuffs at the screen. "Alarmist," she says into the empty bedroom.

She's still at the computer several hours later when the front door sounds—Jen home. Katya closes the laptop, gets up, and finds Jen in the kitchen, filling the kettle with water. "It's late for tea, no?" she says. She rubs a circle on Jen's back. "Why don't you come to bed?"

Jen turns away, pulls a mug from the shelf. "I'm cold. I couldn't sleep now anyway."

"I'll drink with you, then. The movie was good?"

Jen sighs. "I didn't see a movie. I just went to dinner. With Tom. We talked."

"Oh?" Katya says, though her stomach drops. It's dark in the kitchen, the only light coming in dimly from the hallway, and she cannot see Jen's face well enough to read it, to read what she is sensing beneath Jen's words.

"I'm not having an affair with him, if that's what you're thinking."

"I wasn't thinking that. My god, should I have thought that?" All the blood in Katya's body seems to rush to her bowels, hot. *Flee*, she feels her body thinking. *Fly!* She fights the impulse and forces herself to stand perfectly still.

"I just—. I don't think we're working anymore, Kat."

"I don't understand what you're telling me."

On the stove, the kettle blows a high, wet note, and Katya rushes to remove it from the burner. The cirrus of steam issuing from the spout scalds her hand before she can think, and she drops the kettle, pulls her hand close to her chest, cradles it.

"Jesus," Jen says, righting the kettle. "Are you okay?"

"I want you to tell me what you're saying. What your meaning is. I think I'm misunderstanding."

Jen shakes her head. "Don't do that. Don't play that game. Your English is perfect. You're not misunderstanding."

They drink their tea sitting side by side on the couch, not speaking. In her mind, Katya still sees the Tasmanian tiger pacing its square pen, turning, opening and closing its soundless mouth. It occurs to her that when the film was made, the animal was already the last member of the species. Everyone watching him circle his artificial den knew what the animal could not know—that there would be no more of him. He was the end.

"Why?" Katya says to Jen. "Have I done something wrong?"

"Oh, Kat." Jen's voice floats, disembodied in the dark room.

"It won't feel like home here without you."

"For a little while maybe. Not forever," Jen says. "You're barely ever here anyway. You'll get used to it."

"That's not fair," Katya says.

"No, it's not."

Katya gets up and crosses to the kitchen, dumps the last of her tea into the sink. "I should never have let myself become comfortable," she says.

"Stop it," Jen says. "Don't make yourself a victim. You've never been comfortable here. You've never acted like my partner in this—"

She nods at the apartment. "It was never really what you wanted anyway. I saw it the other night. You couldn't even sit through a dinner party. You can't do it."

"That's not true," Katya says. "I did want this. I do."

Jen stands. "I'm tired," she says. "I'm going to bed."

Katya watches her go. She feels the whole night rushing through her like wind down a vacant street. She cannot catch it. She cannot pull it back.

"You'll be fine," Jen calls from the bedroom. There is the *click* of the door shutting.

．．
．●．

The next morning Katya wakes to find Jen already up and packing a suitcase. She'll come back for the rest of her things, she says. She's going to stay with Tom until she finds another place. It's best not to drag things out. They say goodbye at the door—a stiff embrace—when Katya leaves for work.

At the hospital, Katya arrives to the news that Simone's weight has dropped again and she must attend to the intubation before seeing any other patients. But, of course, the girl is stubborn. She refuses the NG tube. She refuses the sedative offered. She refuses to lie still. A second nurse appears at the bedside, then a third. One nurse holds Simone's right arm, one her right foot, one her left. She's given a sedative by injection. When Katya squirts the lidocaine into her nose, Simone turns her head and vomits a spill of yellow bile onto her pillow.

"Enough," Katya says. "This is enough, Simone. You must calm down." A nurse hands her a cool cloth, and she touches it to Simone's face. Another nurse brings a clean pillow and removes the soiled one. Simone's breath slows.

"That's it," Katya says, encouraging. "That's it, *dragi moj.*" The endearment comes out of her mouth before she thinks—a hush, fluttering up to her tongue from the deep of her mind. Her mother used to whisper it to her when she woke from nightmares as a child. It startles Katya, but she doesn't pull away. She strokes Simone's forehead. "You'll be fine," she says. "You can trust me."

"I never wanted any of this," the girl says.

"Look at me," Katya tells her, and when Simone does, she recognizes the dark gaze of feral panic, determined fear. "Just hold my hand now. You're not alone." The girl complies, her hand frigid, shaking, and Katya closes her own around it.

It takes no time after that. Katya is good at this part of her job. This is something, she tells herself—this steadiness in the midst of crisis. This is something not every person can manage.

"Lie back," Katya says when it is finished. She props another clean pillow behind Simone's back. "You need to rest now."

"Don't leave yet," the girl says, and Katya nods.

Through the fabric of her shirt, Simone's clavicle is a blade, a brace, a buttress. Her skin has the fragile, filmy look of tissue. Her lips are the pale gray of a winter sky.

Katya says, "You know, after you showed me your work, I looked for your friend, your tiger. I watched his movie, online."

Simone's eyes are heavy with the drugs, the exertion of her struggle and her submission, but Katya sees her listening.

"I've been thinking about him," she goes on. "He was beautiful. I've been thinking they should not have locked him up."

The girl moves her hand inside Katya's—agreement.

Katya thinks again about the tiger pacing round and round its square cell—about that look of fury and fear in his eyes when he faced the camera and opened his mouth. She wants to attribute virtue to it—emotion—but she knows better. There is purity in an animal's desire, though; there is benefit to following instinct. The tiger could not have grieved or yearned—could not have known that nothing waited for him beyond the fence. He could only know what kept him alive in the wild—self-protection, hunger, isolation. It was not his fault that his body, his mouth full of teeth, left him unsuited to the human world.

She looks again at the girl, but Simone is sleeping, her head dropped to one side, her jaw slack. Her breath smells with the sweet stink of wasting, and Katya is called back to her mother once more, her mother at the end. This same smell in the little room with the sloped ceiling. Owl's wing and turtle's shell. That bow of branches seen in double—the thing and its reflection—at the pond in Maksimir Park. Fine stone Xs of the stone-boned Zagreb cathedral ceiling at Christmas mass. These visions are in her. She carries them, just as the girl carries the facts she has gathered about her extinct species, her examples of life lived on the margins and in the gaps. Katya thinks: *Without the body, the world extinguishes.* She thinks: *Without the body to catch it, the world drains away and is gone.* This, maybe more than anything else, is what we are meant for—not our own survival, but this devouring. And perhaps the isolated, the lonely, the left-behind—those least suited to peaceable adaptation—are best at this particular kind of hunger. Perhaps, like the tiger, it is this hunger that always ends them alone.

The room is warm and still; and in the bed, the girl has begun to snore softly. Katya releases her hand and stands. Later, she will speak to Dr. Moore. Later, she will call the girl's parents. Now, however, she has other patients to attend to, other work to do.

DEAR MISTRESS

Dear Mistress,
You are the cancer in my family's gut, our bleeding ulcer, a bile we
cannot swallow.

This is the letter I write you about my father's infidelity and my mother's rage.

Dr. R, who last week suggested I try writing myself "letters of positivity," frowns when he sees I've written to you instead. "Your anger is justified, Elisabeth," he says. "But we cannot let our anger own us. The Buddhist thinker Thich Nhat Hanh says that anger is like a knot. We can't untangle it until we recognize it, smile at it, treat it with tenderness. Can you do that, Elisabeth?" Behind his wide desk, Dr. R folds his hands and fixes his eyes on me. It's something he does—a therapist trick for breaking you down, like some sort of superhero deathglare. I think it's starting to piss him off that this has no effect on me.

I refuse to blink until he does. "Sure," I say.

He stares. I stare back. The clock on his office wall sounds like tiny knuckles cracking one by one by one.

"Good," he says, shifting in his seat. "Okay then. Why don't you try something else for me this week? A simple spoken affirmation every day to reset your focus?" He stands and raises his hands to the ceiling, closes his eyes. "Today I choose acceptance," he says. He brings his arms down and crosses them over his own chest, a "you-hug," he tells me, and smiles. It's awkward to watch—like seeing my mother try on a bathing suit—and I have to look away.

"I'm not doing that," I say.

"Not now, but try it later." He sighs, my cue that our time is up.

At the office door he nods to my parents, who are sitting on opposite sides of the narrow lobby, my mother reading a paperback, my father editing his latest script. At the sight of Dr. R, my father curls the script into a tight tube he tucks into the back pocket of his jeans. "How's she doing?" he asks.

"Remember what we talked about, Elisabeth," Dr. R says. "I'll see all of you next week." He disappears behind his office door, and from her corner my mother smirks over the top of her book.

Dr. R meets with the three of us for one hour jointly, followed by half an hour each individually every Friday afternoon. That's two-and-a-half hours a week, for six weeks now, which means we've spent a total of nine hundred minutes in counseling. Nine hundred minutes, Mistress, just to get over my father's love for you, to resuscitate something we didn't know we had until you took it from us. Honestly, though, I'm beginning to think we're hoping for the impossible.

"Well, that was bullshit," I say to my parents as we walk outside. It's five thirty and the light is going that fragile blue you get right before dusk. It's the color I see behind my eyes when I close them at night—a blue that could be violet in another minute, and pitch black the minute after that. It's the color of the dyed tap water my father says is filling the DeDanvilles' luxury indoor swimming pool on his show, and also of an ocean when seen from an airplane window, like the one I wish I were looking out of now, far from my fucked-up parents and this fucked-up night and every other night like it until we reach what Dr. R calls "the lasting acceptance."

"Language, Elisabeth," my mother says, but she says it bored.

"She's allowed to express her thoughts just like anyone else." My father's voice is liquid patience. Since you, Mistress, he's been taking this tone with us—my mother and me—as if we are both small children, or maybe mental patients. As if we are his anger and he is treating us with tenderness. He reaches for my hand, but I slip past him and let him walk across the parking lot toward our car, while I lag and scuff the toes of my shoes against the pavement.

"Pick up your feet, honey," my father says, looking back, and when I don't, he turns to my mother. "Can you back me up on this?"

She shrugs. "Why don't you try using a 'feeling statement.' Why don't you try saying, 'Elisabeth, honey, when you drag the toes of those hundred-dollar tennis shoes, I feel you wasting my money.'"

My father does the thing where he sighs and closes his eyes.

The only other car in the lot is Dr. R's convertible, a car that has the look of a wet seal—quick and slippery, too fishy to be truly mammalian. I touch my palm to the window, Mistress, so that my five fingerprints appear in one long smudge on the glass, and my mother raises an eyebrow. "Don't scratch it," she says to me. "We're paying for that thing." When we get across the lot, my father has our car running. She climbs into the passenger seat, settles her bag in her lap. "Get buckled," she tells me over her shoulder. "Your father's buying dinner."

He toggles between radio stations for a moment before settling on NPR and swiveling to look at me. "What do my ladies feel like eating tonight?"

"Whatever," I say.

"Your heart," my mother says.

We pull out of the parking lot just as the first yodel of *La Traviata* trips from the speakers.

Dear Mistress,
Today I am choosing denial.

During one of our family counseling sessions my father let slip that what first drew him to you is your devotion to books. "She's a bibliophile," my father said, as if that explained it all, never mind that you're twenty-nine and beautiful and an actress. You're a *bibliophile*. When he said it I thought of a tack, the sound of the word like the knobby head and silver prick of the pushpins my English teacher uses on the corkboard at school. *Bibliophile*, and I saw the triangle of your face bent close to the thick crease of an opened book, Mistress, your black hair fallen forward over your shoulders. Your pink tongue slipped from between your made-up lips to lick the tip of your finger just before you turn a page.

When he told us about you, I started watching the show. I had watched it now and then in the past when my father wrote a big scene, say, like the one in which Lauraline Estaban fell down the stairs after she told Stefan DeDanville he was the father of her children. They were writing her character off the show, so the fall had to break her neck. Getting a death scene is like getting a promotion for a soap writer, so it was a big deal for my father. He made popcorn and let me stay home from school on a "personal day." We sat on the couch, my feet in his lap and the bowl of popcorn between us, and because we were recording it, after Lauraline fell the first time, we switched to the tape and watched her fall again, watched Cassady Walker discover her mother's broken body at the base of the stairs again. And again. My dad mouthed the words he had written as they came out of Cassady's mouth on screen: *Mother! Darling, sweetheart, wait!* It was a Flannery O'Connor reference, he said, but probably he and I were the only *Valley Heights* viewers who would catch that. He winked at me like *it*—intelligence, I guess—was our secret, and I slapped him a silent air-five with my palm. Until you, Mistress, I'd never seen the show without my father sitting beside me.

Here on the West Coast, the show airs weekdays at eleven a.m., right after *The 700 Club* and just before the better soaps—the ones my father calls "the legacies"—but it replays on SOAPnet at eleven every night. I've moved the old TV into my room. I keep it in my closet, the cord stretched beneath the closed door, so I can watch you there in my private darkness, knees tucked to my chest and your voice lifting from the minispeakers to smother itself in the long sleeves of my sweaters and the cuffs of my jeans. I've watched so many episodes now that the rooms of the DeDanville family estate are as familiar to me as my own house—that grand entryway with the black-and-white tile floor and the telephone table by the front door; the living room with the overstuffed satin striped couch that Virgintine DeDanville fainted on when Stefan told her he was actually her brother; the mantel where Aubrey DeDanville hung poor baby Ivy's tiny Christmas stocking the week my father told us you weren't just some distraction but that he was actually in love with you.

After I shut off the TV and climb into bed, I see you walking those rooms behind my closed eyes. You pausing at the foot of the generous staircase, your head cocked like a pet pony's for the sound of Stefan's footsteps on the marble. You with your hand on the front door knob, your dark eyes narrowed in anticipation of an uninvited guest. You doubled in the guestroom mirror, a look of strained remorse on your face just after you've stolen Carmina DeDanville's treasured brooch.

If I could record the shows, I would run you backward across the room, Mistress, away from the mirror, your remorse returning itself in reverse to whatever came before the theft—selfishness, or jealousy, or loneliness, or despair. I still don't know. Motivation, my father calls it—the push that drives a character toward her choice and the viewer toward revelation. If I could, I would walk you back and forth across the plush carpeting of Carmina DeDanville's ensuite all night long just to see the bloom of your remorse wither backward into what, Mistress? I want to understand.

Dear Mistress,
If I learn to smile at my anger, will my parents treat each other with
tenderness again?

When my father raises the issue of the upcoming *Valley Heights* cast party during our next session, I suggest myself as the solution. This after forty-five minutes of my parents bickering about my father's obligation to be present at said party, and my mother's "absolute fucking unwillingness to ever be in the same room as that whore." She says the last word in two syllables, drawing it out like a hair that's coiled itself at the back of her tongue and must be carefully expelled if she's going to keep from gagging on it. *Whoo-her*. I can't take it anymore.

"I'll go," I say, and all three adults look at me like I've proposed throwing myself into a pit of snakes. Maybe I have, but it's too late to take it back.

"I'd love for you to go," my father says. He puts his arm around my shoulder, smiles at me.

Dr. R makes a throat-clearing sound. "I wonder about that," he says. "What would be the outcome for each of you if you take Elisabeth?" He's doing his best Thich Nhat Hanh now, and he gestures toward me with the pen he keeps tucked between two fingers. Pointing the pen while he reflects on our troubles is one of his things. Like the death-glare and the couch—symbols of credibility. When he really gets going he tends to sweep it through the air, wand style. "God," my mother said after our first session. "It's like being counseled by Harry Potter."

She turns on me now and raises both eyebrows in a question. "Don't you think thirteen is a little young for a cast party?" When I say nothing, she looks at my father. "Are you seriously considering this?"

"She wants to go," he says. "You heard her. She wants to go, don't you, Elisabeth?"

My mother shakes her head. "I can't believe you two." She faces Dr. R. "I'm the bad guy, you see? He lets her protect him."

"That's not it," I say.

"What is it then, Elisabeth?" my mother says. She looks as if she might be sick, as if she might cry. "What is it, then? You tell me."

But what can I tell her, really? That she's right—I do want to protect my father? I want to tell her that I've got this now—I'll protect him and her and all of us from this mess she and my father have made of our family. I want to tell her she can trust me. I'll figure out a way to fix everything. I'll go to the party, and I'll remind my father why he should stay with us, and I'll handle it. I can be trusted. I'm not really a child anymore. I can be adult about this. But what does that even mean anymore—to *be adult*?

"God," I say. "Whatever. It was just an offer."

"And not a bad one," my father says. "I appreciate your compassion, Elisabeth."

"Fine." My mother throws up her hands, dismissing us both. "I hope you two have a great time."

"Why don't we all put a pin in this for a few days and see how it feels," Dr. R says.

"At least I won't have to hire a sitter," my mother adds. The crack I heard in her tone earlier has turned hard and cutting.

"A sitter?" I say.

"For your father, dear."

A look of exasperation crosses Dr. R's face, and I wonder again how different we are from the other families he sees. Are they nicer than us? Easier to cure? Happier, underneath all their anger? I imagine another family, our double in looks but our opposite in manners, standing at the door. Dr. R shakes the father's hand as they leave. The daughter says thank you, and the mother smiles politely as they turn the corner of the lobby. They are not broody or cruel to each other. The father doesn't cry behind his office door in the mornings. The mother doesn't ask the daughter why her husband has stopped loving her. Why she can't seem to stop loving him in return. These doubles are good guests in the doctor's pretend living room for their 150 minutes a week. If half of all families break up, they will be the other half—the half that stays together.

Four days later the school secretary calls my name over the PA system during fifth period. The rest of the class watches as I stuff my prealgebra book into my backpack. No one ever gets called out of class for good news.

All the way down the hall I think, *This is it: they've come to tell me he's leaving. They've come to tell me she's kicking him out.* I picture myself across the kitchen table from my parents, a sleeve of Oreos on a plate between us and a big glass of milk in front of me. It's the setup they arranged when they told me about sex, so it fits that they'd stage a reenactment to tell me about divorce.

But when I get to the office, it's just my mother waiting, her work clothes still on and her staff bag with the public library logo slung over her shoulder. "I'm working on administrative stuff from home for the rest of the day," she says. "But first I thought we'd find you a dress for your father's obligation."

"I'm not sure I want to go anymore," I say.

"Oh, you're going." She signs me out and starts ahead of me through the school's double security doors.

Outside it's bright and springtime warm, though it's only just the end of January. The rest of the world is still iced over with what is probably a respectable winter. A better winter than the sort of cowardly season we get in California, where even the weather is a cheat. I tip my face to the sun. "I won't have a good time," I say, and my mother laughs.

"It's not about having a good time," she says. "No one's having a good time."

"Mom." I stop walking, and she turns to look back at me. "I said I don't want to go."

My mother motions to me and waits while I trudge toward her. "Hey," she says when I reach her. "Hey." She says it softly as I lean into her. She kisses the top of my head, her palm cool on my cheek. "It'll be fine. We'll get you a new dress—an expensive one—and then at least you'll look like you're having fun." She puts her arm around me, and we walk together to the car.

At the food court she lets me get a Mountain Dew and a box of churros. I eat as we walk the length of the mall, licking the sugar crystals from my fingers. My mother pauses at one kiosk and then another. She buys herself a pair of earrings and then a scarf and then a box of six perfect chocolates, which she has gift wrapped, though we unlace the ribbon and dig into the box as soon as we're beyond the clerk's line of sight.

At the bookstore she lets me pick a paperback. While I'm making up my mind, I see her slide a copy of *People* from the metal magazine rack and my stomach seizes. She's seen you on the glossy cover, I think, your face beneath the words "Daytime's Hottest Stars Confess," and now we'll have to leave, the afternoon interrupted, soiled by your unwanted presence, just like the rest of our lives. But when she slips the magazine back in the rack and turns to me, she's still smiling, and it occurs to me like a slap in the face, like the glorious and unforgiving beam of a stage light: you're not the sort of star who makes the magazines. Not yet. You're just a bit part—a hired girl, a climber—and for a moment I get the total pleasure of shrinking you down to size.

The thing is, Mistress, it's been difficult to maintain perspective. You've become the star of our family. Bigger than life. Truer the more I imagine you. After my father told us about you, it was as if you had moved in with us. You were there in the empty fourth seat at our table. You were the darkness I used to be afraid of behind the basement door. I could hear you moving through our house at night, peering in on us as we slept, a sour but shared dream, a ghost looking for a body to borrow.

Sitting in my closet late at night, I watched the real you—the pretend-real you—living your other life in the DeDanville estate, and I compared myself to you. *I am a bibliophile,* I thought. I am the sort of person who would take a brooch from a drawer and hold it in my hands just to feel its weight, and then find it a day later, still there in my pocket, accidentally stolen. Or, maybe, on purpose stolen. Sometimes it's hard to tell. The lines between fact and fear, between real and dreamed, between you and me are getting harder to see, Mistress, and there have been times when I've thought it was my body you decided to borrow, my story my father has written you into.

But now, in the mall with my mother, I see that it's her you've got—or maybe also her—and that since my father brought you home she's been wearing you like a mask, her forehead always fretted, her mouth so often sewn narrow around a feeling I cannot name. Is it fear, or loneliness, or desperation? I don't know. I look at her as we turn into Nordstrom, as we ride the escalator to the top floor, where the really pricey stuff is hung like museum pieces—one dress to a rack. I look at her as she fingers the hot pink tulle on a skirt, the crust of sparkling sequins on a bodice. I look at my mother as she stands next to me in the fitting room mirror, my face and hers side by side, so alike. I look at my mother, and I want to undo you, Mistress. I look at my mother. I look at my mother, Mistress, and I want to understand what's gone wrong.

"What do you think?" my mother asks, spinning me around, tugging the zipper on a blue velvet sheath. "You like this one? You think this could be it?" She frowns, and I search her reflection for what it is that's changed in her. "Yes," she says. "We'll get this. You'll feel good in this."

"Okay," I tell her. "This one's fine."

My mother puts the dress on the credit card, squeezes my elbow as the clerk boxes it, the tissue paper crinkling flat like the leaves of an old book going closed as she brings down the cardboard lid.

On the freeway home, I catch her profile in the driver's seat, and a word comes to me, sharp and silver as a hot pin skewering the tip of my tongue. "I feel so *disillusioned*," I say aloud.

"What?" my mother says. She turns down the radio volume. "Did you say you're disappointed? Why didn't you tell me that before we bought it?"

"No," I say. "The dress is fine."

She shakes her head. "Fuck," she whispers under her breath. "Elisabeth, I'm doing the best I can here, you know? I really am."

"Don't swear at me," I say. "You never used to swear."

For a minute I think she'll cry, but she doesn't, and that's the end of our conversation. She puts in a Heart CD and Nancy Wilson's voice rips out of the speakers the rest of the way home.

I look out the window and think about what Dr. R said about lasting acceptance. About anger as a knot, about a knot as just another puzzle to solve, about acceptance as the lasting resolution. That's just more crap. Acceptance isn't resolution. Acceptance is recognizing you can't change anything. Acceptance is being too tired to do anything but give up.

Dear Mistress,
I'm so tired. So tired of us all.

We skip our Friday session, and on Saturday my parents tell me they've decided to stop seeing Dr. R.

"It's not working," my mother says.

My father pulls one of his sighs. "I wouldn't say that. It's just—" We're eating a brunch of scrambled eggs and frozen waffles, and he pauses with the syrup bottle still poised above his plate. "We're cycling. Your mother doesn't feel we're moving forward."

"So you're getting divorced," I say.

"Oh, I'm not divorcing him," my mother says. "I'm not letting him off that easy."

"So you're not getting divorced."

My father looks between us, pity on his face. To me, he says, "I know you want a guarantee, but adult life isn't as clear-cut as childhood." He reaches across the table to take my hand—an apology—but I pull away. "We love you," he tells me. "No matter what, we love you." His voice is round and low and lumpy. I know I've hurt him in not saying that I forgive him. I know my silence is killing him.

Darling, I think, and I see Cassady Walker standing over the hor-

rible angles of her mother's body at the foot of the DeDanville staircase. *Darling. Sweetheart. No.* In my head, the words take the shape of
smoke rings, rise, and evaporate. For a second I think I'll throw up. I
push my plate away, lean back in my seat. I've brought my new book
to the table, and I pull it onto my lap and turn the pages quickly, not
really looking at what's printed on them.

"We love you, Elisabeth," my father says again, insistent. He is crying now; I don't have to look up to know it. The sound of his cry is
choked, restrained, worse to hear than any good thing he's said about
you, Mistress, or any hard thing he's said about my mother. Worse
than knowing he isn't happy in his life with us, and that he doesn't
know what would make him happy, and that his unhappiness is probably just his puzzle to solve—a puzzle for which he will never have a
lasting resolution.

"Here we go," my mother says.

"Stop it," I tell her.

"Don't be rude to your mother."

"Oh, that's rich," my mother says. "*You* giving her advice on good
behavior."

My father begins, "Beatrice—"

"This is such shit!" I yell. "This is supposed to be brunch!" I close
my book and slap it on the table.

"You think I'd have chosen this?" my mother asks. "You think this
is the way I thought life would go?"

"You're allowed to be angry," my father says, and I'm not sure if
he's talking to her or to me.

"Yes!" my mother shouts. "Let's all be angry!"

I get up.

"Elisabeth," my father says. "Elisabeth, we're still a family."

I hear him, but I am already gone, taking the stairs two at a time.

I watch myself open the door to my closet. I watch myself drag out
the dress box. I am out of my body. I am rage.

Under the petals of tissue paper, the dress is folded in a perfect square. I take it in my hands. Its fabric is smooth and soft and fragile. It is the blue of an empty sky. The blue of a glacier. It rips like a dream. I split it at its zipper first, then tear the lining from the bodice, the slip from the skirt. I pop each tiny knot of blue thread, break each precise stitch. Finally, I roll it all into itself again, a tumble of velvet and satin and tissue paper, and I step into the hallway and throw the whole mess down the stairs for my parents to step over whenever they care to get up and find me.

The next week, during my last private half-hour session, I repeat the fight to Dr. R. I tell him I ruined the dress and it felt good to ruin it. I tell him that neither of my parents has said a word to me about it, though the fabric and the paper and the box all disappeared. I tell him I expected more from them.

"Can I ask what you wanted them to say?" My parents fired him during our family hour, so I know we're both just going through the motions one last time here.

Still, this is the question I've been asking myself, Mistress. I think the answer should be that I want them to say we've all screwed up. We've all made some mistakes and poor choices, but it's okay. It's not too late to rewind. I should want them to say we can still cut you from our lives, edit you out of the story of our family. Wouldn't that be the best answer?

What comes to me instead, though, is the memory of my parents' voices sifting into my bedroom through the air vents early in the morning. I wake and hear them downstairs doing their morning things—making coffee and running through their schedules—their voices recognizable but indistinct. Knots of sound I can't untangle into real words. I've been waking up this way my whole life, Mistress, and it used to be comforting—a reverse lullaby—rocking me gently into the day. But now I don't know. All these years I've imagined them happy downstairs, but how do I know what they were before you, really? How do I know that what I think I saw was real?

What if I rewind and replay, and all I get is regret run a new way? At some point doesn't it all converge? Is this making sense, Mistress? Do you understand what I'm trying to say here? Anger isn't a knot. Maybe Thich Nhat Hanh has never been mad enough to know this, but it's the truth. Knots have beginnings and ends. You see what I'm saying, Mistress? Knots can be safely handled. They can be reasoned loose and stripped to single fibers, single seams. Anger is nothing like that. Nothing like that at all. Anger is an electrical fire or a lightning storm. Have you ever seen those pictures of California wildfires, Mistress? That's anger. A whole dry hillside of people's houses—dry for a long time before the spark—lit and blazing like a goddamned bonfire. And, sure, maybe you can put it out, after a while. Maybe. And maybe you can even accept the damage eventually. But accepting the ash doesn't make your house whole again, does it, Mistress? It doesn't bring back what's already been burned.

"Elisabeth?" Dr. R says after several minutes of silence.

"I want them to be quiet," I tell him. "I just want them to stop fighting and shut up."

That night, once my parents have shut off the lights in their bedroom, I crawl into my closet and turn on the TV. I need to see you, Mistress, and there you are. I've come to appreciate your reliability, if nothing else.

In this episode you're outside—or you're supposed to seem to be outside—on the grounds of the DeDanville estate. For a few minutes I watch on mute, and it isn't until Stefan appears at the garden wall that I realize I've read this episode as a script; my father wrote it months ago, before he fell in love with you, or before he knew he was in love, anyway. At least before he told us. You and Stefan are going to walk to the gazebo, where you will fight, and after he stalks off across the lawn, you're going to have a short gazebo scene all to yourself, like Liesl von Trapp, but since this is a soap opera, you'll talk to the air for a while, and eventually you'll cry. My father debated about the crying. He doesn't like to make anyone cry. On the page it's too hard to pull off—too sentimental to seem genuine. And in real life it's too genuine to be sentimental. But he wrote you this crying scene anyway, maybe because he knew you'd be beautiful there on the artificial lawn, the stage lights set to evening blue.

I watch you cry on mute. You put your face in your hands, and your shoulders tremble. Behind you, at a distance, the DeDanville mansion is large and lit white against the deepening darkness, and though I know it's just an illusion, that you're actually on a set and what I'm looking at is a backdrop, on my TV your world looks impossibly real.

I know your lines well enough to know what's coming next, but when you raise your head and speak, I don't turn up the volume. Instead, I revise my father's dialogue and speak new words for you—the ones I wish you'd say, or—if not you—someone. "I'm sorry," I say in a whisper. Your mouth moves in only slight misalignment with mine. "I'm sorry," I repeat, louder now. The camera is close enough that I can see the line the makeup artist has drawn just above your actual top lip. "I'm so very sorry, Elisabeth."

I make you say it again, dear Mistress. "I'm sorry, I'm sorry, I'm sorry"—the words unwinding from my mouth and yours together at once. "I'm sorry, I'm sorry, I'm sorry."

I make us say it to each other again and again, even after it's all just indistinguishable sound.

THE WOMAN
WITH THE RED SCARF

It was announced at the weekly community meeting that a new person would be joining the house: a woman, arriving from California that afternoon. They would all need to welcome her but not forget to give her room to get familiar. Anders, who had by then been at the Unity Center for nearly two months and had just concluded a silent retreat, was selected to greet the newcomer, and so after Common Lunch he went out to the porch to wait for her. Lying on the hammock, he had a view of the road, and he saw her car—or rather the dust cloud that rose with the car's motion—from a long way off. He smiled to himself as he watched it approaching—a white Fiat, ridiculous in this landscape. A car like that was as suited to the desert as a groomed lapdog.

The Center got this sort sometimes—people expecting a spa vacation and not a spiritual stripping down. They never lasted even a full week. This woman should have stopped in Phoenix, Anders thought, got herself a nice hotel room with white sheets and cable. She should have stopped in San Diego for a week at the sea. He rolled out of the hammock's hug, shaking his head, and walked around the house to the parking lot just as the woman opened her car door.

As it was, she turned out to be exactly what he was expecting: two or so years younger than he was—not quite thirty, he guessed—with artificially fair hair and a figure slim to the point of angularity. She wore an expensive-looking sheer blouse, the blush of a red tank top visible beneath it. From the trunk, she pulled a leather purse, which she slipped over her shoulder, and a hard-shelled rolling duffel. The car let out a shrill beep as it autolocked when she turned away.

Her eyes took him in with an open up-and-down sour appraisal. Anders had stopped shaving when he arrived here. He had cut off the legs of his jeans in acquiescence to the heat and had taken to wearing shoes only on long walks. No one at the center bathed more than once a week—a frugality of communal living—and most of them lost weight. After his recent week of silent retreat and fasting, Anders had lost enough that he could now feel the stays of his ribs beneath his shirt. He was a warning, a human caution sign. *When I got here, I was one of your sort*, he wanted to say. *And now look at me: a commune cliché, a dirty hippie. John the Baptist come from the wilderness, stinking of piss and honey and his own delusions. This place will wreck you.* But only people who were already wrecked came seeking here anyway.

"*Bienvenida*," he said, raising his hand in a wave.

The woman frowned. "*Qué todo el mundo habla Español aquí?*" Perfect college Spanish.

"No, no. I just meant hello," Anders said. "Sorry. I was being casual. That's all." He looked over his shoulder. "The border's about fifty miles from here."

She squinted at him. It was bright out—the usual midafternoon desert glare blanching everything. "Casual?"

"Don't worry about it."

"But I don't follow."

"It doesn't matter," he said. She was as uptight as she looked.

He took her bag and led her up the porch steps, held the metal

screen door for her, and let it slam shut at his back when he stepped
inside. The temperature was noticeably cooler indoors. The house the
Center occupied was old—a midcentury two-story built by some
survivalist lunatic, then left to dilapidate when he died. It had been re-
furbished to meet code now, though only to just meet code. Still, the
end-times foresight of its original owner had some use; it had been
built to withstand the wild fluctuations of desert climate: thick adobe
walls and tile roof, heavy wood shutters on the windows to keep out
the afternoon sun, a bomb shelter below used to store canned foods.
For cold nights there was a wide-mouthed fireplace at the center of
the house, and the outbuilding that had once been an armory was a
sturdy arts studio.

"You'll get a full tour later," Anders said. "Someone will find you
before dinner. If you're hungry now, any food on the kitchen counter
is up for grabs between meals."

"I'm not hungry."

He led her through the shadowed kitchen anyhow. A pile of loose
vegetables from the back garden sat heaped in a wooden bowl near
the sink—a bunch of arthritic-looking carrots, a jicima bulb, three
fat yellow peppers—and beside them, a glass dish of red grapes and
a pitcher of water. "We eat together three times a day. Dinner is at
dusk."

"That late?"

"Time unwinds differently here than anywhere else I've ever been.
The day won't seem as long as you'd think."

"You talk like a native. How long have you been here?"

"A while," Anders said.

The woman nodded. A sheen of sweat had broken out on her forehead and her blouse had wilted around her small frame, a damp on-
ion skin.

He left her at the door to her room—a narrow dormitory, the
same as everyone else's, furnished with a cot, a bedside table, a single
lamp.

"Is that it?" she asked, as she dropped her purse to the floor, a look of blanched worry on her face. "Will someone else be coming up to show me around?"

"Later," Anders said. "Or, if not, just come to the kitchen at dinner time."

"But that's hours from now."

"Yes," he said and smiled. "Settle in." He could have stayed to reassure her, but he turned and took the stairway up to his own room.

Later, he saw her through the open bedroom window, a wide-brimmed straw hat on her head and a white sundress swimming at her ankles as she walked. He watched her open the garden gate. Watched her choose the exposed path of the wash rather than cutting through the shade beneath the stand of pines rimming the yard. The sun hit her square and she kept going, straight out across the desert, looking wholly out of place.

How he had ended up at a spiritual retreat center in Arizona was a story Anders didn't tell everyone. It was usual to be asked—a part of regular dinner conversation at the Center, where people took an almost lustful interest in others' tales of self-destruction and grief and failure. A truly good turning-point story bought its teller credibility here, the way an evangelical's fiery testimonial could grant him proof of God's favor, or an addict's most heinous confessions could earn him the respect of a room of NA members. Anders couldn't stomach it—the self-conscious construction of a history, the vanity. Wasn't the point of coming out here to escape all that? The stories struck him as a kind of pornography, and he'd learned to give just enough to satisfy without having to strip himself truly bare. "I lost my way," he'd say, his tone somber. "I could only hear the noise, you know?" The omissions created his own brand of bullshit, of course, but he didn't figure he owed anyone anything more.

Despite this, people read his silence as pain. They assumed drugs, death, mental illness. They assumed he was running from real demons and not just ordinary life. What he was leaving out was just that, though—the banality. His reasons for leaving home were the stuff of sitcoms, not salvations: a muddled love affair, a tedious job, the messy leftovers of an only typically dysfunctional childhood. That was the whole of it. Nothing truly traumatic. At least nothing that appeared traumatic from the outside.

He had a certain guilt about it all, and in low moments resolved to grow up. Get his shit together. Stop acting the part of the wounded kid and just get back to his adulthood. He'd taken unpaid leave from his tech job in Seattle. What expenses he still had he was paying with his savings, which would eventually run out. He was burning through it all—the money and the leave and everyone's patience with him—but still he had no answers. Most of the time he wasn't even sure he had the right questions yet.

And while he was looking, Jane had kept sending him letters. They were bundled and held by the Sierra Vista post office until whoever had kitchen duties could get into town to pick up the center's groceries and everybody's mail. It was worse to read them this way—a fistful all at once—a torrent of whatever emotion Jane was feeling that week, and then several days of nothing. Jane wrote them by hand in beautiful, lush cursive, which Anders knew was her way of proving she'd won the ridiculous argument they'd had for years about technology's degradation of human relationship. She was studying to be a historic preservationist and tended to extend her affection for crumbling Roman architecture to everything old and dying and irrelevant to real life. Still, even in her antiquated penmanship, the first letters were all fresh rage, her tone hard, and her accusations on the page more difficult to ignore than they had ever been in person. He was a child. A coward. Unfaithful and condescending. A man just like his father before him.

Lately, though, almost inexplicably, she'd softened. She'd begun asking how long he'd be gone. When was he coming home? She wrote about spring in Seattle. The crocuses were up. The cherry trees bordering the university's quad were thick in pink petals. He loved that—didn't he? And he was missing it. He was missing everything. Was he missing her? She was missing him.

He read the letters and folded them and tucked them into the suitcase he'd brought, beneath the clothes he'd been wearing the day he arrived at the Center—clothes that didn't fit anymore, not physically or otherwise.

The truth was that he did miss her, sometimes badly. Most nights he lay on his cot and could not stop himself from conjuring her face above him, the weight of her body on his. Here, the slope of her waist beneath his hand. Here, the hang of her full breasts with their pale pink areolae. Her shoulders with their freckles just a shade darker than her skin, like spots of rain on a page of ivory paper. He could not stop himself.

When he could think freely again, he reminded himself that this was not about her; this was about isolation. Loneliness was inevitable and not a reason for real guilt. Certainly not a reason to return home yet.

One afternoon, not long after coming to the Center, he had called his father and told him everything. He didn't think he could marry Jane. He didn't think he could go on as he had been—bored, unhappy. It was such a predictable crisis. It made him nauseous to hear himself talk.

His father listened, and when Anders finished, he said they'd been worried. Jane had told the family he was in rehab.

"Not rehab," Anders said, though he wasn't surprised by Jane's misinterpretation of the place. "A communal retreat center. And, yes, I know how that sounds."

"No, it's a relief. I'm jealous, actually. Maybe I should come down there after all, but not to bring you home, which is what Jane suggested."

"I'm honestly not sure what I'm doing here, though."

"Yes you are," his father said. His voice was steady, sure. "You're taking the time you need. Don't second-guess that."

"I'm trying to do the right thing."

"You are. You are doing the right thing. Jane is angry now. She won't always be. And you need to know what you want, so take the time. Loneliness is nothing compared to regret. Believe me."

For an instant, the familiar tension stretched tight between them again. Anders put his head against the wall where the phone was mounted. "You regret marrying Mom?" he asked. He heard his father's breath.

"I'm not saying that."

"Leaving her—us, then? You regret that?" Anders had wanted to ask it for more than a decade—ever since his parents had split up when he was a teenager—and here it was, a prickling in his throat, a thistle, a scab picked.

His father sighed again. "I think the body gets used to certain certainties. It's bound to crave company. You're bound to want what you know. That's what I think. Sometimes I still miss how it used to be."

"God, Dad."

"I'm just being frank with you. Desire doesn't disappear just because it's irrelevant."

They said goodbye. His father promised to let the family know Anders was fine, and Anders promised not to let Jane push him.

In the next bunch of mail, then, there were more letters from Jane, these heavy with blame, but also one from his father. "You'll come through this," his father wrote. "You will."

Anders had resolved to stay another week, and that had turned into two, and two more. Jane's letters had eased up. It had become a little easier for Anders to stay away without guilt, though more difficult to find a reason to return at all to his life at home—or to any life other than this one of stillness, isolation. He'd begun to think of the desert as an island floating free from the rest of the world, disconnected, and leaving it—crossing back over to the mainland of regular life—would require a kind of drowning.

This was when the woman arrived—in his eighth week, into the midst of his confusion.

Several days later, when Anders was out walking, he saw her again. It was midmorning, bright already. She had a blanket spread beneath a willow tree, a book in her hand. She looked up when he stopped, and he asked if she'd settled in well. She said she had. She offered him the edge of the blanket, and he sat, folding his legs under him, aware of the dirty undersides of his feet. She still looked like the outside world—her hair pulled back in a braid, her skin not yet as browned as his had become. She was wearing again the white dress, the hat. She had a canvas bag, and she pulled from it a tin of shortbread cookies.

"My contraband," she said.

"Nothing's really illegal here. You know that, right? No one cares what you do, so long as it doesn't disrupt the community." He said this as he took one of the cookies. It was buttery, sweet. He hadn't eaten anything packaged since arriving at the Center, and his tongue had forgotten sugar. His mouth watered as he chewed.

"Still," she said. "It would be frowned on, wouldn't it? Cookies? I'd be judged."

"How long will you stay?" he asked.

She smiled. "I'm supposed to say something like 'as long as feels right,' but the truth is that I have a month off work. I don't plan to quit my job."

She tucked the cookies away in the bag again, closed her book—a paperback copy of a novel, the title printed in the disorienting backward and upside down letters of the Russian alphabet. When she caught him looking at it, she slid the book into the bag, too. "My grandparents were from Saint Petersburg. This seemed like a good time to brush up on the language. I've forgotten more than I'd like."

Anders thought again about her little white car, his first impression of her as someone who had hoped for a weekend at the spa and had only mistakenly ended up here. "So coming to the Center, this is a study break?" he asked. "A time-out from real life."

Her expression hardened. "Everything about me seems to offend you."

"Not offense, just curiosity."

She looked away from him, shook her head. "This place is supposed to be open, but so far I've found it exactly as narrow as everywhere else in the world."

"I think you've misjudged me."

"It doesn't matter." She got to her knees and motioned for him to stand, then began gathering the blanket. Anders stood back while she shook it, a glitter of dust rising and sparkling against the bands of sunlight coming through the willow branches. He watched her fold the blanket into a perfect square and tuck it under her arm, slide the straps of her bag over her shoulder. She looked at him. "I'm going back. If you want to walk with me, you can, but I don't need a lecture."

He nodded. "I'll be polite," he said.

They walked the rut of the wash. Under the cottonwoods, like guard dogs, squat, blue-green agave plants grew in the shade, their spikes rigid and toothed.

"They look unforgiving," she said. "That's what I keep thinking about everything here. That word—*unforgiving*." She pointed across the stretch of dry grass to the distance, where a crowd of cholla cacti stood, all arms raised and bristled. "Like that," she said. "It makes me think of a book I read as a little girl about the settlers coming to the West. At one point in the book, they see a tribal gathering. The dancing and the songs sound threatening to them. Harsh." She turned her face to him, lifted a hand to her forehead to shade her eyes. "I don't mean that the native people of the West were harsh but that the settlers perceived them that way. You see what I mean? To me, this place looks unforgiving."

"Weren't you just reading about Russia though?" Anders smiled. "All snow and ice. That's an unforgiving landscape."

She shrugged. "It's not though. Not at all. But I learned Russia first through someone else's memories, so it's a fairy tale to me." Her voice had rounded, the edges of the earlier irritation gone. She walked close enough at his side that now and then her elbow brushed his.

"Those cacti," Anders pointed toward the cluster of cholla, "they have these beautiful skeletons. You'll find them sometimes if you keep walking here. The wood left when the spines and flesh rot away looks like lace. Full of tiny holes. It's intricate, but not actually fragile."

"I'm trying to see that, but I can't picture it."

They stopped at the garden gate, and Anders opened it, let her step ahead of him into the yard. "I didn't mean to be judgmental," he said. "I've been here too long. I'm losing my manners."

She paused and frowned. "That's not a good apology," she said. "That just means you'd be a better liar if you met me in the real world." She went ahead of him across the yard and into the house, and he watched her go without another word.

The next day, though, he met her again, this time reading on the porch. Again she put her book away when she saw him, invited him to sit and talk. Her name was Anna—Annie. She'd come to the Center from San Francisco. She didn't say why. When the lunch bell sounded, they arranged to meet the following morning to walk. Anders would show her a cave he had found in a rock formation not too far away.

This was how it began, their unlikely alliance. That's how Anders came to think of it—she was a companion here where so much of the day was spent in actual isolation or in silent side-by-side work. Of course he knew some of the other residents—the woman from Texas who had just sent her youngest child to college and was searching for something of her own now; the retired Episcopalian priest; the ex-junkie whose parents had detoxed him when he flunked out of UCLA and then sent him out here; Mick, the guy who ran the place. Anders had met these people, but he didn't know them. Annie was something else.

One afternoon he took her farther out than they had walked before. A stand of willows fenced the length of a narrow creek bed. The creek was nothing but a dry gulch now; only in the summer, when the monsoons came, would it fill. Overhead, however, the willows were full and trembling with a movement like wind, though the air was still.

"What is it?" Annie asked.

"Hummingbirds," Anders said. "They're called Anna's hummingbirds. Watch, and you'll see their pink throats."

They stood still. He found himself holding his breath. Above them, flashes of green movement dipped between the trees. The birds nested here, he told her. He'd stumbled on the little grove one day not long after he'd come to the Center. Sometimes there were hundreds of hummingbirds in the trees, whole branches alive with the motion of their bodies. Before coming here, he had never seen a hummingbird in rest. It was startling.

"Why Anna's?" she asked.

"I don't know. I thought you'd appreciate it, though."

"I do. Thank you." She took his hand and held it.

"We're violating the rules, you know, touching."

"I thought you said there were no rules here."

"There is that one. Romantic entanglements cloud things. We're all here to get clearer."

"You want me to let go?" She tipped her head up to watch the movement in the branches, and he took her in. Something had shifted in her. She looked relaxed, comfortable. Flecks of light filtered through the willow branches and freckled her face and shoulders.

They walked back without speaking, hands still clasped until they neared the yard. At the gate, she dropped his hand and turned to him. "I want to ask you to come to my room." Her face had drained of its little color with the question.

This startled him. "We'd both have to leave if someone discovered us."

She looked away. "You don't want me."

"I do. I do want you," he said. There was an unexpected charge in saying the words aloud, and he stepped ahead of her through the garden and led her into the house.

In the kitchen they stopped for food, found two plates and a bowl of grapes, a quarter section of a watermelon that they carried down the hallway to her room. The space was small and close once Annie shut the door, and the air inside smelled floral and feminine. On the bedside table there were several bottles of lotions and sunscreens, and he imagined these as the source of the smell, but once they were both undressed, he understood that it was also on her skin and the sheets, the taste of her on his tongue bitter with perfume. Wearing fragrance here was a vanity, or maybe a luxury, and he wondered again at who she was and why she'd left her life for this place.

As he touched her, he thought of how cloying and artificially intense Jane could be—how different this was. Jane had not been wrong when she'd called him unfaithful. Many times he had come close to going home with women he knew from work; and once, not long before coming to the Center, he had gone home with a woman he'd met at a bar. She'd worn a green negligee, slick as a snake's skin, beneath her dress, but she'd been a cheerful and good-natured lover, easy to leave when it was over. He thought later that he ought to have been guilty. He ought to have been ashamed. It was surely a defect in him, an inherited flaw, that then—just as now—he felt only relief.

What Annie felt was unreadable to him, her face guarded. She did not speak at all while they made love, but gripped him. He came away from her hold with the red marks of her fingers on his arms, his chest—the heat of her breath humid in his ear.

Afterward, she got up and pulled on a thin robe, and they sat on the floor, their legs out in front of them and their backs against the frame of the cot. It was late afternoon. The light coming through her small window was already heavy with evening.

She settled the two plates they'd brought from the kitchen in front of them, dished from the bowl of fruit. As she did, he leaned forward to kiss her again, and she pulled away. When he touched his fingertips to the flat of her chest, she closed the collar of her robe.

"What is it?" he asked.

She sat up. She looked suddenly anguished, full of remorse. "I should have given you the truth: I'm married. My husband is in San Francisco, working, living in our apartment."

"Why didn't you tell me?"

"Would it have changed your mind, knowing this?" Again her direct stare, her way of cutting quickly to the heart of things.

Anders stood and began to pull on his pants. "I'll leave," he said.

"Please don't leave."

"What do you want, then? Why tell me at all?"

She sighed, touched the spot on the floor at her side, and he sat again. "I don't know what I'm doing. You must think I'm terrible." Her face had gone sallow, her expression stiff. The robe had fallen open to the tie at her waist once more, and there was an intimacy that hadn't been there before in seeing her naked chest.

He shook his head. "You should have told me when we met."

She looked away. "You're disappointed."

"I'm the last person you want to be your conscience." He bit into the watermelon, wiped the juice away from his mouth with the back of his hand.

"We're having problems," she said. "My husband and I, we're struggling. It's part of why I'm here. I needed to get away. To figure it out."

Anders dropped the rind onto the plate. "I don't need to know. I told you—I shouldn't be anybody's confessor."

"You think I'm confessing?" She looked at him.

"It's useless, that's what I'm saying. Remorse, regret—whatever it is you're trying to get off your chest. It doesn't matter. It doesn't change anything now, does it?" He was disgusted suddenly—with himself and with her. He wanted to tell her to close her robe.

"You're angry. I knew you would be."

"Not angry. Just honest. You said you didn't like a liar."

"You should go."

"Yes," he said.

Outside her door, he moved along the hallway in a hurry, took the stairs to his room two at a time, anxious now to get away from the narrow room and from her—anxious to be alone again.

Several days passed. At night, unable to sleep, he took out Jane's letters and reread them. What was his obligation to her? Was he less guilty than Annie because he wasn't married? That's what he'd always told himself—they were not married, and so he was not betraying her. This was an easy lie, though, and he needed to be honest now. He needed to commit himself to honesty, at least, if he could commit to nothing else.

He began writing a handful of apologies, each one wrong, the same excuses reclothed in different words. He threw them all out. Finally, a week after his afternoon with Annie, it came to him clearly: He did not love Jane. He wrote to her with harsh focus: He was not going to come home. He could not be what she needed. He had realized at the Center that there were certain traits he could not change in himself, certain lives he could not live without hurting others. Perhaps this was a weakness in him, a pattern he could not unlearn. Maybe it was beyond that—an inborn inability. It didn't matter, really. The point was that it would be better for them both if he did not come home.

He sealed the letter and left the house. Outside, the air was cool. It was not quite dawn, and the sky was still dark blue, starred, far away, the mountains furred in purple shadow. The desert was nearly silent. It was just under ten miles to town, and he figured he could be there in a couple of hours if he ran, if he didn't stop. He'd get breakfast—a real breakfast—at the diner, and then find the post office, mail his letter before starting back. After that, he wasn't sure.

All the way there, he tried to empty his mind as he had been encouraged to do since coming to the Center. It was another of his deficiencies that he was unable to do this. His head buzzed more loudly when he tried to quiet it, his attention to every detail only sharpened when he tried to see nothing.

As a kid, he'd seen a school counselor for a few months during his third-grade year, and she, too, had tried to coach him through meditation. "Close your eyes," she'd hush. "Count your breaths. Let every thought that comes into your mind just float away." But he heard the heater in the wall click on and whir, the even thunking of the copy machine in the office next door, spitting out copies. He thought: *I am warm in my clothes. I have spit in my mouth. I have heavy feet.* In his mind, he saw his friends back in the classroom, working at their math problems while the teacher slid a new transparent film sheet onto the overhead projector. It was a racket, all this. He could not slow his thoughts—could not sit still—which was why he had been assigned meetings with the counselor in the first place. He was a failed case from the start, and eventually even the counselor recognized this, and Anders was permitted to stop seeing her.

Maybe, he thought as he walked now, some people are just restless. Maybe some people are truly unable to sit still—no matter what form that stillness takes.

He recalled the last meal he'd eaten with his parents before their divorce. It was June. A late supper. His mother had fixed salmon and had pulled and cleaned green beans from their own garden for a salad. The thick-gold light of such summer evenings was pouring into the house through the wide front windows, and when Anders sat down at the table between his parents, he'd felt an overwhelming spill of comfort, contentment. Only looking back now did he recognize his father's restlessness during that meal. The way he'd fidgeted with his napkin while the rest of them talked. The way he'd risen for more of the beans, a new fork, a second glass of wine. His mind was elsewhere already, though he would not actually leave the house for another month.

Anders wondered now how much of his father's life with their family had been a sacrifice of the self, a loss. And could Anders be angry with his father for leaving the family when he so closely understood that leaving was a method of survival? Could he hold it against Annie if she now wanted a respite from her own unhappy marriage?

It was not yet nine when he arrived in town. He found the diner, sat by the window, and watched the first of the morning's traffic passing in the yellow street while he ate his platter of peppered eggs and sausages and fried corn cakes shining with grease. He took out the letter and looked at it while he drank his coffee, then put it back when he got up to pay the check.

All the way through town, he kept his hand on the envelope in his pocket. It gathered weight while he walked, and when he finally dropped it into the mailbox at the post office, it felt like he was dropping an enormous load—a rock he'd been carrying too long, a planet on his back. As soon as he reached the Center again he went to Annie's door.

They spent the rest of her time at the Center together, meeting quietly, always in secret. His need to be near her surprised him. When she went out on errands alone, as she now and then did, her little white car pulling away from the Center's parking lot with a ruff of desert dust, he missed her. When after sex she became pensive and lay on the cot with the sheet pulled to her shoulders and her back turned to him, he grew anxious, his heart racing with the thought that she was considering breaking things off, choosing her husband. He didn't even know this man—Dmitri—but he hated him, and hated himself for the hating. Annie had told him that she'd married too young, but that she'd known her husband since childhood. Their families were close, both active in the same Russian Orthodox church; and Dmitri's father had long been like a brother to her own. She had loved Dmitri genuinely at one point—and she loved him now, in some sense, though she was no longer sure they should have married. That's all she would say. She wouldn't speak badly of Dmitri, and she never shared anything from his letters to her, though Anders saw that she was reading them. They arrived every few days in rubber-banded bundles, bricks of paper that she held against her chest as she carried them from the mail bin up to her room. Anders wondered what they contained—what professions of love or longing or obligation. He wondered how Annie felt when she read them. Guilty, maybe. Trapped. Or, worse: beloved and needed.

As Anders saw it, though, neither Dmitri nor Jane had any idea about the people they'd rooted themselves to, and there was something unforgiveable in that innocence, wasn't there? There was something blameworthy in being so blind.

"Leave him," Anders said one night. He would quit his job and move to California to be nearer to her. He could go back to school maybe, or just do something to pay the rent on a cheap apartment— clerk at a grocery store or drive a cab. "Or don't leave him, but don't stop seeing me." She could get away on weekends, he proposed. She could make up excuses about where she was going.

Annie touched his cheek. "I do have a friend with a vacation cottage in Santa Cruz. She's always looking for a tenant." It was an abstract statement, the house appearing briefly before them both, a bit of ephemera. Nothing would come of it, Anders understood.

Then, at the start of her last week, a call came for her: Dmitri was in the hospital. He'd had a migraine, which had happened before, but this time his vision had gone black and hadn't returned when the headache waned. They were running tests. It could be nothing—temporary; or it could be something serious. He was asking for her.

She explained this while she packed her bag. Anders sat on the cot and watched her clear the room of her things. The jars of lotions, the books, the white dress—she swept them all into her bag with a reckless indifference. Her face was tight again, as it had been when she'd first arrived at the Center, her expression piqued. But why? He wasn't sure. Anger at Dmitri for forcing her home early, or at herself for making it so difficult to leave? When she finished, he followed her out to her car, stood with his hands in his pockets while she loaded everything.

"I don't have your address," he said.

"I think that's best." She turned to him and frowned against the sunlight. "I feel like we did this to him. I did this to him. It's my punishment."

"You don't believe that really, do you? Life doesn't work that way." He bent forward to kiss her, not caring now if anyone inside the house saw them, but she turned her face from him.

"I don't know what I believe," she said.

He didn't wait to see her pull away but went inside, climbed the stairs to his room, and shut the door.

That evening he began packing his own things to leave.

It occurred to Anders only once he was on the road that the home he'd left was no longer his—he'd cut his ties there. He'd sent the letter to Jane.

He drove north with the aimlessness of a traveler, not a resident, unsure where or when to stop. He didn't want to return to the job he hated, but without it, he had nothing. He didn't want to beg forgiveness from Jane, but where else would he live?

Anders thought of his father and the little island house he lived in alone, and for the first time he considered retreating there. His father would take him in. There'd be long days on the beach, nights up late poking the campfire in the yard and looking for stars between the deep banks of blue cloud that always rolled in from the Pacific after sunset. It would be the safety for him now that it had been for his father just after the divorce.

But no—he couldn't go there. The house had become a symbol of his family's unraveling, and going there would be an admission of empathy for his father. He'd made a fragile peace with the past, but he was not ready to just accept the symmetry between himself and his father, or to forgive it in himself.

In the end, he drove to the house he'd shared with Jane and knocked on the door. As he expected, she took him in without any resistance. He'd just been lost, she told him. She would help him find his way again, and everything would be fine.

He fell back into the old routine: work, short evenings of numbing distractions, sleep, work again. Summer came and went, and then fall, and soon Seattle was steely with winter, the sky as thick as the gray, gray Sound, the city draped behind layers of gauzy fog that drifted inland smelling of fish and cold water. Anders didn't mind winter, actually. It was sleepy and permitted isolation without questioning. You could walk from office door to bus stop briskly, hands sunk into your pockets, eyes down, and everyone would presume you were avoiding the drizzle, not company. You could decline invitations to go out by claiming a head cold, or by simply saying, "the rain." You could convince yourself to a certain degree that your own malaise was due only to the season, the lack of sunshine—that it was the psychic equivalent of the constant damp drip of the sky and muddy choke of the landscape.

All this time, Anders couldn't stop thinking of Annie. He wanted to forget her, to put her out of his head, but she was always with him, just there behind his thoughts, the ghost of every moment. Out with friends for drinks one night, he started to mention her: "There was this woman I met when I was in Arizona—"

His friend clapped him on the back and laughed. "There's always a woman, isn't there?" he said, and Anders felt himself retreat, the impulse toward honesty slithering inward again like a snake back into its hole.

At night, after Jane had gone to bed, he often looked Annie up online, searching for evidence of what exactly, he didn't quite know.

He didn't want to wish another man dead, but what if it had turned out that Dmitri was seriously ill? Or what if Annie's unhappiness had got the best of her and she'd left him? What if she was alone now, one way or the other? What would Anders do then?

He found proof of nothing, though, just old images of her, and not even her own—photographs culled from someone's Twitter account and another person's Facebook page: Annie as a younger woman, sitting on a dorm room bed beside two other grinning coeds; a teenage Annie standing before Saint Petersburg's Winter Palace at night, her bright red scarf flying loose in a breeze, and the whole, massive palace lit a swollen gold at her back against the darkness. Anders saved this last one to a file on his computer, hid the file on his hard drive.

Each time he spoke to his father, he nearly confessed everything, but what good could come of that? What advice could his father offer that he could take? *Stay*—but his father had not stayed; he had chosen his own happiness over everyone else's. *Leave*—but Anders knew what loneliness leaving brought. As it was, he decided his father would be of no help, and so he said nothing.

Only Jane was suspicious. Once he caught her scrolling through his phone messages. Another time he was certain she'd gone through the drawers of his dresser while he was at work, the clothes inside disordered somehow, though he couldn't be sure. Many times, in the dark of their bedroom when they could not see each other's faces, she asked him what had happened during those weeks he was gone. Why had he sent the letter? What had brought him back to her?

"Nothing," he said. "I don't know."

"If there was someone else, you should tell me," she said. "You have to tell me." Always the same plea, and always he responded with silence, rolling toward her, laying his palm on her back, physical reassurance taking the place of the answers he could not give.

Still, despite Jane's anxiety and against his own better judgment, he went on looking for Annie. It was just after the turn of the new year when he finally thought to search her husband's name, and once

he did, he quickly found their address. He booked a flight, told Jane
he had an out of town business meeting, and packed a bag. SEA to
SFO. In three hours, he was stepping into a clear, bright California
morning.

He got a hotel and spent the day walking. He'd been to San Francisco as a little boy, but not since then, and he took in the city with a
strange sense of déjà vu, the place a foreign familiar. Certain sights—
the red-roofed military buildings of the old Presidio, the pink-pillow
dome of the Palace of Fine Arts—sparked in his memory like little
firecrackers as soon as he saw them.

By midafternoon he could take his own restlessness no more. He
gave a cab driver the address he had noted in his phone, just a few
blocks from his hotel. He paid the driver, got out, and stood before
the house. It reminded him of her—neat, angular, charming. A four-
story wooden Victorian that sat shouldering its neighbors. From the
row of mailboxes beside the front door, he gathered that hers was
the third-floor apartment, and he looked up, tried to make out any
distinguishing features through the windows, but they were opaque
with gauzy white drapes, nothing but reflective shadows on the glass.

For a long time he stood in front of the house before walking once
around the block. His body was all adrenaline. *I could just leave*, he
told himself. *I could go back to the hotel right now.* But he circled the
block once more, and then again. It was getting late, and the light was
fading. Overhead, the streetlamps came on. Just then, though, her little white car appeared at the end of the block opposite him, the dark
shape of her behind the wheel. His stomach seized, and he raised his
arm in a wave.

She told him her husband was not home, wouldn't be home until
late, but she felt uncomfortable inviting Anders into the house, and
so they drove to another neighborhood where she wouldn't bump
into anyone she knew. They found an Indian restaurant for dinner.
The place was small and overwarm, the walls and ceiling hung in tap-
estries, the smell of curry thick.

"Why did you find me?" she asked once they were seated.

"I need you to understand something," he began, but she cut him off.

"I'm unhappy here." Her hand was cold when she reached across the table and took his wrist. "I'm so unhappy, and now you've come down here and made it worse." She looked as if she might be sick, her face gray-white and all of the color gone out of her lips. "You should never have come."

They ate without speaking. All around them, Anders heard the sounds of the restaurant as if from inside a tunnel.

"What will we do?" she asked at one point. "What are we going to do?"

At the end of the meal he called a cab to carry him back to the hotel. On the sidewalk, before the cab arrived, she stepped close to him, and he pulled her into a long kiss. When she turned away, Anders watched her walk down the street and get into her car. She would drive home and park in her garage, climb the stairs to her apartment, change her clothes, and get into bed, just like any other night. When her husband came home, he would find her there waiting as always. And he—Anders—would go back to his hotel and call Jane, as he had promised to do, and she would tell him about her day on campus, about her progress with the dissertation chapter she was writing, their conversation no different from those they had most nights. He and Annie were both, he saw, living two lives—one thin and transparent, open for everyone to see, and one shrouded. Here again, he thought, was his father's life tucked inside his own. All those years, when he believed he knew his father's happiness, his worries, he'd been only half right. He'd known half of the man, half of the life his father was living—the half his father wished to have known. Whatever else there was—the truly personal—was unseen, a fragile skeleton just beneath the skin. This is how everyone must live, Anders saw. The inner workings that make a man most human are sewn below the surface, secret, where they can remain safe and unscarred. This is why his father had left and why Annie had made herself invisible on-line—to preserve the personal. This is why he himself had so long re-sisted writing to Jane: everything intimate was more easily exposed in writing, the private ghost of every word excruciatingly plain there between the lines.

The next morning, Annie called him from the hotel lobby. She had taken a personal day at work, could she come up to his room? When he opened the door she was there, wearing the red scarf he remem-bered from the picture of her as a young woman in front of the Win-ter Palace.

"It's cold out," she said as she unwrapped herself from the layers of scarf and coat and sweater. "The fog is full of ice crystals." She reached for him, and her face against his—her mouth against his mouth—was cold, too, though her skin quickly pinked with the warmth of the room.

"What are we doing?" he asked.

She moved to sit on the edge of the bed. "I've thought of every reason not to do this, but I love you." Her tone was hard, almost defi-ant. "I don't want to feel like a criminal anymore."

Anders put his face in his hands. He could not stop himself: he began to cry. He thought she might get up and leave right then, dis-gusted with him and this naked show of need, but she hushed him.

"You're fine," she said. "Go on. We'll be fine."

When he had control of himself again, they sat talking and mak-ing plans. For the first time in months, Anders felt free and happy and certain. They would leave their lives for a new one together. They would start over. The worst was behind them, and they would live a long time together, in love. It suddenly seemed wonderfully impos-sible to either of them that anything but this could be true.

WHEELING

In the month since he came to stay with her, Janie's grandson has turned sixteen and failed the driver's licensing exam twice. Thanksgiving has come and gone, and with it the first fine snow, which fell and quickly melted away. Today, when Janie wakes at six to the sound of the phone on the bedside table ringing, the sky on the other side of the bedroom window looks unmistakably wintry, night just beginning to thin with dawn and the moon still out, though far away and made transparent by the light, as inconsequential as a smudge on the wide plane of darkened glass.

"It's early," Janie says into the phone.

"This is the only time we're permitted calls." Her daughter Caroline's voice is tinny with the bad connection. They only have one landline at the retreat center, she tells Janie, and the phone is a rotary dial. "It's sort of charming, though."

"I'm glad you're enjoying yourself." Janie catches the barb in her voice, takes a breath to stop herself from saying more.

"How's Devon?" Caroline asks.

"He misses you."

The silence between them circles like water rounding a drain.

"We're both fine," Janie says, relenting. "We'll be fine. And how are you?"

"That's why I'm calling." Her tone is hesitant. "I've let the lease go on the apartment in Connecticut. I'm going to stay here. At least for now. I put the furniture into storage last weekend, so there's nothing for you to worry about."

Janie holds the phone closer to her ear, the receiver hard against the hollow there. *Except your son*, she thinks. *Nothing to worry about except your son.* She says, "You were in Connecticut last weekend? You flew home?"

"I had to pack before I could let go of the lease."

"But you didn't come to Montauk."

"I miss Devon. It's not that I don't."

Janie swallows. Her tongue is a bit of bone in her mouth. "Fine," she says. "We'll be here. Whenever you're ready to come home."

After the call Janie lies looking at her ceiling for several moments before getting up, then she dresses in her sweats and makes her way to the kitchen, her sneakers and a pair of mittens in her hand. She is surprised to find Devon awake before her on a Saturday. Already, he is sitting at the table over a bowl of cornflakes, the white threads of his earbuds sprouting like vines from his ear canals, and his fingertips drumming the vague rhythm of a song on the tabletop.

"Morning," Janie says. "Couldn't sleep?"

"The test," he says, and she remembers—he has a ten o'clock appointment to retake the driving exam.

Janie fills a water bottle, takes the day's vitamins—still, happily, the only things she takes, though she will be sixty-eight later this year—and wolfs down a piece of buttered toast standing at the counter.

Only when she sits in the chair across from him does Devon pull the buds from his ears. A riot of electronic sound shouts from the tiny speakers for an instant before he reaches into his sweatshirt pocket and silences it.

"Don't shut it off on my account," she says to him. "You're free to listen to whatever you like." She lets out a stiff huff of breath as she bends over her knees to tie her shoes.

Devon hangs his head low over his cereal bowl and shovels in several mouthfuls before pausing to chew. His hair is dark, like his mother's, but so straight that it hangs in a flat sheet—too long and a little dirty. He reaches up to sweep it out of his eyes.

"You sure you want to do the test again today?" Janie asks. "The roads are probably icy. You could wait until spring. I don't mind driving you to school."

"I already made the appointment." He spoons more of the cereal into his mouth.

"Those first two drives were just chokes anyway," Janie says, winking at him.

"It wasn't me. That examiner is a prick. I'm asking for the other one today."

"Watch your mouth."

The house is quiet, but for his chewing. The furnace kicks on and there is the blown hum of the vent, a shushing. A bubble of trapped air gurgles in the waterline under the sink. Devon swallows.

"Today will be better," Janie says. "Sometimes anxiety is a motivator."

He meets her eyes. "I want the license before my mom comes home. She doesn't think I'm ready for it."

"Great. Prove her wrong and we'll both be happy." Janie pushes up from her chair. "I'm going for a bike ride, but have your things together when I come back and we'll go. And could you make me some coffee? You know how to use the pot?" He nods and she touches his shoulder as she leaves the room.

Outside, she pauses at the end of the drive and turns to look back at the house. Devon is there on the other side of the kitchen window, making the coffee, just as she asked.

Grief, unlike anger or joy, often has a long gestation period. Janie knows this. Two years ago her husband, Alan, died suddenly one morning, a heart attack seizing him just as he was about to lift a forkful of eggs to his mouth at breakfast. He hadn't shown any signs of weakness before the attack, and was, by all appearances, a healthy man. Even that morning he'd seemed himself. When it happened, he simply stopped, midbite, a look of strain crossing his face. "O," he said, his wet mouth forming the letter, a fleck of egg on his lip, and he slumped forward against the table.

Afterward Janie did the things his death called for with stoic and efficient urgency—arranging for a service and reception to be held at St. Mark's Episcopal, where they'd long been faithful members, then smiling dutifully as relatives and friends embraced her before carrying themselves forward to the buffet of cut fruit and canapés and deviled eggs she'd had catered. She succeeded better than anyone might have expected at managing the legal and financial tidbits of widowhood. She navigated the endless paperwork of his pension and filed her own taxes for the first time in her life. (It had felt like such a victory, she'd taken herself out for a glass of wine after dropping the IRS envelope into the mail.) She even sold the old house in Yonkers where they'd raised Caroline and bought this little one out on the beach in Montauk, where she'd always wanted to live.

"You sold our house?" Caroline asked when Janie called to tell her.

"You didn't expect me to go on living there forever, did you?"

"I guess not, but, it's just—" Caroline stumbled, went quiet.

"What would one person need with a four-bedroom house?"

"Nothing. I understand. You just don't make decisions like that when you're in grief."

"I'm not in grief. *In grief* makes it sound like grief is a bathtub you can climb into or out of. This is my life now, Caroline. I'm a widow." Janie chuffed, rolled her eyes to herself, standing alone with the phone in her hand. "It was my house to sell."

But the first morning in her new house she awoke in a panic, sat up in the dark and unfamiliar bedroom struggling for breath, her ribs as tight as if someone were sitting on her chest. It took a full day before she could talk herself out of her bed, get dressed. A panic attack, the doctor said when she drove back to Yonkers for an appointment. Not uncommon when a person is *in grief*. Janie went home feeling ridiculous and irritated, indulgent at having wasted her worry on something that was ultimately just in her head.

But, still, no matter how she dismissed it, she couldn't fully shake the presence of that panic—that grief—there below the skin of each moment, restless and ready to collapse her. Some days it was only a malignant apathy; others, she was wracked with an obsessive homesickness that left her wishing she'd kept the old place and all of Alan's things—all of his blue oxford shirts and the pair of stale running shoes perpetually sitting by the garage door for her to trip over, the little red Swiss Army knife that had inexplicably turned up in the kettle of the washing machine a few weeks after he died, clattering there against the metal rim as the towels churned. Months after Alan's death her grief was still there, not even truly attached to the loss of him anymore. It had to do with him, yes, but it was something else, too—a spur, a shoot of guilt and loneliness. A coiling fear (*Of what?* she demanded of herself—the worst had already come and gone) that she could not root out.

And so she had understood, more or less, what her daughter Caroline was going through when her own husband died unexpectedly the following autumn, his car overturned in a ditch on the road he'd taken to work five days a week for over a decade, his body still inside, nothing to be done and no explanation. "Maybe a deer jumped out

and he swerved," the officer they first spoke to said. "Maybe just a distraction. Sometimes we don't get answers."

Janie wanted to cradle Caroline and carry her away from the officer and his condolences, from the hospital waiting room and its
bright and determined going-on-ness. "You'll get through this," she
said, stroking Caroline's hair as she hadn't done in years. "You're
made of strong stuff."

Caroline wouldn't let her come to stay when she offered to those
first few weeks, and so Janie tried to be supportive from a distance.
When Caroline decided to move herself and Devon into an apartment to save money, Janie said it was a brilliantly responsible choice.
When Caroline, who had quit her teaching job after Devon's birth
and had not worked outside the house since, took a position filing
records and answering phones at a doctor's office, Janie congratulated
her. Though she would never say as much to her daughter, a part of
Janie could not believe that Caroline, who had spent much of her
teenage years wallowing over minor high school dramas and falling
into weepy anger at Janie's every little criticism, was adeptly handling
everything.

In April Janie called to invite them both to the beach for a weekend of rest.

"It's busy here right now, Mom," Caroline said.

"No one's that busy. Just come home and let me feed you and
Devon for a couple of days. Then you can get back to it all."

From where she sat near her back door, Janie could see whitecaps
on the easy waves, a pale blue sky, the first green tips of the tulips
she'd planted in wooden boxes on her back deck. She liked the idea
of Caroline and Devon coming out. They hadn't been but once, just
after she bought the house, and only then just for the day. If they
came she could make soup, buy a loaf of good bread. They'd all go
to a movie maybe, or out to dinner. She hadn't been to dinner in
months.

"That's not home," Caroline finally said, her voice threaded with irritation. "And we can't come now."

"You know, I remember how it was after your father. It was very hard at first, but I managed. And you will too."

"Don't compare us," Caroline said. "That was different. You had a whole life with Daddy."

"I'm not comparing. But you have a life with Devon. And you have me. You say you need me and I'm there."

Caroline paused. "Devon's a child, Mother." Her voice was quiet now, stilled. "If anything he makes this all the harder."

"Oh, now. Don't say that. He's a good boy."

"He's been difficult."

"He's just lost his father."

The sound of the connection hollowed, as if Caroline had set the phone down or turned her face away from the receiver. Janie heard her let out a breath. "This is what you always do—how you make everyone feel smaller. You've done it to me for years. I've wondered how Daddy put up with it, but I really just can't. Not now."

"What?" Janie said. The line of her breath caught like a hook in her chest.

"I can't talk to you about this, Mom. I'll tell Devon you say hi." She said goodbye and hung up.

Janie resolved not to call again—to wait for Caroline to call her with an apology first. But weeks passed and no call came.

In June Janie bought a bicycle in an effort to begin to whittle off the few pounds she'd gained living alone. She'd been indulgent, eating ice cream directly from paper pint containers (who was there to know?) and avoiding the ridiculous emotional wreckage of cooking for one by microwaving Hungry-Man (what a terrible name!) frozen dinners. The bike was a good idea, she thought, a means of both exercise and whimsy, and she certainly needed more of both.

One long afternoon she got out the bike and rode a few wobbly loops in the sand-and-gravel driveway to get her footing again before

taking it down the sandy road toward town to the grocer's, then rode
back with a canvas sack swinging from the crook of her elbow, in it a
bunch of cilantro, a lemon, and a single pink salmon filet wrapped in
brown butcher paper for supper that evening. She let the bike coast
where the road sloped toward her house and the low dunes of the
beach. The bike picked up speed as it cruised downhill, the wheels
spinning a giddy buzz, and as if the memory had only been curled
up asleep somewhere in the recesses of her body all these years, Janie
lifted first her feet from the pedals then her hands from the handlebars. Like that she was cut free, flying. The air whipped against her
face. The road rushed beneath her so that she was both part of it
and unconnected to it, and a surprising vertigo lilted in her stomach
with the pleasure of thrill, a sensation so near desire—something she
hadn't felt in so long—that she actually laughed out loud.

She only set her palms solidly on the grips again when the sack of
food slid to her wrist and threatened her balance. But even then the
feeling didn't quite evaporate right away. It lingered, that lightening.
It lifted her just slightly as she wheeled the bike back into the garage
and stepped up to the house and in the front door.

With the joy of the ride still humming through her, she called
Caroline that evening. The standoff had gone on long enough. But
when the phone rang it was Devon who picked up. He spoke in
one- or two-word phrases rather than complete sentences. How was
school? *Same.* How were he and his mother? *Fine.* Janie imagined he
was probably spread out on the couch, the TV on. It was six p.m. on a
Tuesday and his mother ought to have been home to be sure he was
eating dinner, doing his homework.

"She doesn't have a date, does she?" Janie said.

Devon seemed to sputter at the thought. "God, no. She's at her
church."

"On a Tuesday?"

"Tuesday is her group. She goes to worship Saturday nights." *Worship.* He said it as if the word were a rotted peach in his mouth.

"And what about you?" Janie asked.

"She doesn't make me go anymore." He sounded tired. "Do you want her to call you later?"

"Devon, why don't you come out for a visit? I've bought a bike. There are some nice rides out here on the beach. You could bring yours and we could go together, before the weather changes again."

"Yeah. Maybe." The line hung slack between them for a moment. "I haven't really ridden a bike in years, Grandma. I don't even have one now. I got rid of it when we moved."

Janie nodded, aware of the quiet of her kitchen. Her reflection was there against the dark glass of the back door. "Are you two getting along okay—you and your mother?"

"It's fine."

"You know I love you," she said.

"Yeah, okay. Talk to you soon, Gram."

Afterward, the conversation nagged at Janie. She made popcorn and stayed up, sitting in her bathrobe on the couch, watching a tedious movie on a cable channel. The sunset outside the windows mingled with the darkness, the sky the red-black color of wine, of deep seawater. When she looked at it through the window she saw herself looking back.

She thought of what Caroline had said: that she made people feel small. That she'd done it to Alan. What had she meant by that?

Once when Caroline was maybe four or five she had walked in on Janie and Alan fighting. It was late. They were in their own bedroom, the door open only a crack. Caroline had gone to bed hours before, so they'd believed she was sleeping; in those days they often argued after she went to bed. In the end, theirs had turned out to be a solid, mostly happy marriage, but during that period, when Caroline was small and demanding and Janie was home with her all day with few distractions beyond the domestic ones, Janie's anger was a constant, aimless presence, exorcised only by fighting with Alan. It was inexcusable, she knew; still, her anger followed her like a shadow all day—while she sopped up milk from the tabletop and wiped Caroline's bottom and folded endless baskets of laundry. And then, at night, when Caroline was safely in bed and dreaming, it erupted. Sometimes she felt herself stalking excuses to let it erupt, in fact, though when it did, she shrank like the stone of a plum into the center of herself, where she watched on with loneliness and ineffectual disgust as she went on saying horrible things to the husband she genuinely loved.

Who would remember now what they were fighting about that particular night?—Alan forgetting to drag the garbage cans back in from the curb, or whose turn it was to take Caroline to a birthday party on the weekend; those fights were all the same, all the grievances utterly unimportant, and yet impossible to let go. But that night, when Caroline had interrupted, peering around the bedroom door, Janie had lunged forward to slam it shut again. "What do you think you're doing up? Get back to bed."

"Jane!" Alan snapped. "You nearly took off her hand." He went to Caroline, who had blanched and looked tiny standing in her little pink footie pajamas in the dark hallway. He lifted her to his shoulder and stroked her hair. "It's okay," he said. "You didn't do anything, sweetheart."

"Of course she did. Or she will," Janie said. "She's exactly like you." She had wanted to wind the words back into her mouth immediately, but she'd stood rigid before her husband and daughter. It had all gotten away from her.

She hadn't apologized, and they'd left her to herself for the rest of the night, Alan making up the couch after he got Caroline to sleep, and Janie lying awake in the bedroom, fuming and lonelier than she'd been even in the midst of the fight itself. In the end it was always that loneliness that made her angrier than any of the rest of it.

"Oh, Alan," she said aloud now, remembering all of this in the emptiness of her darkened living room. "Alan, do I make people feel small? Was I an unbearable wife?" But, of course, he was no longer there to defend anyone, and so she got up and went to bed.

After the conversation with Devon, the rest of the summer passed with no word from him or his mother, and in the end it wasn't until October that Caroline finally phoned to say they'd be coming out to the beach—she, Devon, and someone named Ina, from her church. Caroline left this all on the voicemail while Janie was out on a ride. "We just decided," Caroline said on the message. "I hope it's okay we're coming. We're already on the road." The message stalled in silence, no goodbye, and clicked off.

Janie showered and changed, got in the car and drove into town for groceries, spent the afternoon readying the little house. The day was fair and blue skied, the air clarified by the first true fall storm, which had drenched the beach the night before. She opened the windows so the smell of the tide would drift in. At four o'clock, the last light over the water looked rinsed, the water glistening and shining. At five she pulled a perfect roast from the oven and set it on the table to wait.

But they were late. Janie ate by herself at six thirty, cleared away the table settings, and sliced up the roast for sandwiches. She put on a pot of coffee. It was eight when they pulled into the drive.

"There was traffic coming through the city," Caroline shrugged as she opened the car door. She looked tired, but good. Her graying hair was short, cropped around her face the way she'd worn it when she was a teenager, and it flattered her. She was pretty still. Under all the years of mothering and the loss, here she was.

"You might have called from the road," Janie said, but when Caroline bristled, Janie simply leaned forward to kiss her daughter's cheek. "You're here now," she said. "Doesn't matter."

Devon got out of the back seat and opened the trunk, took out a single duffel bag and a pillow and a cardboard box with open flaps, and stood with this luggage at his feet, his hands in the front pocket of his sweatshirt.

"Is that it?" Janie asked.

Caroline stepped away. "I should have said something on the phone, but it didn't seem right to leave it on your voicemail. It's just Devon staying, and I'm hoping he can stay a little longer than the weekend." She folded her arms across her chest. "It's cold out, isn't it? Maybe we should talk about this inside?" Caroline nodded at Devon and stooped to pick up the pillow he had dropped on the sand. He shouldered his duffel, heaved up the box of books, and followed his mother inside.

It was dark, just the porch lamp's narrow beam lighting the drive. The friend, who hadn't climbed out of the car, sat with her face turned away, not looking at any of them. "Aren't you coming in too?" Janie said, poking her head into the opened car window.

The woman turned and smiled but didn't get out or offer her hand. "I'm fine here," she said. She was stout, plump bosomed, older than Caroline by probably ten or fifteen years. Her dusty-colored hair was frizzy and short and she wore no makeup but a poorly chosen shade of rose lipstick that had crept up into the wrinkles that fringed her lips. "I'll just get a catnap out here while you three talk." She smiled again, a pleasant, docile look on her face, and leaned back against the headrest of her seat, shutting her eyes.

"Suit yourself," Janie said.

Inside, Devon had flopped down on the couch and turned on the TV. His mother hovered behind him.

"What's with your friend out there?" Janie said. "Is she on drugs?"

"Please, Mother."

Janie ignored this. "I'll bring you a sandwich, Devon," she said.

"We ate on the way," Caroline told her, but Devon nodded, and so Janie went into the kitchen and took the sliced roast and a head of lettuce and the mayonnaise from the fridge.

Caroline sat at the table. "I would have been clearer on the phone, but I didn't want to ask about leaving him over voicemail."

"No. That would have been rude, you're right."

"Turn that off, Devon," Caroline said.

On the TV, a group of young people in summer clothes lay about on several velvet couches, all of them watching as a dark-haired boy in a tank top gesticulated and yelled.

"Watch whatever you want, honey," Janie said as she handed Devon the sandwich she'd made.

"Mother, I told him to turn it off."

Devon looked between Janie and his mother, put the TV on mute, and began to eat.

Janie crossed the room and sat down across from Caroline. "So, where're you going that you can't take your son?"

"It's a spiritual center in the Catskills," Caroline said, scowling at the television.

"Spiritual center," Janie said. "I don't know what that really means, Caroline. Is this place prayers and fasting, or white robes and Kool-Aid?"

Caroline made a sound at the back of her throat. "The church runs it."

"The place you've been going to since David died?"

"I'm not talking about David right now, Mother. The center is an opportunity for quiet and contemplation. That's why I'm going."

"And Devon will be here," Janie said.

"If you'll keep him."

Janie folded and unfolded her hands on the tabletop. They ached suddenly. Suddenly they felt arthritic. They looked to her there on the flat surface of her kitchen table like the hands of someone very old. Too old to have a teenager under her roof again. "He should have come to me when David died," she said though. "You're still in grief."

Caroline smiled a mean little grin Janie recognized from the adolescent years. "You're probably right about that," she said.

Janie looked away. Here it was again: that coil of fear, leaping up in her. She felt her face flush, her chest go hot with—what? Embarrassment at finally having to admit her own mistake? Regret at not having admitted it to her daughter sooner? "It doesn't end, Caroline," she said, her voice steady now, serious. "Believe me, I wish it did. Leaving your child so you can go looking for spiritual catharsis won't change that. You are a widow. Forever." She reached across the table and took Caroline's hands in her own. "And I'm sorry to have to say that to you. It hurts me to have to say that to you."

Caroline looked for a moment as if she might cry, her forehead puckering as it had when she was a little girl, but she pushed back in her chair. "I leave tomorrow," she said. "I need to be in New Haven tonight if I'm going to get a ride. I guess I'll figure out something else for Devon." She turned her face to him. "Come on, Dev. We're going."

"Caroline," Janie said, standing too. "This is ridiculous."

"Mother, I need to go."

Neither of them moved. The light of the front porch lamp Janie had left on for Ina beamed a cold yellow on the other side of the kitchen window.

"Okay," Janie said. "I'm happy to have Devon for as long as he wants to stay."

"I appreciate it," Caroline said. "I do." She crossed the room to kiss Devon, all rush and brusqueness now. "I love you," she said. "Be good for your grandmother." He didn't turn away from the television to look at her. And Caroline said nothing to Janie as she left. There was just the start of the car in the drive moments later, the sound of soft compression as its tires backed over the sand and gravel.

Janie put away the food and shut off the coffee pot. She closed the window she'd left open over the kitchen sink and looked out for the two bright spots of Caroline's headlights far off down the road, but the darkness was one wide, undisturbed pool beyond the house.

"Come on, Devon, honey," Janie said. "Let's get you settled."

This morning, when she leaves Devon making the coffee, Janie goes to the garage and wrestles with the bike to free its back tires of an old hose that has wound itself around the spokes, wheels the bike over the uneven sand of her yard, and climbs on at the end of the drive. She rides a few circles to warm up before pedaling out onto the open road. The road is sheened in frost and her tires slide here and there. She slows, though this makes the climb up the hill more difficult, her breathing heavier. The chill air is barbed with fine motes of ice that nettle the back of her throat.

At the top of the hill she drops her feet and drags them to stop the bike. When she reaches for her water bottle she realizes she's left it behind. She can see it sitting where she put it on the kitchen counter, full and cold and exactly what she needs right now. "The first sign of dementia," she says aloud.

There's a field between her and the slope of the dunes, and she rolls the bike along the footpath that cuts through it. In the spring the field was a frail green, the beach plums pretty purple dimples against the sand. Now, with the frosts, the cordgrass is the color of potatoes, the sand the color of a pumice stone. She drops the bike on its side at the crest of the dunes and sidesteps down to the beach. The water is steeled, the waves narrow and rigid, corrugated like the pleats in a suit of armor.

She has the beach to herself. She walks toward the water and thinks about stepping in, but it's too cold. The sand is a frozen crust. The pebbles at the wrack line knackle against each other with a chilled sound as the waves jostle them.

It is only when she turns away from the water again that she sees it: a body, lying just hidden behind a pile of driftwood. She strains to see. No, it is two bodies. Teenagers—a girl and a boy, she sees now. They are a knot of limb and clothing. The boy's hands have disappeared beneath the girl's white shirt, and her legs seemed joined to his hips. They've both kept their shoes on, though the boy's toes are dug into the sand. At their centers they might be one body. It's all very familiar, if far away.

Janie steps forward and then again back. She means to look away, but before she does the two separate and the boy sits up and sees her standing there, watching. "What the hell?" he says.

The girl stands too and tugs at her skirt, tucking her white shirt into the waistband. Her blond hair has come loose from its braid. "How long were you going to stare, lady?"

For a moment Janie thinks the girl, who is big, really, now that she's standing, and who has the hard, wide face of a bully, is going to stalk across the sand and come at her. Instead the girl puts her hands on her hips and laughs. "Lonely freak just likes watching," she says to the boy.

He hooks his arm around the girl's waist and pulls her toward him, leans his face into the dip of her shoulder, and puts his mouth to her neck. The girl closes her eyes and opens her mouth in the O of a false gasp. Her breath is a billow of milk in the watery air.

They both laugh as they part and climb away over the white-washed logs. "Bitch," the girl hollers over her shoulder at Janie as they start up the beach.

"What?" Janie calls to them. "What did you call me?"

They laugh again. They're sauntering. His arm is around her waist.

"I'm talking to you!" Janie yells. Heat has risen behind her ribs. She feels it climbing the ladder of them, working its way to her face.

"Fuck you," the girl calls.

"Hey!" Janie can hear the rapid knocking of her pulse in her ears. They are several yards ahead of her. This time they don't even turn their heads.

She takes off up the beach after them. Up the shore and over the driftwood. Running on the sand is like plowing through knee-deep water. She stumbles once and nearly falls. There are looks of dismay on the kids' faces when they hear her and look back. They seem younger now that she's closer, their faces pinked at the cheeks and still round like children's. Janie can remember Caroline at this age— all swagger and fire one moment, insecurity the next. The intensity of her need for mothering as transparent as if Janie could see through her skin, and her unwillingness to be mothered like a thick glass shell around her.

"She's following us!" The girl grabs the boy's hand and pulls him behind her up the dune.

They're too far ahead, but Janie chases them as far as the footpath. From her distance, she sees them throw her bike off the path and into the grass in their haste to get away and when she reaches it, she has to pull it from its awkward tangle, the grips of the handlebars sunk into the sand and the front wheel in a violent right angle to the ground. They are a hundred yards down the road by the time she is on the bike's seat again.

"You don't treat people like this!" Janie yells at their backs. "I'm talking to you. Don't run away from me!" She means to put her feet on the pedals and catch up to them—but then what? They're nearly adults and she caught them doing little more than being impetuous and rude. Hardly crimes. What can she possibly do? She lets the bike rest against her thigh, her chest heaving as if the wind has been knocked from her. Here it is again, grief, that silent, circling dog; that knife blade tossing in her belly. She stands until she catches her breath, and then she rides home.

At the house, she leaves her bike leaning against the garage wall and goes inside. Devon is drinking a cup of coffee and watching cartoons when she opens the door. She is still flustered, her face damp and hot, her heart still pounding with anger and with the exertion of the ride home. "You ready?" she says. "Let's go."

"Right now?" Devon turns his head. "It's only nine."

"Just get your bag."

She starts the car and waits for him. How long can it take to grab a book bag? It's thirty-five degrees out, but she is sweating. She runs the air conditioner, leaning forward into the steering wheel and the stream of cold air pouring from the air vents, letting it blow down her T-shirt against her chest.

"Ready," Devon says when he gets into the passenger seat.

She backs out and drives down the road out of the beach neighborhood, her eyes on the lanky stretches of grass along the roadsides, still looking for the kids, though she knows they're long since gone. Still, she can imagine spotting them, there in the field, the two of them hand in hand, and then steering her car right off the soft shoulder of the road toward them. She wouldn't hit them, of course, but she'd like to see a little fear on their faces, a little humility. That's what it was about them that infuriated her—their bravado. As if they refused consequence. As if they didn't have to listen to her or to anyone. As if nothing bad could ever happen to them.

"You're mad," Devon says, interrupting her thoughts.

"What?"

"You're angry. I can tell."

"Oh. Well, not at you," she says.

He withers into his baggy sweatshirt. "I'm sorry, Gram, about all this."

Janie shuts off the air conditioner. The windshield has beaded in condensation and she reaches forward to wipe it dry. "What's that? It's nothing. You're not the first one to fail the driver's test."

"I didn't choke the other times. I just pulled over." Devon looks out the window as he says this. "I just stopped."

Janie slows, pulls to the roadside and puts the car in park. "Why?"

"I don't know." He touches his index finger to the fogged passenger window, draws the outline of a puppy, then a skull and crossbones, then his own name in bubbled letters on the glass.

There's a breeze blowing up the beach to the road as the tide comes in, and the points of the tall grass tousle. A skiff of sand whisks up a few feet ahead of the car and swirls before dispersing, flying off.

"She's not coming back, Devon," Janie says. "Your mother called this morning. She's staying out there at that commune."

"Right."

She looks to him. "Are you angry? I'm certainly angry, mostly on your behalf, but for myself too. The way she's abandoning us." In the seat beside her his eyes are still fixed on the window. "Aren't you angry at her? You ought to be."

He frowns, slumps in his seat, and pulls his hands into the cuffs of his sweatshirt as if he is cold. "Yes and no. She's scared, I think. She's been scared for a long time."

"Scared of what though? I'd like to know."

He shrugs. "The normal stuff, I guess. Being alone." He turns to her. "Same as everyone."

Janie nods.

"After he died, you know, she was kind of a mess. She's not like you were after Grandpa. She needed my dad. She's not getting over it."

Janie sits back against her seat as if she's been walloped, a fist to the chest. "I needed your grandfather," she says. "I was a mess, too, in my way. Your mother must have known that."

Beside her, Devon looks uncomfortable, his hair hanging now over one side of his face again, his whole frame seemingly sunk in the folds of his sweatshirt.

They sit a while, neither saying anything, and then he reaches across the parking brake and takes her hand.

"You're cold," Janie says, and she flips on the heat so that it whirs and begins to blow on their feet and faces. The heat smells like dust. The inside of the car warms and Janie can smell the dank scent of her running shoes and the dog-hair-and-sweat teenage-boy smell of her grandson.

She opens the car door and gets out, rounds the hood and knocks on his window. "Hop out," she says through the glass, and he opens the door. "You're driving."

"Me?"

"Go on. Drive us. It's good practice."

She waits for him to climb over the brake into the driver's seat before taking the passenger side. He shifts the mirrors, moves the seat into the right position, tests the brake in anxious taps.

"Don't go too fast," she says as he eases it onto the road, but this turns out to be unnecessary, as he drives more like an old man than a boy, keeping the speedometer needle hovering just under the speed limit and slowing far in advance of every stop sign.

He drives all the way into town and they park and get out at the DMV. There's a long line of other people ahead of him, one slow-moving employee behind the counter. It is past ten thirty when he's finally called up for the drive. He nods at Janie as he and the examiner walk out, and she holds up her crossed fingers and mouths him a *Good luck*, and when he is gone she gets up and buys a cup of coffee in a Styrofoam cup from the vending machine.

"Waiting on a driver?" a plump redheaded woman in the next row of seats asks.

"My grandson."

"My daughter," the woman says. "I mean, what happened? Am I right? It's all so terrifying. They're driving now. Ack!" She pulls a crazed face and laughs. "Next she'll leave for college, and who knows what after that." She shakes her head. "I'll never sleep again."

Janie sips her coffee. "No," she says. "You don't ever stop worrying about them." She looks across the room, out the tinted plate glass window at the parking lot. Somewhere beyond here Devon is driving a stranger up 495, Manhattan-bound, nothing but the spread of the Atlantic Ocean at his back and the vaguely hazy expanse of the heavens over his head. Janie sees Devon gathering speed as he nears the freeway, pushing the gas pedal so that the car tires spin anxiously to catch up to the flow of traffic. She feels for him the fear of that moment when it all seems like chaos before the merge, the same vicarious fear she'd once felt for Caroline standing before a similar window at a DMV in Yonkers. That same churning sense of loss.

She remembers when Devon was born, how like his mother he looked. Holding him in the hospital, Janie had had the happy sensation that slipping back in time might be possible after all, back to when her own family was new and motherhood all ahead of her, one rosy possibility. She had held onto Devon then as if it could remake her.

She turns around now, her coffee in her hand, and the red-haired mother has already gone. Janie is alone. She crosses the room to the window. The frost on the parking lot is melting now, the pavement glittering only where it is shadowed. Soon enough the frost will stick, there will be snow, and Devon just licensed and out on the roads in it. She touches the glass and lets out a breath. The road near the DMV is flanked by grassy fields on both sides, little clapboard houses like her own perched off in the distance, precarious looking, dangerously teetering there at what from this angle seems to be the blue break between the earth and the sea, though that's just a trick of the eye, she knows, and not the truth at all.

She moves to walk away, but before she does she sees a formation of geese appear in the wide sky, a perfect V of birds, rushing and squawking, anxious to get out of town before the worst of the cold. They rise and fall in what seem random patterns, and now and then their line goes slack for a moment, reconfigures. It's a wonder, this. It's nothing out of the ordinary, of course; but still, it's a wonder. So many birds all flapping in unison, all flying toward some unseen home as if strung to one another by an invisible thread.

THE REMAINDER SALVAGED

WELLINGTON, WASHINGTON, 1910

Nils scoops away the snow carefully at first, with a trench shovel, then desperately, finally getting down on his knees and scraping with his hands at the thick stratum of ice when he believes he's found another body. Twice what he has uncovered has been not a body but someone's luggage—the olive-green duffel of a soldier the first time, and now, an hour or maybe two hours later (time has become hard to measure out here in the dark and the cold), a lady's brocade valise. He sits back on his heels and breathes the rimy air in ragged gasps. The fabric of the bag was so certainly a woman's overcoat an instant ago, the round shape of it her curved back. He kicks at the bag with the toe of his boot and pulls off his gloves.

It is March, but there is no sign of spring here. Snow is still falling, and Nils's fingers are stiff with the freezing temperature. He works at the buckles and the bag opens; when he shines the beam of his lantern inside he sees the cream-colored satin of a woman's underslip, a

pair of gold-rimmed reading glasses in a soft drawstring pouch, a silver compact with a clamshell design on its case and a mirror inside,
the glass clean and unbroken. He snaps shut the clasp on the compact
and drops it into his pants pocket, tosses the bag aside, and pulls on
his gloves again to keep digging.

Here and there flares poked into the snow fizz and hiss, their sul-
furic halos trembling and bright against the white drifts. In their odd,
low light the wreckage of the avalanche seems imagined, too strange
and awful to be real: trees snapped to raw splinters, and the whole,
wide swath of the mountainside cleared; metal sheets ripped from
the train cars' sides, the frames twisted and freed of their axels and
carriages, shards of window glass and the steel cages from the train's
internal light fixtures tossed out onto the snow. Near the tracks,
where the train had stopped to wait out the weather, the rotary plow
and both engines sit mangled and half buried, wheels upturned to the
sky. Two of the three passenger cars that were once hitched to one
another have been flung apart and lie on their sides, farther down the
mountainside—one only a hundred yards from the tracks, the other
picked up by the tide of snow and ice and swept a quarter mile downhill. Both look as if they've been exploded from the inside, the metal
roofs blown out by the force of the snow, their wood siding broken
and strewn. And everywhere precarious collisions of logs, evergreen
needles, and bits of gravel and dirt churned up by the slide.

There is also what the searchers have uncovered as they've dug: a
silver coffee carafe, and nearby the book someone on board had been
reading, its pages open and face down, the paper softening now. Nils
comes across suitcases and purses; checked blankets and white pillows, stamped "Property of Great Northern Railroad"; and several
shoes and boots somehow separated from their owners. As he walks,
he spots a single seat ejected from the train and detached from its
aisle mate in the accident, sitting upright between the shorn stumps
of two fir trees as if waiting for a passenger to amble up and sit down.

The snow underfoot here is wet and dense and grainy. It was compacted in the rush down the mountainside, and a rigid crust has formed beneath the inches of loose, new snow, making it hard for Nils to keep his footing. There is a strange, mineral scent in the air too—stirred up by the slide—something like the smell of a river. Nils realizes he will smell this odor again when the thaw begins in the spring and this year will think not of new life but of destruction.

He passes a new mound every few feet that looks the size and shape of a body. Sometimes he stops and digs. Sometimes he just plunges his shovel into the snow and hopes the blade won't strike anything solid; he sighs his relief when it goes in cleanly, pulls it free again, and keeps walking. There are drifts taller than men, wider than the train cars, and the task of unburying whatever lies beneath them seems impossible and useless. This is already the second day of searching—it took Nils a full day just to arrive, with the tracks blocked by the avalanche and the only way to get up the mountain by foot. No one else will be found alive.

He recalls his mother telling him about the midwestern blizzards of her childhood. Cows out to pasture suffocated when their own breath froze in their nostrils. Farmers caught in a storm and lulled to their deaths by the monotony of white and the chill of hypothermia. He imagines children curled like rabbits in burrows beneath each mound of snow here, their eyelashes coated in tiny grains of ice, their lips sealed, their skin marbled blue.

"Here!" a man's voice yells from several feet down the mountainside. "Here! Here!"

Nils lunges forward against the snow, breaking the ice shelled just below its surface. He feels as if he's running through deep water; every step requires double the usual exertion. His boot tops fill and the snow melts with the warmth of his legs and soaks through the canvas of his pants, the wool of his long underwear. He sweeps the beam of his lantern across the white drifts, the kerosene inside sloshing, and catches the shadowed columns of evergreen trunks, the shadowed bodies of other men straining to run. The men at his back holler to one another as they plod forward; one man in front of him carries an axe and a shovel, their blades clanging together as he moves.

"Where are you?" Nils yells in the direction of the voice. His exhalation is a bright cloud in the sphere of his lantern's light. Snow whirls and kaleidoscopes as it passes through that round of light.

"Down here!" calls a man up ahead, and the others join him. They've been in a small meadow, Nils sees now for the first time; the railroad track is at the top of a short rise above them, and the voice hollering for help is thirty feet below, at least, down a steep incline.

He uses his shovel to steady himself. Some of the men use pick-axes they've brought, and there is the rhythmic pitch-and-stick sound of their blades cutting into the snow and holding, then dislodging as they make their way down the grade. The snow glints and shimmers inside the rails of light extending from their lamps. Overhead, most of the snow clouds have cleared, but there is no visible moon, and it is as if a lid has been screwed onto the jar of the world. The circle of sky is a hard, polished black, punctured only by the tiny, pale holes of stars.

By the time Nils reaches them, the others have already uncovered the body of a man and are lashing it to a toboggan with rope. Nils looks on and feels nothing, and then is guilty for this nothing.

The man's skin is gray with the cold. They've wrapped his body in a checkered wool blanket, his face and feet sticking out at the ends of the sled. He's still wearing dress boots and hand-knit socks. Someone takes off his own hat and puts it on the dead man's bare head. The gesture seems ridiculous out here, an unnecessary show of warmth that can't possibly matter. The man's face is frozen in a grimace. His eyes are shut.

"Jesus," someone from the back of the crowd says. "They're all just icicles."

Two men take hold of the toboggan's ropes and start up the mountainside to the tracks. They'll take the body into the station town to be counted, and once the rails are cleared, onto the train, which will take it west, over the pass, to the morgue in Everett.

The others stand for a moment. They pull flasks from their coat pockets and take off their gloves to slap their hands against their thighs, warming their fingers again before slipping gloves back on. Someone has brought a pail of sandwiches and passes it around. Nils takes one and eats quickly without tasting what's between the bread. He crumples the waxed paper the sandwich was wrapped in and stuffs it into the top of his boot.

"It's two a.m.," the man next to him says, and so they pick up their shovels and start up the incline again, hiking with high steps, casting the beams of their lanterns up the rise, toward the blue-black stand of evergreens at the top of the ridge, and back and forth across the angle of the mountainside, looking impossibly for anything salvageable.

.●.

He is in her bed. Her sheets smell like summer to him. When he says this, she tells him she cut lavender from the garden in August and dried it for sachets to keep in the linen cupboard.

It's October, two years earlier, and the house is chilled, though it is late afternoon and there is still sun behind the thin drape at the window, lighting the collection of potted plants she keeps on a side table beneath the sill—spider plants and ferns, a white-blossomed amaryllis on a slim stalk, and a geranium with petals colored an oxidized red. On the floor sits a pot overcrowded with a spiny bed of hen and chicks. "I think you'd bring the whole yard inside if you could," he says.

"Not the weeds. Not the bugs. I can honestly say I don't miss a single aphid or wasp all winter." She lays her head on the pillow beside his.

Eva grew up in California and winter here makes her homesick. "I remember the air at home smelling like persimmons. But maybe I'm misremembering. My memory is an optimist. In my memory of this moment you'll be younger and I'll be prettier."

"I've never seen a persimmon," he says.

"How can that be true?"

"Are they like apples? Because I've had my share of apples and yours too, probably."

"Here I thought you were worldly. What else have you missed?"

Eva is thirty-four—eleven years his junior—and plain, really. She wears her dark hair cut as short as a man's, the bare stretch of her neck exposed even when she's fully clothed. She was widowed suddenly last spring, after only nine months of marriage, when her husband's appendix burst. He'd been the librarian in town, a fisherman on the weekends. He left her a very small savings, a wide bookcase of books, and this house—a one-bedroom bungalow a mile out of Wenatchee, with a little outhouse in back and a porch overlooking the river and mountains.

"What will you do in the winter here, alone?" Nils asks.

"I'll be fine. There's the stove, and I'll buy wood."

"You'll have to walk the mile in the snow alone."

"I've done it before. It doesn't bother me."

"What does bother you?"

"You pestering." She chucks him on the chin and he pulls her toward him, kisses the flat of her chest.

"Don't worry," she says. "You love to worry." Her body is warm against his. She lies still long enough that he wonders if she has fallen asleep, but then she sits up.

"Look away," she says, and she reaches for her robe at the foot of the bed.

"I won't. That's ridiculous."

"Fine. Have it your way." She is thick across her hips and has a round, white belly into which the rose of her navel disappears when she bends to pull on her socks. Her breasts swing forward matronly.

She's never had a child. Now that she's alone, she's told him, she's glad of this.

"I do worry about you," he says. He wants her to meet his eyes, but she doesn't. "I want to keep worrying about you."

"Don't," she says. Then turning away: "Persimmons look like pale tomatoes. Orange, not red. But they taste like apples, you were right. Nothing special, really." She pulls a sweater over her head, swifts her fingers through her short hair. "You haven't missed anything."

At five the sky flushes pink along the white and jagged eastern crests of the Cascades and a man dressed in a parka and holding a record book appears at the top of the ravine to call out that it's time for a shift change. He's brought with him a new crew of men—some of them company men, like Nils, dressed in winter coats with Great Northern patches on the breasts, and some members of volunteer search crews from Wenatchee and Everett and the other surrounding towns. They start down the ravine as Nils and the others who have been out all night tromp up.

The man in the parka gives them a verbal report of the search, taking a small pad of paper from inside his coat to read off the numbers. Ten bodies recovered alive, eight of those injured, all ten recovered in the first hour after the wreck. Since then, thirty bodies recovered deceased. Various luggage and personal effects will remain on the mountain until the missing persons search has concluded. There are fifty-two bodies still missing, he tells them. And the third train car still hasn't been found. "We'll keep at it." His voice turns falsely bright. "Thank you all for your efforts," he says, releasing them. "Go get warmed up and rested."

They make their way along the railroad grade. Usually the tracks would have been plowed already, but there were smaller avalanches to the east and west that have blocked the pass from both sides. In some spots the tracks are buried beneath twenty-foot drifts. The temperature is still frigid, and Nils's fingers and feet, knees and hips have long since numbed. He seems to be moving forward without willing it and has a sensation of dislocation from his own body that makes him question for a moment if he is not maybe among the dead.

"You look dazed, Riis," the man walking beside him says and slaps Nils on the back. The man's familiarity startles him. He's seen him at the rail yard in Wenatchee—he's a mechanic, maybe, but Nils can't think of his name. He offers his flask, but Nils declines.

"I'm fine. Just a long day."

"Long night, you mean."

"That's right. That's what I meant."

"You need a hot plate and a warm bed." The man takes a swig from the flask himself and Nils can smell the alcohol like a tremor of heat on the cold air.

The town is small, and they arrive at the west end, the railroad tracks suddenly opening onto a wide valley in the crotch of two ridgelines. Slaggy cliffs rise up on either side of the town, and a narrow creek with water so emerald green it looks like flowing paint runs parallel to the railway on the other side of the one paved street. It's a company town, run by the railroad, with one grocery, one hotel, a post office in the railroad station, a single building to stand as both schoolhouse and church, and a few saltbox houses lining the few dirt roads off of Main Street. The avalanche swept into the far end of town, plowing through a set of barracks set up to house railroad crews. Five men asleep inside at the time of the slide were killed.

With the barracks gone, search teams have taken over the hotel: the injured being tended to in first-floor rooms, and the crews sharing beds upstairs. When they arrive, Nils and the other men stand on the front porch stomping snow from their boots and lining their tools along the wall before entering the dark lobby.

There's a crowd filling the dining room already, and the noise of conversation and the clatter of dishes being passed seem chaotic and louder than usual after so many hours in the cottony quiet of the snow. Nils finds one of the few free seats in the room, next to a man still wearing his gaiters and scarf. "Pardon me," he says. The space is tight, the chairs pushed close to one another along the table's long sides, and the other man is big, his elbow on the table where Nils means to set his plate, his knees sprawled wide under the table so that Nils has to ask him again to make room when he pulls out his chair to sit.

"You gentlemen have left me no place to eat." A tall woman still dressed for the outdoors stands near the table with a bowl of stew and a mug of beer in her hands. Melted snow has beaded on the wool of her coat and large leather gloves gape from her pockets where she has stuffed them.

A man across the table from Nils looks up. "You can have my seat, Sister." He hunkers over his bowl and shovels the last spoonfuls of stew into his mouth in rapid succession, then pushes back. "I'm done anyway."

She walks the long way around the table and the man holds the seat, nodding at her as he lifts his coat from the chair and leaves.

When she takes off her own coat, she reveals a man's sweater, the brown wool loose on her narrow frame and the cuffs rolled. Her face is ruddied with the night's work in the cold air, her hair straying in gray-blond wisps from the braid that circles her head. Around her neck is a wooden cross on a leather cord.

"Morning," she says, brightly greeting the table of men, and then she bows her head and says a silent grace before taking up her spoon.

"What do you do when you're alone?" Eva asks.

"What do you mean, what do I do? I eat and sleep and read and work—what everyone does."

"No. I mean, do you ever get tired of yourself? Do you ever say anything? Just to keep yourself company. I do, sometimes. Not because I mind being alone, but because it just seems so quiet."

"I never feel obligated to talk."

"I've noticed. It's one of your faults."

He laughs at this.

They sit at the table in her small front room, eating the doughnuts Nils has brought from the bakery downtown.

In his mind, he places this moment earlier than the memory from the bedroom. This is September, not long after they met. He recalls with certainty the doughnuts, the dark and buttery perfume of coffee in the room. Through the cracked bedroom door he can see just the foot of the bed, the yellow-and-blue quilt hanging lopsided as if she never pulled up the blankets after waking.

Most of the specifics of the morning are frustratingly foggy though—what she is wearing, what she does with her hands when she speaks—and trying to force his memory to clarify is like trying to draw an object and then looking down at the paper to find the image vaguely familiar but also lacking the shadows or peculiarities that make the real thing real. And so Nils fills in the gaps with what is likely: Her shirt is blue, big—probably one of her husband's. Her hair is uncombed, wild still from having slept on it, and she touches it again and again, trying to smooth it down as they talk. A novel lies facedown on the tabletop, still opened to the page she was reading when he appeared at her front door. He wasn't invited, but she doesn't seem surprised to have him across the table from her now, her face as placid and content as it has been each time he's seen her.

"I wouldn't know what to say to myself," he tells her. "What do you say when you're in here yakking to your shadow?"

She runs her thumb along the rim of her plate, collecting the sugar crystals that have fallen from the doughnut, then touches her thumb to her tongue. "Me and I, we talk about the weather. The cost of flour. Sometimes I complain about men. We have a wonderful sense of humor." She grins at this. "No, actually, I mostly just sing."

"I bet you do whole routines. Where are your tap shoes?"

"I *can* tap," she says. "You'd be surprised. Come over for dinner sometime and I'll do a little soft-shoe for you while I cook."

"I'd like to hear you sing now."

"What would I sing? You'll just laugh."

"I won't. Sing something I'd know. Sing 'Oh! Susanna.' Everyone knows that."

"No, I've never liked that one. It's too sad. I'll do 'Red River Valley.'" And then she sings a few lines, keeping the rhythm against the table, waving him on to join in. Her voice is high and round and clear.

After this he notices her singing all the time—as she makes coffee in the mornings, as she leans over the washbasin to rinse her face at night. Once he catches her singing as she works in the yard, her figure bent toward the ground, a pail of pulled weeds at her knee.

"Come on," she says. "Don't leave me out here on my own. Join in."

His voice is a buzz in his throat. He hasn't sung in ages.

She drops off a few beats before him, letting him hum the last notes of the song alone, then claps when he's finished. "Bravo! Well done!"

"I never sing," he says.

"I can tell." She picks up her novel, and he sips his coffee, and they sit at the table together in quiet.

.•.

He watches the sister as she eats. She is ravenous. She gets up to re-fill her stew bowl and returns also with another hunk of bread in her hand, a slice of apple pie on a plate balanced on top of the bowl. A man down the table offers her the last glass of beer in the pitcher, and Nils is surprised when she accepts. The men pass the pitcher down, hand to hand, and she takes it and fills her glass quickly so that a thick white froth forms at the top. She licks this, then drinks in gulps. He has never seen a woman eat so much and so hungrily. The other men seem to find it just as startling, as they pause in the midst of their conversations to look at her.

"You worked up quite an appetite," Nils says.

"Didn't you?"

"Of course." He refills the coffee cup in front of him from a carafe on the center of the table. "I've just rarely seen a woman enjoy her food so fully. That's all."

"Maybe you've known only joyless women."

"I'll give you that," Nils says. "You're mostly right about that." He nods. "You're part of the search?"

"I'm a trained nurse. Though it turns out nurses outnumber patients up here three to one. They're stumbling all over each other trying to be useful." It's true: Nils has noticed several young women in nurses' uniforms darting in and out of the lower hallways and lobby. "It's wonderful to see so much compassion when there is a tragedy," she says. "But too many ladles in the pot ruins the soup, if you see what I mean."

She forks the last bite of pie into her mouth, stacks her plate and bowl, and sits back. "That was good," she says. "The cold did make me hungry."

"You'll acclimate. And you can always stay in if it's too much—the cold. There are plenty of us out there."

"I'm here to help. I volunteered. And, as I said, another nurse is the last person needed, so I'll go out again, cold or not, where I might be at least a little useful."

"What order?" Nils asks.

"Sisters of the Holy Names. You're Catholic?"

"My mother was."

The sister nods. "It's not for everyone."

"I'm surprised you'd say that."

"If anyone could have turned your mind, it would have been your mother, would it not?" Her face softens when she smiles. "But I'll pray for you if you like." She pushes back in her chair and collects her dishes.

"No, that's fine. Thank you."

She leaves, and in a moment Nils gets up too and goes to the desk in the lobby to inquire about a bed. The men are taking shifts, and when he gets to his room upstairs, he finds the last man has left the bed unmade, a pair of damp socks hung over the foot rail. The sheets smell like kerosene. He lifts his hands to his nose and finds that he smells kerosene on his fingers too. Everything smells like kerosene and wet wool and that gray, elemental scent of the snow. He's losing his mind up here. He shakes his head at himself, tucks under the quilt, and is quickly asleep.

⬤

Some dreams come in scenes: he is a character of his own mind and watches himself. Here he's walking around the orchards just beyond his childhood home. Or here, he's at work in the rail yard office, bent over a record book; it's any routine day. Sometimes he's back in her bed, her body just a warmth beside him. In another dream, it's his childhood bedroom: he is sick and his mother is in the chair beside his bed knitting, the quiet tick-tick-tick of her needles registering in the deep nautilus of his ear as he dreams, so that when he wakes he actually sits up and looks for his mother in the room with him. He is both inside the dream and very definitely outside it, sleep separating him from himself like an orange peeled of its skin.

But in many dreams there is no double, no order. Sometimes there is just chaos, the wreckage of fuller memories washing up against the shore of his mind. The heavy metal scoop of his trench shovel slicing again and again into the snow with a metered, pitching sound. A white teacup whose reassuring weight he can feel in the palm of his hand, though there is no hand, no palm, no him. That bucket of her weeds. A windowsill piled in an inch of snow. The disembodied smell of his childhood house—so strong!—like soil and clean linens and fresh ashes in the fireplace—but no accompanying vision of the house. In one dream, the pincushion on her night table, stuffed with hair pulled from her dead husband's brush.

And today: twenty flares, lit and hissing like a nest of snakes, burning up the dark landscape of the dream, burning red against the ceiling of his head, burning up the backs of his eyes with their red incandescence.

．●．

The sister is at the front desk when he returns to the lobby at two o'clock. He's slept only five hours, the exertion of the search leaving him strangely too tired to sleep well.

"Hello again," she says. She has combed and rebraided her hair, pinned it up wreathlike around her head.

"Can't sleep either?"

"We keep a routine of prayer at home. The day begins at five a.m."

"Well, it's not exactly morning, but I'm looking for coffee, if you'd like some."

"I would, thank you. I can't seem to get warm."

"Sit by the fire. I'll bring you something."

Nils fills two mugs from a carafe in the dining room and brings them to the lobby, where the sister perches on the stone ledge of the fireplace hearth, her back to the fire. She thanks him and takes the cup, holding it between both hands and closing her eyes for a moment before taking the first sip. "Thank you," she says again.

"I found a photograph while I was out there last night," she says. "It was of a man with a heavy mustache, and beside him a little boy holding a toy drum." She smiles. "He must have been carrying it in his pocket."

"Sometimes you can almost see their lives from their things," Nils agrees. He remembers the mirror and nearly takes it from his pocket to show to her, but doesn't.

The sister raises her cup to her mouth and drinks. Steam is still rising from the coffee, and she looks contented, the way she pauses after swallowing. "I've ridden this train route," she says. "Have you?"

Nils shakes his head.

"You feel every jostle of the tracks. It's unsettling."

"I haven't traveled much."

"You should. Just the going changes you." She looks at him. "That sounds romantic, but I believe it. You are changed."

"We're changed even staying as still as possible."

"Yes. Stillness is important. That's true, but it's not exactly what I mean."

"That's not what I mean either."

"Tell me what you do mean then, Mr. Riis, if I'm getting it wrong." She sets her coffee cup down on the hearth and looks at him. Her expression is so earnest for a woman who has known him only a few hours.

"Sister, I'm not young. Neither are you, if you don't take offense to me saying that. And in my experience, most of life just happens to us. It's not as if you have to go out looking for it."

"You sound grizzled. I think your mother would have told you to remember providence."

"Providence. Of course." Nils puts down his cup and buttons his coat, fishes his gloves from his pockets and pulls them on too.

"I can see I've upset you," she says.

"No, but we've come to the fork in our agreement."

"You are upset."

"Sister, I've finished my coffee. Any more standing around next to the fire would look like idleness. You'll have to excuse me now."

Outside the temperature has risen slightly and the light is thin and tinny, the sky over the mountaintops the color of water in a glass pitcher. Icicles hanging like stalactites from the edge of the porch roof drip hollows into the mound of snow below. Nils stands on the porch taking deep breaths, then collects a shovel and lantern from the line of them leaning against the porch wall and, feeling steady again, starts back toward the wreck.

Spring now—March maybe, or early April, and the weather not bad for walking. He's still far from her house when he hears the dead thuds of the axe. It's a heavy violent sound, and he can't place it exactly, though it sets his heart racing, turns his stomach over. "Eva?" he calls.

The sound continues. He is running now, and in a moment he can see her. She swings the axe again and again at the tree, cracking heavy blows into its trunk, her body bending with the weight and motion of her swings. The bare branches above her quiver.

"What are you doing?" he hollers, picking up his stride. He cups his hands to his mouth and yells again. But she doesn't hear him. Her face is pinked with fury and she pulls back again, swings a loose, wobbly arc at the tree. The triangular head of the axe embeds itself again and she yanks to wrest it free.

"Whoa!" Nils calls as he jogs into the yard. "What are you doing?" He reaches for the axe when she swings back again and the force of her motion nearly knocks him to the ground.

"Let it go," she says. "I've got it done already." He steps back and she lunges with the next swing so that the noise of the axe in the wood resounds around them. In two more blows she's cut through. There's a sound like bone breaking, the fraught pause as the tree sways then crashes. Its branches snap and splinter as the tree hits the dirt. It's a crabapple, and there are berries everywhere softening, leaving behind their rust-colored pits in the dirt.

"I've hated this tree since I married him," she says. She swipes the back of her wrist across her face. Her cotton housedress is stained with a deep V of sweat. "And I'm sick of its mess. The crabapples attract the birds." She drops the axe and stands catching her breath. "And then the birds get into my garden."

"You could have waited for me. I would have done it."

"I couldn't look at it anymore."

She's barefoot, he sees now. The last of the winter's snow has just melted and the earth is soft and wet, the pads of her feet caked in mud. She wears a dishcloth around her waist as she does when she's cooking.

"What were you doing before I got here?" Nils looks toward the house. The front door is open.

"What does it look like I was doing?" Her face is still flushed, and she flashes him a look.

"This is crazy." He reaches to put his arms around her, but she walks away from his embrace and back toward the house.

"If you want to do something for me, cut that into firewood," she says over her shoulder. "Or don't. It doesn't matter. I just wanted that tree gone." She disappears into the house and the door slams at her back.

Nils picks up the axe and begins cutting away the branches, piling them to burn. It takes him all afternoon to chop and stack the wood, and by the time he's finished and knocks on her door, she is herself again, her dress changed, her face washed, a fire going in the cook stove and a pot of potatoes boiling furiously on the stovetop for dinner.

.●.

"What did he look like?"

"I hardly think of him anymore. He seems like someone else's husband, not mine. Or I was someone else then, maybe."

"I'm trying to see your life then. What did he look like?"

The room is sunk in the blue of midnight. There's ice on the window glass, and the thin strains of moonlight coming through it are wobbled and distorted. He shifts to reach the water she left on the bedside table and pulls long sips from the cup. She brings water to bed every night; there is a white ring on the table's surface.

"Not like you. Is that helpful?"

He gets up, walks across the room. There's a mirror the shape of a large egg mounted to the wall and he stands before it. In his reflection, he can see his breath coming from the dark hole of his mouth in gray bursts. "Then I guess this: full head of hair, and body wide as a tractor. Or else he had red hair. Soft gut. Piggish eyes." He turns around to face her. "Which is it?"

He can't see her, but he hears her sigh. "You're either laughing, or I'm wearing you down," he says.

"It's both," she says. "Come back."

He gets in bed and she puts her hand on his face so he knows she's looking at him. "Don't ask me again."

"We'll see."

She falls asleep curled into him beneath the weight of the blankets, her knees in his stomach, her nighttime breath a little sour on his face.

. ·.
. ●.

But before it all, there is this:

She is sitting at a back table eating a plate of roast and mashed potatoes, wearing a yellow blouse, a book open on the table in front of her.

He is in his usual spot.

The waiter brings him his sandwich, his coffee. He eats dinner here after work most nights before going home. He has a newspaper rolled in his bag to read over eating but doesn't reach for it. Instead, he catches her turning her pages, stirring the potatoes on her plate.

He sees her close the book and sit for a long minute with her hand on top of its cover and her eyes fixed in thought, as if the story is still unspooling in her head.

He argues with himself, then just gets up and carries his plate to her table. He's never so forward, he tells her—she'll have to forgive him—but he'd like to sit down.

"Go ahead," she says. And he does.

It has taken only this small rise in temperature to start a thaw, and the mountain groans and creaks as it warms. Snow sloughs from the boughs of the evergreens in wet slumps. The branches still under mounds snap and sigh with the burden. Far off, at a higher elevation and across the valley, there is the muffled thunder of the snow tumbling down the mountainside: another slide. Nils finds himself digging faster. The sun slips from behind a raft of clouds, flares one last time as the clouds part, then falls behind the mountains, bleeding a spill of bright yellow light, like an egg yolk broken across the lower reaches of the sky and gilding the mountains' edge and the boat-bottom undersides of the clouds.

Nils stops and fishes a match from the box in his pocket, strikes it until it sparks, and lights his lantern.

The search has focused now on finding the third train car. He hears voices farther down the incline and starts moving toward them, his heels gouging deep holes in the snow as he descends.

It's a long way down, and at the bottom the ground levels out again. Through the blue stalks of tree trunks the beams of other lanterns flicker and shine.

"You again," the sister says. "I wondered if I'd see you." She stops working to lean on her shovel, wipes the back of her glove across her wet nose.

"Any luck?"

She shakes her head. "You?"

"No. We're at the end of it. They'll call us in soon and end the search until spring. Whatever is still under snow will have to stay that way until then."

"I don't like the idea of that."

"Of leaving it unfinished? Some of these searches turn up nothing, ever. This one's been productive, really." Nils uses his teeth to pull his gloves from his stiff fingers, then cups his hands around his mouth and blows onto the blanched skin. There's that kerosene smell again in his nose; it's begun to make him sick. He takes a deep breath to quell the twinge in his stomach. He's lost feeling in his fingertips already, and his knuckles ache when he bends and straightens his fingers to get the blood moving again.

"No, of bodies staying lost. I don't want to abandon them here."

"I don't quite see the difference. They're buried here or someplace else. Someone somewhere will miss them, whether we find the bodies now or not."

"Why are you here then? If it doesn't matter?" She looks angry for a moment, and Nils nearly apologizes, but he's too tired to start in with her again.

"I work for the railroad," he says. "I do what they tell me to do. But I didn't say it doesn't matter."

The sister sniffs at this answer. "Well, you do as you wish, Mr. Riis, but I'm going to keep moving."

"Don't get proud and go wandering off. I never said I was quitting." He looks toward the other lights, still a fair distance away. "If you want to follow me, it's probably better we stay a pair. The temperature's going to drop again, and it's already dark."

"I'm sure I'm fine."

"I'm telling you not to go alone." He works to stuff his dull fingers back into the gloves. "Please. Just follow me."

As he works his way horizontally down the side of another slope, he hears her a few paces behind, her breath coming hard. She doesn't speak, though, and he doesn't turn to look at her.

May—over a year ago now, unbelievably. When she tells him, she's already sold the house. "This has never really been my home," she says, and when he presses, when he says he'll go with her and they'll make a new home together somewhere else if she likes, she says only no.

"I have money saved," he says. "I've been saving all these years for something without knowing what." But, no, she tells him. No. She's made up her mind.

He lies beside her on her bed. The bedroom window is open. Outside, the goldfinches and robins in her garden chirrup and flit, singing at one another, squabbling over scraps and seeds. The river down the hill is overfull with runoff from the mountains. It moves with a sound like boiling water. It turns up all sorts of flotsam onto its banks, spits out a bubbly brown froth that rides on top of its current.

He gets up and stands looking at her. "Are you afraid of me?" he asks.

"No," she says.

He picks up her hairbrush with the silver handle and throws it at the mirror. The mirror breaks. The glass scatters in shards across the wood slats of the bedroom floor.

"You knew all along you'd leave," he says.

"I didn't know. I stayed longer than I might have if I hadn't met you."

"Are you in trouble? Are you not telling me everything?"

"There's no child."

"How can I trust you?"

"I'm not a liar." She meets his eyes. "Sometimes there's no reason. I need to leave this place, and that's all. You can't understand that?" She is crying now, but quietly. She gets up from the bed and kneels on the floor, sweeping the bits of glass into her palm.

"You're running away from a dead man, is what I think."

"Stop it," she says, her voice even. "You've never been cruel. Why are you doing this now?"

"It's not meanness. It's fact. I should have seen it earlier."

"Fine, then." She raises her face to him. "You need a reason? You're too much. You and this place. You need too much."

"You're all excuses."

"Stop it now. I won't argue with you. I'm tired." She sits back on her heels. "It's decided. And you should go now."

He gets his clothes and begins pulling them on. He tries to keep his balance, but stumbles putting his leg into his pants, steps back and feels needles of broken glass embedding themselves in his bare foot. He curses under his breath.

"I'm sorry it's all turned out so badly," she says. "I am."

"You're making your choices."

His foot is bleeding; he pulls his socks and shoes on anyway. He leaves the buttons of his shirt undone.

When he goes, he slams the front door hard enough that the windows rattle at his back.

.ᐧ
ᐧ●.

I'm asking you to reconsider. I want you to say something. I want you to stay. He writes this on a piece of paper, slides it under her door, and walks back to town.

.ᐧ
ᐧ●.

He allows himself to walk past the house once, after she is gone. The stump of the crabapple is there, but the new owners till over the garden. They put up a chicken coop where she planted strawberries and squash. The white and red chickens stalk around their fenced square scratching at the dirt, bobbing their heads at each other.

As he stands watching, two of the birds take up a fight. They circle and charge each other. They flap their wings and kick sprays of dust that rise from the ground then shower back down on their heads. In only a moment the scuffle is over, the dispute—whatever it was—settled, and the two amble away from each other. The other chickens, who paused to watch the fight, resume pecking at the ground as if nothing has happened, though their patch of yard is littered with shed feathers.

For the rest of the day he thinks of how she would hate the ugly coop, hate the chickens and all their mess.

He is unused to sleeping alone then. He stares at the wall of his bedroom until the square of light from the window brightens, brightens, and finally goes white with morning. He gets up and his thoughts float like fluffs of cotton through his mind. He feels like a sleepwalker, lurching through the day. He goes to work in the railway offices, comes home. There is summer and then fall again. A fine crust of first frost on the bedroom window glass and the color of morning pale blue now, or gray. Snow then. A new year. Winter. The river calcifies with ice. A flock of starlings roosts on the roofline of the building across the street—so many dark bodies all in a line. They rise all at once and circle overhead, once, twice—a knot tying and untying itself in the sky—before they are gone. He taps the window with his forefinger and beads of condensation slide down the glass. Everything comes at him as if he is lodged far beneath the surface of his own perception. His body is layers of bundling, and somewhere beneath skin and muscle, bone and gristle, he is half awake and listening for what?

. .
. ●.

It is nearly seven o'clock—long past dark—when the third train car is found a quarter mile down the mountain and far to the west of where searchers expected it might be. There is hollering, cheering and clapping, and Nils and the sister raise their heads and move toward the noise. Far off, the lights of many lanterns throw a faint halo around the site where the other men are digging out the car.

The sky is clouded over again. The clouds are heavy and big bellied, full of more snow and looking less like tufts than like something wet and solid. *Like soggy newspaper*, Nils thinks. *Or sacks of wet feathers*. He says this to the sister, and she makes a sound that is something between a chirp of laughter and a snort.

"I have an awful memory of plucking the ducks my father raised one winter, so we could all feast on Christmas Day," she says.

"We kept geese and chickens. I remember it being awful."

"My mother saved all the feathers to stuff bedding and pillows. But she wanted to wash them first, to get rid of the dust and mites. There were wet feathers stuck everyplace. My hair, my sister's arms, all over the dirt. We had to throw them out. There was no good way to dry them."

"She didn't know what she was doing," Nils says.

"No. She'd been raised in the city. But my father let her do it. He didn't tell her it wouldn't work. It was better she find out by experience, or she'd never have let it go. She'd have gone on worrying about mites in the beds till kingdom come if he'd told her she wasn't to wash the feathers."

"And you didn't have Christmas ducks the next year?"

"No, we did. But Mother and Father did the work themselves. We children got in the way, they said. And I don't know what happened to the feathers, but they weren't washed, I know that."

"Do you miss them? Your family?"

"My parents died years ago."

"But when you first left."

"Of course. Isn't that true for you too? Don't you miss your mother since she died? Your dad? Sometimes I get nostalgic and even miss the girl I was when I was young. As if she was someone not me. That's silly, yes?" She pauses in her walking and Nils stops too to wait for her to catch her breath.

"Not silly," Nils says. "I've had a similar thought. I've come across shed snakeskins before and have thought what a thing it would be to do that—get outside your old skin as easy as taking off a jacket."

"We're saying different things again, I think. I'm talking about nostalgia, not regret. But maybe that's the gift of my life: my devotion keeps me in the present. For that I'm still grateful, even all these years later."

She shifts her weight and clasps her gloved hands together. Nils pulls his hat down over his ears.

"I'm ready," she says, and starts ahead of him. "It's getting cold standing here, and I'm talking too much for you again, I can see by your silence."

"I was rude earlier."

"You were," she says over her shoulder. "But it's fine. We've made up now. Let's go."

Nils lifts the lantern and follows her.

They don't get far before the sister stops him again. "Have I been out here too long, or am I seeing something there?"

Nils treads through the snow toward the spot she's pointing out. The slide seems to have come to a stop down here, and there are more trees still standing. They are not far now from the others. The sounds of the men shoveling out the inside of the train car have grown louder, and just ahead there is debris from the car still on top of the snow— what looks to be a piece of siding, a strip of metal from the car's undercarriage, bent and curled up at an odd angle.

Nils stops near a fir tree and tilts his lantern so that it illumines the sunken round of shadow beneath the tree. He gets down on his knees and moves snow aside with his hands.

"What is it?" the sister calls. "Is it anything?"

Nils hesitates. "It's a dog," he says.

They clear the snow away from the animal's body. The dog is male. His white fur is matted with ice, his legs folded close to his abdomen in awkward, unnatural angles. The pink pads of his feet have gone gray-blue, and his nose is spongy, his eyes open and their stare waxy. When Nils lifts the dog's body a dark blot of blood is revealed in the snow beneath him; the dog's right ear is gone, sheared off completely, and that side of his face is crusted brown with frozen blood.

"Oh, no," the sister says. She puts her hand over her mouth as if she may be sick.

"Someone's pet," Nils says. He sets the body back down and begins to cover it with snow.

"What're you doing?"

"They're not going to haul a dog out. There's enough to do with human casualties."

"Don't do it yet," the sister says. "Please." She's crying quietly, and Nils looks away from her. "I'm going to pray."

Nils sits back on his heels and waits as she bows her head. She keeps her voice low, her words materializing as a continuous strand of chilled exhalation. When she finishes, she leans over and touches the dog's face with her own, puts her hands on its flank, her forehead to its ribs.

"I'm starting to feel like everything I've ever lost is under here," she says. "Like if we looked long enough we'd find the brooch my grandmother gave me when I turned seventeen, and those ducks, and my parents. Maybe they're all here." She turns to Nils. "When I was young, a neighbor woman lost a baby in the middle of a very long winter and then drowned herself when the pond between our farms thawed in the spring."

"My mother was sick in bed several days before she died," Nils says. "Her priest came at the end to perform the last rites, and when she went, he told me she was needed more above than here on earth. 'She's been called by her maker to join Him in heaven. Take solace in knowing that her Redeemer needs her now more than you do.' I remember he said that."

"That's a horrible thing to say to someone in grief. He should have known better."

Nils smiles. "I can't say I appreciated it much."

"They try to be reassuring. I'm sure that's what he meant to do. But he should have thought better of it and said something else."

"It wouldn't have made any difference. I wanted him to say nothing. I wanted every noise to stop without her there to hear it." He pushes back and stands. "But that kind of thinking is as useless as his consolation."

"She wouldn't want you to stop your life."

"She wouldn't have, but that hardly matters. What you'd will doesn't matter. There's no stopping. And that's all. I didn't see that then, but now I do."

Nils buries the dog, digging first beneath the snow to bare ground, then a couple of feet deeper into the frozen dirt. The soil comes up in solid chunks, and he's clumsy with the shovel. The exertion warms him though, slowly, and soon his hands and feet tingle with sharp needles of pain as they begin to come back to life. When he lifts the dog, he brushes the snow from its flank, fingering its leather collar for a moment and rubbing his thumb over the mirrored oval of its tag before lowering the body into the hole and covering it.

"We should see how the others are doing and then head back for the night," he says.

They walk without speaking toward where the others are still digging out the third train car in the growing dark. Several more flares are lit, poked into the snow and throwing a low, trembling light on the wreck; some of the men have also strung their lanterns from the limbs of the evergreens and these sway and bob as the breeze moves the boughs, their warm glow bouncing against the trees and drifts, their long files of light stretching across the shadowed mountainside.

Nils takes off one glove and tucks his hand into his pocket to feel for the compact. Still there. It's a heavy, round weight in his palm, its solid heft and curve reminding him of nothing so much as the skipping stones he collected as a boy. He's not sure now why he took it, nor what he thought he'd do with it, this token of so much lost; but it would seem wrong to toss it away, into the snow, where it would be just another thing gone. And so he holds onto it instead.

"Are you okay there, Sister?" Nils asks.

"I'll be fine," she says.

He nods to himself and keeps walking through the snow, toward the noise and the lights just ahead.

RETREAT, RETREAT

It's Sylvie's friend Cath who mentions the couples' retreat. Mentions and then pushes. They meet for lunch the first week of the new year. Cath picks the place—a restaurant that has just opened downtown in the space that used to be a children's ballet studio, then a high-end boutique, and most recently a shop selling dog treats and froufrou pet collars. That was before the recession. The short blocks of the downtown center went mostly dead during the last three years, but things are looking up now. As Cath scans her menu, Sylvie watches through the restaurant's overlarge front windows at people passing, ducking into and out of the bookstore and tea shop and the new coffee roaster across the street. She imagines that at the end of the block Mark must be getting at least some traffic in his shop too, though no one walks in and buys something as large and expensive as a kayak on a whim. Still, it's good. He'll come home cheerful, chatty. His faith that things can turn around again is proving right, and nothing makes Mark happier than being right.

"You want the quinoa or the millet?" Cath is asking when Sylvie returns her eyes to the table. "I'll get whatever you don't, and we can split."

"Don't they do any normal sides, like mashed potatoes?"

"You'll like the food. I promise." Cath slumps back, folds her arms across her chest, and smiles, self-satisfied. "Jem and I found this place last month. We've been here twice already." Jem—Cath's boyfriend. (*Jem?* Sylvie had asked, skeptical, after Cath's report of their first date. *Like "and the Holograms"?* But now they've been together six months—are living together, in fact—and Sylvie must keep all such remarks to herself.)

Cath's eyebrows tick up—a wicked, suggestive look. "We're doing date nights."

Sylvie reaches into her purse for her glasses. The menu's print is small, calligraphic, meant to look hand done, though the effect is illegible. "Isn't every night date night when there are no children to interrupt you?" she asks.

"You'd think, but no."

Sylvie decides on the salmon and sets her menu on top of Cath's at the edge of the table, trying to signal the waitress, who's been perched at the service counter for the last five minutes, her back to the dining room. It's her turn to pay, and if no one shows up to take their order in the next five minutes, Sylvie will knock a solid 10 percent off the tip.

"Not lately, anyway," Cath adds.

"Things not going well at home?" Sylvie asks. "You have to arrange romance now?"

"Something like that. We're trying to fix a few things between us before they become boulders."

"*Boulders?*"

"It's a keyword from this retreat we did a couple weeks ago." Cath lurches forward, sets her elbows on the table. "You wouldn't believe this retreat. It was fantastic." She beams at the memory. This is one of the things Sylvie envies in Cath—her visible, live energy. Cath will turn forty in a couple of months, and there is something still wired in her, still excitable. Lately, she's stopped coloring her hair pink or blue as she has for many years, and—surprise—a natural stripe of white has appeared right in the front, as perfect as if Cath had planned it. Sylvie isn't sure she herself is aging all that well, but even midlife, it seems, will be cool on Cath.

Sylvie restrains an eye roll. "A keyword," she repeats.

Cath grins. "Sounds terrible, right? I know. But, god, Syl, you and Mark should do it. The whole thing was so powerful for us."

Sylvie has a vision of a roomful of middle-aged couples in yoga pants, all sitting knee to knee, crisscross applesauce, as her son's kindergarten teacher said. She snuffs back a laugh. "Yeah, because couples retreats are right up Mark's alley."

"Also pedicures and talking about his period, right?" Cath shakes her head. "You make him out to be such a dick sometimes. He's a good guy, you know."

"Of course. I know that. He's just not prone to public outpourings of emotion, that's all." Sylvie hears the defensive edge in her voice, but she's right. She's known Mark forever. She might see the benefit of something like a couples retreat, but she'd never be able to drag him along. "Should we order?" she asks. "Shouldn't we be ordering already?" She raises a hand to get the waitress's attention.

"Seriously, though," Cath goes on. "The guy who leads these gets you to do so much important work."

"I do enough work at work—and on the weekends, come to think of it. I don't need to pay for more of it."

"You know what I mean. Internal work. The real stuff. You pinpoint the central boulders on your relational path."

"Yuck," Sylvie says, but she's smiling. "Are you hearing yourself?"

Cath winks, leans across the table, and whispers: "Ours is sex."

This catches Sylvie off guard. "No," she says. She lifts her eyes and scans the room to see if anyone is listening to them, then sits forward. "You and Jem? Really?"

Cath slouches back again, nods, shrugs. "True."

"I don't want to know about this."

"Yes you do."

"Okay, yes I do. But maybe not here."

The waitress arrives—a college girl who, up close, looks familiar enough that Sylvie wonders if she's had her in class. It'd be English 101 most likely, this girl one of the hundreds she's taught. Or maybe a total stranger. How could she tell? It happens more and more often—mistaking people she's never met for former students, going blank when she bumps into an actual former student out in the world somewhere. They blend together. The longer she teaches, the younger the students look, and the more similar. Girls with long ponytails and candy-colored lip gloss. Boys in baseball caps. Most of them share a face, a voice, a single set of ideas that they all believe to be revolutionary. She thinks of her father, who still always had an entourage of eager students tagging after him in his last years of teaching, and wonders how he found the energy.

Cath orders champagne. They toast the new year, eat around their own flurry of meaningless chitchat. Sylvie's boys are out of daycare and school for one more week. They're bickering endlessly. Cath's mother spent the holiday with her and Jem, was judgmental (as usual). Etcetera. Around them, the noise of the other diners takes on the unified, frenetic vibration of many people speaking together in a small space. Overhead, light pours thin and white from several hanging, caged bulbs; and under their feet, the blond planks of the wood floor have been waxed to a thick sheen (the overglossed shine of a high school gymnasium, Sylvie thinks). The tables are all done in rough white linens, no candles, and the chairs are faux-seventies schoolhouse—metal frames and orange vinyl upholstery. The only fixtures remaining from the old ballet studio are the floor-to-ceiling mirrors. They give the building a deceiving width and depth the owners must love. Sylvie looks from one mirror to the next and sees herself replicated—her double here against the wall at her side, and also there behind the service counter, and there across the room. She watches from the corner of her eyes as her sisters move in synchrony with her. At first this is charming, the trick of it. But as she eats, she keeps looking up. There she is, lifting her fork to her mouth, chewing. There and there and there. Across the room, she pulls her face into a stiff, two-dimensional grin. When she moves to dab her napkin to her mouth, she catches her own eye watching. She can't get away from herself, and when lunch is over and the bill has been paid, she hurries to push through the front door and out into the stiff brace of the January air, where she is just a single self again.

"So, the sex," Cath says now as they walk. She tugs one of Jem's lumpy knit hats onto her head, links her arm through Sylvie's.

"I'd have guessed money, if you'd asked me what it was between you two."

"Oh, I know. It should be, right?" When Cath and Jem first started dating, Jem was an "unemployed bartender." Later Jem worked at a record store for a while, and now he introduces himself at parties as an unemployed music distributor.

"This retreat changed your lives though, and now it's all bells and whistles in the bedroom and peace in the universe." Sylvie smiles. "I have that right, yes?"

"Such a cynic, but exactly. That's it exactly. And you'd find out how right I am if you'd just sign up for a weekend, too."

They reach Cath's car, and she fumbles in her satchel for the keys.

"Lost again?" Sylvie says, and leans her hip against the car's flank. Just before the winter break, she had to drive to campus when Cath called to say that she'd locked herself out of their shared office after dark.

Cath comes up with the keys in a moment this time though, and shakes them over her head like a prize. "Lucky day," she says. "I need to graft these to my hand."

"But you found them. Like I said, the universe loves you for your good sex life."

Later, as Sylvie stands at the kitchen sink washing lettuce for their dinner salad and Mark stands beside her stirring a pot of pasta on the stove, she mentions Cath's "coital bliss." That's how she puts it. The whole thing is awkward. How many personal details can you know about someone else's relationship before it's impossible to be friends? But it isn't the sort of information she can keep to herself either, so she cushions the image with language. It's apparently a habit of hers. Just before the holiday break, a student wrote an end-of-term evaluation of Sylvie's teaching that said, *Uses too many bullshit elitist words.* Sylvie's first impulse was to appreciate that the student had spelled *elitist* correctly, but the barb of the comment stuck. She revises herself now, thinking of this. "Cath told me the retreat improved their intimacy," she says, and only as she says it does she hear herself making the same mistake twice.

Mark laughs, pauses in his stirring. "Wait, what are you telling me about Cath's sex life?"

"Just that Cath said it's all resolved between them now—her and Jem—whatever it was that wasn't working in the first place."

"I know exactly what wasn't working," Mark says. "Cath's standards are too high." He has his back to her, his eyes on the bubbling pot. His hair looks windblown, and Sylvie can smell the salt air of the bay on him as she always can when he and Jason have been test paddling their shop's new boats during the workday. Tonight, when they go to bed and she leans to kiss him before shutting off her bedside lamp, she will still be able to taste the salt on the skin of his neck.

"What are you talking about, high standards?" she asks. "Cath's flaky sometimes, but never like that. You're saying she's demanding?"

"Wasn't she dating a massage therapist a while ago? You don't come back from that." Mark looks over his shoulder at her, winks.

Sylvie dismisses this line of speculation and goes on. "She didn't say what the problem was—and thank goodness, right?"

Mark turns. His face has pulled suddenly into a look of almost grief. "That's right—I forgot to tell you. Jason's divorce is final. He's throwing a party. We're invited."

"A divorce party? Is this something people are doing now?"

"I don't see how we can get out of it."

"I don't want to toast to that, do you? And what will we talk about? How horrible his marriage was? What a witch Christy turned out to be?" Sylvie shakes her head. "Tell him we're busy."

"He doesn't talk about Christy. I think the party's mostly a maneuver to get this woman he's been seeing over to his place. But still, it's Jason. I have to go."

"Yes," Sylvie nods.

"And by that I mean that we should go."

"I don't think so. You have to go—I see that. But I'm not going."

On the stove, the pasta pot hisses, a heavy froth of foam rising over its lip. "Shit," Mark says. "I can't talk and stir." He lifts the pot just as the water boils over. "Hot, hot, hot!" he says. Spilled water spits and fizzes on the stovetop. "Let me drain this before I burn myself."

She steps aside as he swings the pot into the sink and dumps a rush of water. A thick billow of steam wafts up. For a moment, Mark's head is swallowed, and he is nothing but a body—legs and torso— and a cloud. Sylvie thinks the phrase twice, clearly: *A body and a cloud. A body and a cloud.* And her own head feels pleasantly light at the strangeness of this vision—her husband divorced from his head. But then the steam is gone just as quickly—cooled and dissipated into nothing but a fine, damp humidity between them in the narrow kitchen, and Mark is himself again, and she is herself once more too.

"That was nearly a disaster," Mark says. He tips the pot back onto the burner, swirls the noodles in the last saved measure of their own starchy broth, and smiles what Sylvie knows to be his private pleasure at the whole process. He's good in the kitchen. Better than her. Cooking is logical, methodical, physical—just like him. Before the boys were born, she left all of their meals to Mark, but now, with the boat shop running at full speed all the time just to stay in business, it's rare for Mark to make dinner, and rarer yet for the two of them to be in the kitchen together.

"What are you making over there?" she asks.

"I haven't made up my mind yet. Just marinara, maybe. Or do we have bacon?" He crosses the kitchen, and she hears him shifting containers in the fridge.

"Bottom shelf," she says.

"Where?"

She lets out a breath. "I'll get it."

"No, just tell me." His voice comes out thin from within the cold cavern of the fridge.

"Left," she says without looking. "Under the butter."

More rummaging. "It's not here."

"You're not looking." Sylvie turns, frustrated, and peers around him, but she doesn't see it either. "It was right there," she says.

For a moment they stand side by side before the fridge, and then Mark claps his hands once and leans in. "Aha. Got it. Top shelf, not bottom." He slides the flat package of bacon from beneath a tub of yogurt, grins at her, gloating. "I told you."

It's nothing, but it irritates her, and she goes back to her chopping flustered, lays the blade of the knife into the ribs of the neat stack of lettuce leaves so briskly she nearly slices the tip of her own thumb. "At any rate," she continues, "what I was saying is that, according to Cath, the retreat they did was amazing."

Mark sighs. "Look, Syl, I see where this is going, but if you want a retreat weekend, let's just get your mother to take the kids, and we can sit on our own floor and sing 'Kumbaya' to each other here for free."

She raises her eyes to him, uncertain if this is still a joke, but he is leaning over the pot again, two halves of a cracked egg shell in his hands, a glisten of egg white on his fingertips. *Carbonara*, she thinks. To him she says, "I didn't mean anything about us going, and, anyhow, I have no idea how much the thing costs. Cath and I didn't get into it that far."

Mark shrugs. "Better yet, let's take the kids to your mom and then just spend the whole weekend in bed." He grins and flourishes a fork in her direction, pokes the air. "'Heal thyself,' right?" He returns his attention to the stove, and before Sylvie can say more, the boys are in the kitchen, too—Nick talking without breath about some playground altercation from the day, and Benny spluttering wet car noises as he pushes his little Matchbox Corvette over Sylvie's bare feet.

It isn't until much later—after they've eaten and washed up, bathed the boys and read the stories and sung all the lullabies twice; after the house is finally quiet, and they have climbed into bed themselves for the night—that Sylvie says into the darkness, "What did you mean earlier?"

"When?" Mark lies facing her, their knees touching, and she can see even through the shadow their bodies make together at the center of the bed that his eyes are already closed.

"When I told you about Cath. You said we could just stay home. 'Heal thyself,' you said. What did you mean?"

"I was just being funny."

"But the way you said it. That implies something about us."

"Not really."

"Do you think we're not connecting like we used to?"

"Is that a euphemism? Because I'm happy to connect."

"Stop. I'm trying to ask you something real," Sylvie says, but she doesn't go on.

For a long stretch they lie still. Sylvie watches fiddleheads of light curl in through the split between the curtains. A car passes and they

unfurl and retract, unfurl and retract in the dark pool of the bedroom. "Why did Jason and Christy break up, really?" she asks.

Mark's breath is slow, and for a moment she thinks he is sleeping,
but then he says, quiet, "They were never going to make it."

"No. They weren't," she agrees. They've discussed this already, she
and Mark, in the months since Jason and Christy's separation. "But
how could we tell? What was the sign, I mean?"

"We're not Jason and Christy," Mark says.

"Of course we're not. I wasn't saying—"

"We're not your parents."

Beneath the blanket, she feels Mark's hand searching for her, and
she leans closer. His palm finds her hip and rests there, warm. The
heat of his body is always amazing to her. He radiates it, wakes in the
middle of the night sometimes to throw off the quilt. It's a trait he's
passed on to their sons, who both slip the clutch of the blankets she
tucks in around them at bedtime and end up on top of their covers,
their legs and arms sprawled wide on the bed tops, and the fine hair
at the napes of their necks and temples curled with the sweat of their
dreaming. In contrast, Sylvie feels every draft on these winter nights
when the sky is clear and the old house seems to let in every gasp of
wind.

"I'll do the retreat, if you really want to," Mark says.

It surprises her, this compromise. She says, "I wasn't angling for
that, you know. Really."

"It's fine. Just promise me no role playing or trust falls, okay?" He
pats her hip once, a goodnight, and rolls to his other side, away from
her, already drifting off.

Classes begin again the following week, and on Monday morning Sylvie drops the boys off at their separate schools and drives to
meet her mother. For the last year—since her parents' divorce—she's
joined her mother three mornings a week to walk the gravel path
that rounds the lake on which her mother's condominium sits. Her

mother is still young—just sixty-one—and healthy, but there's a nig-
gling worry at the back of Sylvie's mind that her mother might fall
in her bathtub someday or have a sudden and massive heart attack
alone in her bed, and that without these regularly scheduled walks,
her mother's body could go on lying there in her empty condo for
days, unnoticed. She'd never mention this worry to her mother, who
would just laugh at the way her oldest child's mind works, at the silly
proclivity Sylvie's had since childhood for seeing the very worst pos-
sibilities in every scenario. Instead, Sylvie simply waits at the lake's
trailhead and breathes a silent sigh of relief when her mother appears,
bobbing down the path.

This morning her mother is easy to spot even at a distance, her
graying hair tucked up under a white, knitted cap, and her green
windbreaker wildly bright against the fog and the damp shadows of
the wooded lakefront. They make it half a mile before the conversation about the pie her mother has made for the annual library board
luncheon and the novel she's just finished reading fizzles out and settles into quiet, the only sounds between them the measured chuffs of
their breath in the cold and their matched steps on the gravel.

"Mark's business partner is throwing a divorce party," Sylvie says
into the gap.

Her mother huffs out a syllable of amusement. "That's the way to
do it, I guess, if you have to. Douse your sorrow in champagne. I wish
I'd thought of it."

"Mark says there's some new woman Jason's aiming for, so I don't
know that he's trying to drown his misery at this point."

"I think it's hard for anyone outside the marriage to see the
grief."

Sylvie looks at her mother, but nothing has shifted in her expression. Her face has pinked, a raw flush at the cheekbones and nose,
and a dew of lake mist nets her cap in silver beads, tiny as fish eggs.
She walks with her arms pumping at her sides, a pedometer clipped
to the tongue of her sneaker.

"I told Mark to make an excuse, but he's right—we'll both have to go. It's Jason. There's no polite way out of it."

"You liked the wife?"

Sylvie pulls a face. "She's shrill, no filters. Terrible."

Her mother nods. "No one ever likes the wife."

"Even you wouldn't have liked Christy. Still—a divorce party. I don't know."

"Well, dear, it's not your divorce, so just go and have a good time," her mother says. "Have a drink. Have two drinks. Don't be judgmental about the sorrow of someone else's lifetime." This silences Sylvie for a moment, but her mother goes on. "You can bring the boys to me for the night."

"I'm not judging, you know. It's not that," Sylvie says.

"Of course not."

They cross the footbridge over the creek that marks the south edge of the lake. When Sylvie was a teenager, there weren't any condos on this lake yet, just a few big houses along this south side. The rest of the lakefront was treed and untended, wild. On weekends, kids came out to party unchecked in the woods, and the one time Sylvie came with a friend, the party ended up in the water—fifteen or twenty stoned high schoolers swimming in their boxer shorts and bras in the middle of the night. She thinks of it every time she walks here—the cold water, the slippery thrill of weeds slicking her bare calves. There was a rumor about a little boy swimming out and getting tangled in the weeds, drowning, and though even then she was fairly sure it wasn't true, the lake had felt believably dangerous that night—not because death seemed like a real possibility, but because of the darkness of the sky and the water, the unmeasured depth of the lake and softness of the silt below her feet where she could touch ground. She swam out blindly, not knowing how long it would take to sink to the lake's dark bottom, nor how far she was from the shore. Thinking of it now, when she would never do something so stupid as strip to her underwear and swim out to the center of a dark lake at night, the memory echoes with longing. Her whole body remembers the charging freedom of that fear.

"Do you want to come in for coffee?" her mother asks as the path returns them to the trailhead and they stop to catch their breath.

"I should get home. I have work to do. Class prep."

Her mother kisses her forehead, pulls away with a look of concern. "I can see that I've bothered you with what I've said."

"I just thought you'd take my side."

"What side? This is no different than when you were little and couldn't decide between the blue skirt or the red. Just make a choice and be happy." Her mother smiles, waves a hand in the air as if Sylvie's concerns are all vaporous, no weightier than the filaments of mist lacing the air just now. "You don't want to go to some party, then tell Mark you don't want to go. You feel you must go, then go." She shrugs. "It doesn't have to be a big deal."

Sylvie disagrees with this, but she nods. "I just find the whole thing—I don't know. Gauche, I guess."

"Divorce, you mean." Her mother sighs. "I know you feel that way. Your father and I did that to you, and I'm sorry. It *is* gross."

Sylvie snorts. "I said gauche, Mother, not gross. And I meant the party."

A sudden look of hilarity crosses her mother's face and she laughs. "That's funny. I would hear it that way, wouldn't I? After everything."

"I don't know if I'd say *funny* is the right word."

"Oh, now. You know what I mean." Her mother pauses, turns sober. "It is gross, though, honestly. Divorce." She squeezes Sylvie's arm—something like a little nudge, which Sylvie understands is meant both to punctuate what she's saying and to comfort. "No one wants to divorce," her mother says. "I'm sure of that. It's a failure." She peels the cap from her head and shakes her hair loose. A soft lift of steam rises from her head. "No one ever expects it will be them. I know your father and I didn't. Nearly forty years together and still we couldn't stick it out. We never thought it would be us." She shakes her head. "Intention is flimsy, though, as it turns out. You can't build a life on intention."

Sylvie walks her mother back to the condo.

"I didn't ask," her mother says when they reach the low wooden gate at the back of condo's yard, "do you have to take a gift to this thing?"

"God, I hope not. What does one take to a divorce party?"

"A lawyer," her mother says, and laughs.

"Right. Or a gift certificate for therapy."

"No, actually—and I mean this in all seriousness, Sylvie—if you want to give him something genuinely useful, I recommend condoms. A nice box, but none of the fetishy sorts." Her mother wrinkles her nose. "Those are too personal for a party gift."

"Okay, Mother. Thank you for that."

"Just my advice." Her mother lets herself into the yard, the gate snicking shut at her back, then she turns and heads across the yard. Once at her door, she raises her hand to wave goodbye. "See you!" she hollers. "I'll keep the children Friday night!"

Sylvie opens her mouth to say something more, but what is there to say?

The fog has risen, coalesced as a thick, muzzy wool in the low boughs of the trees, a muddling cloud. She makes her way through its drizzle, back to the car.

That night, when Sylvie finishes readying the boys' next-day school lunches and setting up the coffee pot for morning, she finds Mark already in bed, a trade magazine open on his lap, a glossy photo of a wooden kayak filling one page. She has given him stacks of novels to read over the years, but they always sit uncracked until eventually Mark fits them into the bookshelf, where they remain. It never used to bother her, but now she's unable to stop herself from adding it to the growing tally in her mind of things that might possibly indicate their potential incompatibility in the years to come. Also on the list:

the fact of his being here reading while she was making lunches; the dish he left on the counter above the dishwasher—rather than in the dishwasher—this morning; the way he seems to be supporting Jason's ridiculous party as a legitimate way to recognize the close of a marriage. He said over dinner that he told Jason they'll both be there. Eight o'clock, Friday. No children, so could she call her mother? She didn't say anything, just nodded, but she knows she will not be able to bite her tongue all week.

One side of her thinks this is nothing—watching friends divorce is just another of the unpleasant realities of middle age. Her mother's friends are all having surgeries, so it could be worse. She knows she should just go to the party, have the couple of drinks her mother suggested, and let be what is. But the other side of her cannot abide the pretense. Already she knows that this lesser self will win. Already she knows what will happen: between tonight and Friday, she will say something barbed about the party, Mark will look irritatingly confused by it, as if he hasn't seen it coming, and that oblivion will prompt from her a second cruelty. She won't be able to stop herself. Friday they'll leave for the party without speaking to each other, drive to Jason's in rigid silence, spend the evening standing stiffly near one another. It will all play out with a tedious familiarity, a re-enactment of every fight they've had over their nearly twenty years of knowing one another. There's a rigidity even now, the space between them in the bed starched to a static snap with her anticipatory resentment.

She asks, "Did you like that memoir I gave you for Christmas? The man at the bookstore said you'd love it."

Mark raises his eyes from the magazine and frowns. "Did you give me a book?"

"Maybe you missed it." She reaches to shut off her lamp. "I don't think I wrapped it."

"What was it about?"

"Doesn't matter."

"Hey," he says, soft, closing the magazine and leaning to turn off his bedside lamp. "Sorry. I'll look for it in the morning."

"It's fine."

In the dark, she feels him reaching for her, his hand on her waist beneath the blankets, his hand on her hip, her breast. He kisses her just below her ear. "Boys asleep?" he asks. His foot finds hers between the folds of sheet.

"What're we doing here?" Sylvie asks, her voice low as she leans into him.

"I don't know. What're we doing here?"

There's the sound of rain on the roof once they stop talking, and the thin notes of the lullaby CD Benny still insists on at bedtime chiming down the hall. The shadows pooled on the ceiling above the bed recede with the passing of a car in the road outside the window, then swim forward again.

"Slow down a little," she says after a few moments.

"Sorry."

She shifts on top of the sheets, closes her eyes. A flood of end-of-day thoughts, all tedium and distraction, wash against the front of her mind for a moment until she is able to let them float away.

"You okay?" Mark asks.

"Yes. Sorry. Focusing."

She puts her cheek to the warm slope of his shoulder. The smell of the bay and the wind—deep green, cold, mineraled. She sees him on the water, the dip and rise of his paddle, a swirl of churned bubbles glittering in its wake. She tucks her nose into the curve of his neck. *Mark*. Familiarity. Comfort. "Remember," she begins, and then pauses to draw a sharp breath. Starts over: "Remember that time we took the kayaks to the cabin. We paddled out to that island and camped—I don't know where—"

"I remember," he says.

"It was in the fall. Before the kids."

"It was Patos Island. We were the only people for miles."

They've had this conversation before. It's certain kindling. She says, "Remind me."

He begins slowly. Her mind reels backward, and she sees herself as a younger woman. Slowly, she remembers herself. Slowly, she remembers desire. For a few moments she waits for time to constrict, and then she is lost in it. When the story becomes unnecessary, she kisses him into silence, just the taste of his mouth grounding her to him— grounding them both into their own bodies and each other's—for a few seconds. And then, just as swiftly as she left it, she is returned to the present of the bedroom, to the four walls and the solid night shadows on the ceiling overhead.

She turns toward him and lays a leg over his hip to pull him close. "Now I'll tell you what I remember."

This is their arrangement—never spoken: her turn, his turn. A fair trade every time. Marital equality is always easiest for them in bed.

And then it's over, and within a moment he is sleeping, and it is just another workweek night. This worries her a little, the habitual rhythm of their life now. She recalls again that camping trip to Patos Island. Rake-headed pines and yellow shrubs thinned and burned by wind rather than heat. Stiff scent of salt water. A lighthouse on a rocky point velveted with moss. It was years ago, but it's still so vivid. She and Mark were young when they took that trip—still childless and jobless, free without realizing their freedom, and she worries that the heat of the memory has more to do with that than with Mark. That their ritual telling of their early stories has more to do with a retrieval of that freedom than with each other. She worries that this might be the sign—the indication that something has burned out between them. Or is this simply marriage at its midpoint? Life at its middle? Every interaction an echo of an earlier one. All the old grievances and glories fingered and fingered again, like polished stones, until you are eventually walking forward with your pockets weighted? And maybe this was it for Jason and Christy. For her parents. Maybe they never held onto anything. Or they held onto too much, and the seams simply split eventually, torn, irreparable.

Beside her, Mark sighs in his sleep, and she lays her palm against his bare back, feels the expected heat.

Wednesday morning, she opens her office door on campus to find Cath already at work. "Coffee now or later?" Cath asks.

"Now, please." Sylvie drops her bag, and they cross the damp lawn to the cafeteria. The boxy, brick buildings look drab this time of year, with the gardens between them vacant and the trees stripped naked. There's nothing to ornament and hide the public college economy, which gives the whole place a feeling of depressing desperation that Sylvie never notices in the fall when the leaves are flushing or late spring when flower beds are full.

"We need better weather," Sylvie says. "I'll drown in cloud cover."

"I know. We're only three days into the term and I'm fucking exhausted," Cath says.

"I looked at my freshman essays last night," Sylvie says. "First of the term. I kid you not—three of them wrote about vampire books, and another four about the same zombie romance novel." She turns to Cath. "Did you know there were zombie romance novels?"

"What were they supposed to write about?"

"Favorite book, and why. It almost doesn't matter what they write; I just need to see that they can make paragraphs. The question isn't working anymore, though. Half of them aren't reading at all. Most of the other responses just irk me. I should ask about video games."

At the student union building, Cath holds open the door. "I can see the sex appeal of a zombie romance," she says. "What I don't get is how people write them. Not much for dialogue, zombies. What is there to put on the page?"

"Maybe that explains my romance, then—I'm married to a zombie."

"Mark? Please. Mark talks."

"You always defend him," Sylvie says.

"Does he need defending?"

Sylvie shrugs. "I didn't even really mean that. I'm just being funny."

They file into line at the coffee counter, then take their cups to a table near the window. The cafeteria is loud with chatter, laughter. Students sit singly, bent over open textbooks, earbud strings wiring their pockets to their heads; or they lounge around the tables in sprawling, raucous groups. Across the room, Sylvie spots the dean, a tight-faced woman her mother's age. The campus rumor is that last year she went through a horribly messy divorce, though she never missed a day in the office. *She's a workhorse, a ballbuster*, people say, as if this explains everything. Cath has compared her to Sylvie's mother, but Cath doesn't know what she's talking about. Divorce has softened her mother, worn down her edges rather than sharpening them. If anything, the surprise has been how fully she's thrived on her own since Sylvie's father left, how happy she is without him, though a small and childish part of Sylvie hates to acknowledge that. Her mother is a success story, and the dean has become a caricature—a spinster, a prig. Still, the meanness of the gossip riles her indignation. Treatment of women in the workplace, diminishment of women in power, misogynist readings of women's choices, etcetera, etcetera. She meets the dean's eye now and waves, and in return she gets a pinched nod before the woman stands, shoves her seat against the table's edge, and scissors out the door on the points of her black patent heels.

"I don't know what's going on with you and Mark," Cath picks up where they left off as soon as they're seated, "but the solution is a retreat. *The* retreat."

"God, give it up," Sylvie says. "It's just not us, a retreat. It's far too kumbaya for us." She hears the edge of Mark's judgment in her voice—the retreat's gooey spiritualism not even her gripe—but she goes on. "I'm surprised, honestly, that you've gone in for that kind of faux-psychobabble glop."

Cath waves this off. "I don't care. It works. The touchy-feely thing means I'm getting touched and having feelings, so I'm good with the rest of it. I swear to you—if you give it a chance, you'll never be happier."

"I'm happy now."

Cath laughs, one loud spike of skepticism. "Last night, Jem and I planned our future for the next five years. You believe that? Five years. We're on fire, Syl. Fire."

"Good for you," Sylvie concedes. "But my five-year plan is to work on a slow burn. That's all I want now: *slow burn.*"

They finish their coffees and walk back across campus. The sun is splitting the clouds in spots, white fissures in the bunting of gray so bright that Sylvie has to lift a hand to her forehead to shade her eyes. She wants to stop in place and tip her face upward for a moment, into the light, to feel the ache of it behind her eyes for just a few seconds. Class will begin shortly, though, and this winter sun is deceptive; it only looks warm. If she stands still, she'll just give the wind a chance to blow through her.

"I'm not trying to be pushy," Cath says as they near their building. "About the retreat, I mean." She catches Sylvie's hand and squeezes gently. "I care about you and Mark. And the boys. They're family to me, you know. You all are family."

"Of course we are," Sylvie says. "Of course you're family."

"Good. So you'll think about it, then—the retreat? Or marriage counseling?"

A knot of breath constricts in the soft spot between Sylvie's ribs, as if Cath has punched her there. She withdraws her hand from Cath's clasp. "Why are you so worried about us? I thought this was just about you and Jem."

"Maybe I shouldn't have said anything. I thought we were close enough."

"We are close."

"I thought you'd take it differently than this."

"Take what differently?

"The last time I was there for dinner, you argued in front of the boys."

Sylvie fumbles to remember this. Had they fought? About what? It's lost to her. Something inconsequential, obviously, or she'd remember. Water under the bridge. Or not, but not worth fighting about anymore. She pinches the tip of her nose. Her eyes are watering. She says, "I don't want the boys going off into their adult lives with some fairy-tale half-truth about what love really is. Some—" She flutters her fingers before her face, a grasping. "Some coo-coo-ca-choo ideal."

"I don't live in a fairy tale."

"I'm talking about giving the boys a fair sense of reality. We're not going to fake it. How would that serve them?"

"Why would you assume happiness has to be fake?"

"Why would you assume happiness has to be incessant?" Sylvie lets out a breath.

For a moment they stand facing the closed door, silent. The light of the sky is now glaring. It's now a glare like the aura of a headache behind Sylvie's eyes.

"I'm worried for you," Cath says. A triangle of skin at the base of her neck has flushed, a splotch like the bloom of a rash there where her shirt collar widens. Sylvie has seen this before on her: she's angry.

"I appreciate your concern," Sylvie says. Her voice is steady, flat. She hears herself thank Cath for her good intentions. She opens the door to the building, and climbs the stairs, shuts herself into the office to wait for Cath to appear, though she never does. The day passes. Sylvie teaches her class. Students arrive at her office hours, they talk, the students leave again. The sky outside the office window goes brighter, brighter, and by four the sun finally burns off the clouds over the bay as it always does just before dusk, a regular triumph.

Sylvie drives home with the last of the daylight going gold-orange at her back. Going orange-white. Going white-silver-gray. A quick flare-and-fade routine, the same every evening. *Burnishing*, she thinks, as she pulls into her own driveway. *Garnishing. Furbishing. Tarnishing.* The garage door rises, articulated, slow, and she pulls into the darkness of the unlit space. *Anguishing, extinguishing,* she thinks. She turns off the car and waits for the door to wrench itself down again, then goes inside to start dinner.

All week Cath remains vanished, absent from the office without even a phone call or a text. On Friday night Sylvie's mother arrives at six to stay with the boys, tells Sylvie the black cocktail dress she's chosen for Jason's party looks sufficient with or without the red belt, and waves her out the door with a look of pleasant impatience. Mark has the car running—they are late—and they pull off down the street as soon as Sylvie is settled. They debate for only a moment about the route, then take the bay road—the longer way—because Mark says some of the boats in the marina are still strung in Christmas lights and are sure to be lit up. Sylvie keeps her eyes on the window as they move, looking for this—signs of festivity, of cheer, even though there is something wearying about lights up so far into January.

"Only certain people keep their lights up this late into the new year," she says aloud to Mark.

"Maybe they just don't want the holidays to end."

"I doubt that. It's laziness, really. Don't you think? They can't find one hour to take down their Christmas lights?"

"I like the lights."

"I do, too. I'm not saying that. I'm not saying I'm a Scrooge."

"Why complain then? Just enjoy their laziness."

"Was I complaining? I was observing."

They go on like this, quibbling benignly, filling the quiet in the car and warming up for the party chitchat ahead. It's their pattern, this inconsequential bickering. There's no heat behind it. No one has a dog in the fight, as her father would say, because it isn't a fight. In fact, it's comfortable, this back and forth. Easy between them. It's the kind of dialogue they can retreat into when there's nothing else to say, and

no one will leave feeling offended or unheard because the whole conversation has been trivial. *A lark*, Sylvie thinks, though this isn't quite
the right word for what they're doing.

She sees how outsiders might not hear it this way, however. There's
a chance Cath heard exactly this sort of ruffing and mistook it for
real disagreement, a shoot of some deep-rooted peevishness. There's
a chance Cath is wrong, after all, and they aren't in actual trouble as
a couple but have just been mistranslated. The idea lifts in Sylvie, and
she wants to believe it.

"Do you think the boys understand us?" she asks.

Mark looks at her and makes a face. "Actually," he says, "I'm glad
you've brought this up. I've been meaning to suggest that we start
speaking English in their presence." He grins at his own joke.

Sylvie shakes her head. "Be serious. I want to know what you
think."

"Seriously, I think they're not supposed to understand us; we're
their parents. If they understood everything about us, we'd be telling
them too much, depriving them of their childhoods."

"You're missing my point."

They pass the marina and Sylvie taps the glass of her window so
that Mark won't miss the sight: a line of boats anchored to the docks,
all of them bobbing in discordant rhythm in the wash of darkness,
four or five of them lit, bow to stern and deck to sail. They glitter
against the sweep of night above and the black, black swell of the bay
below.

"It is pretty," Sylvie says. "Like candle flames."

"It's prettier from the water, in a kayak. You feel like you're in space.
The lights on the water are stars." Without turning his eyes from the
road, he finds her knee, squeezes. "The boys are fine," he says. "We're
fine. Everybody's fine. But you go on worrying, Syl. I know you will
anyway."

When they reach Jason's, the party is in full rush. Jason has invited
clients and neighbors, college friends who have driven up from Se-

attle and Portland still dressed in their business suits and trim workday skirts. They all seem like reasonable people—people like her—
and it throws Sylvie to see them laughing and chattering on as if a
divorce party were a normal social occasion. Mark recognizes Jason's
brother manning the bar and tells Sylvie he's going over to say hello.
A few moments later he returns with two amber-toned cocktails in
sugar-lipped glasses. The flavor is bright and acidic. It conjures for Sylvie visions of orange popsicles and sunlight. Each sip slides down her
throat and opens like a flower in her belly, first the florid sweetness,
then the burn.

"What is this?" she asks between gulps.

"Sidecars," Mark says. "Jason's idea of a divorce joke."

"I'm going to want another."

He pulls a face at her. "Who are you?"

"Apparently divorce drives me to drink," Sylvie says. "Make a
note of that." She tips her head back to catch the last swallow and
hands him the glass. "One more, please. I've decided you're driving us
home."

He's surprised—she can see it—but he turns and makes his way
again to the bar anyhow. Watching him go, his own drink still full in
his hand, she feels a spark at the sight of his shoulders, his back—still
attractive to her after all these years—and also the small, smoky pleasure of having cornered him into sobriety tonight.

Everyone else is drinking freely. There are empties on the stone
mantle, where, when she lived here, Christy kept a menagerie of faux-
exotic wooden animals. A rough-hewn giraffe. A boxy tiger and its
mate. Beside these, a tribal-looking mask of the sort sold at home de-
cor shops, and a wide-basined silver dish full of plaster pomegran-
ates. As Sylvie recalls this, the room reassembles for her, full in its old
form: a perfect white leather couch along the far wall, an end table
topped with an ivory chess set always at the ready, a thick wool rug
in beige that Sylvie had coveted. This is all gone, the room stripped
of its former self. The taper candles from the bookshelf, the stack of

art books, the ceramic jug lanterns—all of it packed up, presumably, when Christy left and now populating the living room of a clean, new condominium.

In the absence of Christy's things, Jason has moved in an over-stuffed sectional, a boxy coffee table now littered in hors d'oeuvres plates and wadded napkins, a wide-screened TV. The cliché of all this burns at the back of Sylvie's throat, a high, shrill, inappropriate laugh she is only just containing. Jason's using the fireplace now, too, though he and Christy never did—because of the soot, the smell—and Sylvie imagines him inviting women over, lighting a fire to warm the room and the mood. She is seeing a vision of him on his knees with a match in hand just as the actual Jason appears before her, Mark at his side.

"Here's your drink," Mark says, and lifts an eyebrow—a warning, Sylvie knows, or maybe a plea for good behavior.

She chimes the rim of her glass against his, takes two rushing gulps. The first drink is blunting this one's bite, the alcohol less a heat now than a syrupy warmth in her gut.

"Glad you could come," Jason says, and leans in for a half embrace.

Sylvie smiles as he pulls away. "Couldn't miss it, but I don't know what the protocol is for a celebration like this. Should I congratulate you? Offer condolences? What's the etiquette?"

Mark's laugh is uncomfortable. "I don't think we need to follow any protocol, Syl. It's just a party. We're all just having a good time."

Jason seems to shrug this off. He's Mark's age exactly but looks younger—one of those men who has somehow maintained the puck-ish face of cool—until he smiles, and then the lines of wear crack around his eyes and draw down his dimples. She knows other men like this—her brother, for one, who seems to think relationships should be replaced as often as the oil in his car. And Jem, for another, whose only source of stability appears to be Cath. Men who ride out their own middle age as if growing older is of no consequence to them, as if they are not afraid of ending up alone. Men like her father, who live nearly a whole life in partnership and can still walk away at the end. With a feeling of vertigo, Sylvie watches Mark watching Jason.

"No, it's fine," Jason says. "Congratulate me, definitely." He sweeps his arm wide. "I've got the house. I've got the business. I've got this awesome community who'll come party with me. Congratulate me. For sure."

"Awesome," Sylvie says. "Congrats for sure, then." She rings her rim once more, this time against the heavy lip of Jason's beer mug. Her body feels loose and weighted as she raises her arm, her face heavy when she pulls it up in a grin. When she lifts the glass to drink the last sip of this second drink, the light swims in the alcohol for an instant, the iridescent flash of a netted fish, before she swallows it down.

Jason goes on. "I was telling Mark at the shop yesterday, I just feel free now, you know?"

"Mark didn't mention that," Sylvie says.

"He's heard me go on about it for weeks now. He's probably sick of it."

"Are you sick of his freedom, Mark?" Sylvie asks.

"Need another drink, Syl?" Mark's face has gone waxen, his expression still and pale.

"Maybe," she says, a lilt. *Who's free here?* she thinks to herself. "Maybe," she repeats. She feels the meanness hardening around the edges of her words, but she is smiling, smiling, and Jason seems oblivious, enraptured by the narrative of his own escape.

"I was in a cage," he says. "I just couldn't see it, but once I did, there was no looking back."

Sylvie wants to laugh. "That's a little hyperbolic, don't you think?"

"Okay," Mark says. He holds her elbow, a gentle squeeze.

"You know the craziest thing?" Jason goes on, though, leaning in and lowering his voice as if sharing a secret with her. "Since Christy and I split up, I can't tell you how many friends have said they never really liked her in the first place."

"No," Sylvie says in mocked shock. "How rude, right?"

"Can you believe that?" A flash of real hurt crosses Jason's face. "Why wouldn't anyone tell me this before? For fuck's sake. No one said a thing. Not a single thing."

"Divorce is a horrible business," Sylvie says. A muddling heat rises in her chest, her neck. "We're all so horrible."

"Syl," Mark says, but she turns from him, releases her elbow from the cup of his hold.

"I didn't mean you guys," Jason says. "I didn't mean to say you."

"No. No, you're right." Her tongue seems to flip-flop in her mouth. Loose at the root. "We should have been honest. All of us."

Jason looks wounded now.

For a moment the party seems to pulse around Sylvie, bright, loud. The discordant chatter of the others rises and buoys against the ceiling overhead, stuck there. The windows sweat with the heat of so much exhaled breath.

"We're all just so well intentioned," Sylvie says. She looks at Jason, then at Mark, but the alcohol and the overhead lights are affecting her vision, and their faces are hard to pin down.

"Sylvia," Mark says.

She raises her glass again before remembering that it's empty. "*Vive le divorce*," she says, and steps back, wobbles, feels Mark's grasp once more. "*Vive le divorce!*" she shouts, and the room turns to look at her, though only one man—his own face already slack with too many drinks—lifts his beer and echoes her call.

She shakes her head. The drinks and the heat and the look on Mark's face have made her vaguely nauseous, and she can't quite get her breath. "I need a little air. Excuse me." The room slides like a rolling wave as she crosses to the door. "Sylvie," she hears Mark say somewhere far away behind her, but she doesn't stop.

Outside, she tips her face to the sky, closes her eyes, and gulps back the bile at the base of her throat. Her dress is sleeveless, and the cold sluices her bare arms in goosebumps, but she no longer feels sick, just weary. Just foolish. She'd like to reel the night, the day, the week—everything—in backward and begin again. She'd like to retrace her steps until she found the misstep, the kink. Where was the moment when she began to sink without even realizing she was going under? But it's never so easy as that—one knot tied and then untied. It's never just as easy as that.

Overhead, the sky is clear, black as the water of the bay, and clotted with stars it is usually too cloudy to see. Sylvie doesn't bother trying to connect the constellations as she would if her boys were here, and without the effort at assembly, the stars appear more numerous, more chaotic. Immeasurable. She searches for the word for this—a *racket* of stars, maybe. A *startle*, a *choke*, a *thicket*, a *thrill*. But these are all derivative of something else, and that seems wrong in the face of a sky so big, so terrifying and beautiful both. She's only diminishing everything.

And maybe it's this at the heart of Cath's worries about her—this shrinking, this tendency she has to retreat into her own fears. *Yes*, Sylvie thinks. That's it: she's too afraid. She's getting lost, just like her father did somewhere in the middle of his life. Or she could. She could get lost like that.

Behind her, the door opens and the noise of the party floats out.

"Sylvie?" It's Mark's voice. "Are you out here?"

She hesitates a moment before answering him. "Yes," she says, though. "Yes, I'm here. I'm going to be fine. I'm right here."

MATTER

In the middle of the night he knocks on my open bedroom door, one thin rap, followed by a pause. When I look up from my pillow his figure is framed against the doorway. "What's wrong, Matty? Did you have a bad dream?" I ask. He doesn't move, and so I throw back the sheets and get up.

It's hot in the house. The fires trap the July heat, the smoke insulating the city like a layer of quilt bunting. I've been afraid to open the windows with the poor air quality, afraid we'll both die choking rather than burning. I'm sweating though. I pick the fabric of my nightgown from my chest where it clings to my skin and go to him. He's warm too, his hair wet at his temples and his pajamas wrinkled and damp. His sweat still smells like childhood—sweet instead of salty and dank, something like dough and wet grass, though I can't quite name it. He holds his favorite blanket in his hand. Behind him, the hallway is oddly illuminated for this hour, the rectangles of sky visible through the skylights colored an unsettling sickly rose brown—the halo of the fires. When my ex-husband was a graduate student we lived for a handful of years in Nebraska, and this light makes me think of the way the winter sky on the prairie always pinked before a heavy snow, the way the air could smell ominously of snow for hours before the first flake. Last night's news report said there could be flurries of ash from the fires in the next twenty-four hours, and I imagine it will fall like that midwestern snow—heavy and grayed, making a catastrophic mess of everybody's car windshield and floating in wet clots on the surfaces of my neighbors' backyard pools.

I reach for Matty's shoulder and he pulls away. His blue eyes are wide and he looks far younger than his five years. Far off, behind the closed windows, a siren flares and recedes, flares and recedes. A racket of wind shakes the glass of the French doors downstairs and Matty shivers.

"Come on, sweetheart. You can sleep in here," I say. I pull a pillow and blanket from the bed and settle them on the floor. He will not climb into the bed with me, I know this without asking. "Come on," I say again. "Matty." But he crosses the room to the window and slips behind the drapes, only his ankles and feet showing beneath the hem. "You want to see?" I ask him. Behind the curtain he rises onto his toes.

For a moment I wait for him to wail, but when he doesn't, I go to him and pull the cord so that the curtains part. Light spills into the room. Matty touches his fingertips to the glass. Below, the streetlamps are on but dulled, as they would be in daylight. The sky is the color of a muddy lake, and a helix of wind spirals the dry grass clippings that have settled in the gutter so that they eddy up and around like a dust devil before dropping to stillness again.

A day ago there was only smoke, but now the foothills are bright with visible fire. Flames in neon orange have swallowed the tops of the hills, and the charred tree line stands in spiked silhouette. A pelt of smoke rolls skyward from the blaze, thick and felted by the heat. It is impossible to tell cloud from smoke. The gray swath of it blankets the whole horizon, unfurls in woolly hanks, unravels upward and spools down the hillsides and out to the Pacific in brown flumes and rivulets. The world might be ending. It is a scene from a dream or a movie, something unreal.

"Moon," Matty says. I take it as a question, though the inflection is wrong. If he speaks at all, he demands. He hasn't picked up the cadences of English conversation yet, and I'm not sure I'm a good interpreter.

"Moon?" I say, lifting my voice. He and I are locked in our own flawed way of communicating, or, more often than not, left to read each other's silences.

"Speak to him in complete sentences, as if you understand him, even if you don't," the therapist directed me at one of Matty's early sessions. "Eventually, the wires will connect."

I point to the sky now and tap the glass. "The moon is there," I say. "Somewhere. Behind the smoke, it's there. You just can't see it."

Matty slaps the glass with the flat of his hand, once, and then a second time, harder. The window shakes. I'm afraid he'll put his fist through it.

"No," I say. "No, Matty. Come on. Back to bed. You're so tired. Time for bed."

"Moon!" he yells and jerks away from me when I catch his wrist before he can hit again.

I don't want to argue. For just an instant I would like to be complicit instead of fighting him. But it's nearly four a.m. and he'll be wrecked with exhaustion in the morning. "Let's come away now, Matty," I say. I move to pull the curtains shut.

"No!" he says.

"Bed." I touch his shoulder. He hisses. A wet splatter of saliva hits my cheek. "Matvei, now," I say, a stone materializing in my throat. "I said bedtime."

He reaches forward for a handful of curtain and pulls until the rod comes loose from its fixture. It clatters to the floor and he screams— in fright or rage, it isn't clear. I lift him and he kicks, fights to get free.

"Matty, don't be silly. You'll hurt yourself," I say as I set him down and drag him away from the dressing table and the bed. His face is red. He kicks my ankle hard enough that I actually stumble forward and crack my own shin against the bed frame.

"Damn it, Matty," I say.

And suddenly my chest is nettling with anger.

I step away—I have to—step over him raging still in the middle of the carpet. In the corner I turn to the radio on the dresser and fumble through the stations for something, anything—just another voice. I find the news. The reporter's voice is steady, low, monotone, and I sink to the floor and hug my knees.

"More than five thousand acres have burned," the voice from the radio reports. "Residents of Goleta, Isla Vista, and Santa Barbara should prepare for power outages and possible evacuations if firefighters cannot contain the blaze."

Matty is sobbing now, wearing down. This is his routine: rage, destruction, exhaustion. "It's okay," I say over the news.

It is nearly dawn. Behind the brown of the smoke, the sky is pearling with morning. The light comes in the bare window milky and pinked. Eventually Matty puts his cheek to the rug. Eventually he goes quiet and just lies, his eyes wide and alert, but his body still.

"Everything is fine," I say in a whisper. "Everything is fine now, Matty. You and I are fine." He turns his eyes to me as I say it.

Sometimes it seems he exists alone in the glass globe of his mind and only now and then looks out and sees me there on the other side.

"It's all fine, Matty," I say to him. I say it again and again.

⠪●⠊

It was the fall of 2002 when I was first shown into the Los Angeles office of an international adoption agency. A young social worker with a thick eastern European accent I recognized from our several phone conversations sat behind the desk, a stack of manila files in front of her, mine opened on the top. The walls in the narrow office were painted a cheerful yellow and tacked with photos of smiling children standing beside their adoptive parents, some taken on the front stoops of children's homes in China and Russia and South Korea, and some taken later, in suburban backyards and living rooms. There were several Christmas photos: a mother, father, and three children all dressed in red sweaters and seated, arms around each other's shoulders, on an overstuffed couch; a collage of photos of the same dark-haired child doing things like sitting on a plastic sled, cutting out cookies from dough, licking a candy cane. In another picture, a little girl grinned from her seat on the lap of an American shopping mall Santa. The children all looked well fed, happy, clean, adjusted. If I received one of these cards in the mail, I thought, I would never guess at an infancy spent in foster care or an orphanage across the world, and this recognition buoyed me.

The social worker, Vera, a petite mousy-haired woman, recited my profile aloud, her English stiff and impeccable, stating each fact of my biography, asking me questions. "Yes," I said again and again, confirming what I had typed into my computer at home in Santa Barbara: I was forty-two and divorced; I had no living children; I was an editor employed by the University of California, though I would take a leave of absence when I brought my son or daughter home. I had planned for this, I said to her. I had waited and waited, and now I was ready. More than ready. "It doesn't get more ready than this," I said. And, yes, I knew I'd be a single mother—an "older" single mother, though it pained me a little to describe myself in that way, because I didn't feel old and I wasn't sure anymore that single mattered. I was ready for this. Had I made that part clear enough? This was my third go at the adoption process. I was open to a child of any age, nationality, or race. A child with disabilities or special needs. Fine. I was ready. "I am someone's mother," I said.

Vera's face brightened. "You wrote that here, too, in your file: 'I am someone's mother,'" she said and looked up. "You wrote that, yes?"

"I've been waiting a long time for a child."

Vera reached across her desk to squeeze my hand. "Your child has been waiting for you, too, Nina." She patted my hand and I nodded. Vera whisked a tissue from the box on the desk to hand me. "Don't worry," she said. "It's an emotional time." She turned back to the file and signed her name in tight, perfect cursive on the line at the bottom of the page, approving me for the next step in the process.

I drove home to Santa Barbara to wait again.

Then, in midwinter, a phone call. "Thank you so, so much," I heard myself say into the phone, too eager maybe, when the man on the other end gave me a date and a time for a home study. I bought a child's bed and a set of twin sheets printed with red and yellow and blue stars, a red bureau, and a nightlight. I made a trip to the bookstore and brought home enough children's books to fill two emptied shelves. I fit child safety locks on the cabinets in the kitchen and stuck bright orange foam corners to the angles of the glass coffee table. Even with these changes, I couldn't seem to evict the feeling of solitude in the house. The house was too quiet. Too still. For several days I lived around the solitude, trying to pay attention to it, as if it were a feral cat I'd only inadvertently let in and might still tame.

Finally the social worker arrived—not Vera, but a young man with a slow, California drawl, and he was an hour late. I showed him the kitchen, the baby-proofed front room. "Given your file, your child will probably be older," he said. "Not an infant." He gave me a sympathetic look and nodded at the foam corners.

I shrugged. "I might keep them anyway. The orange adds a decorative something, a je ne sais quoi. Don't you think?" He smiled. Perhaps humor could make up for my other faults.

I took him upstairs to see the bedrooms and he marveled at the view of the city and the foothills from my bedroom window—all of Santa Barbara spread out, the green florets of the treetops and the orange tiles of the roofs. Downstairs again, he told me he'd kill for a backyard with fruit trees and a patio like mine. He hugged me when he left, and I couldn't help but feel that was a good sign, an A+ in the way of home inspection grades. "You seem really genuine," he said at the door. "Really authentic. I'm putting that in my report." He squeezed my forearm.

In a week a letter arrived: the house was approved. I was approved. More waiting.

It was March when the next letter arrived. They'd found a child. His name was Matvei—Matty—and he was four years old, though his exact birthday wasn't known. He had blue eyes and blond hair, a speech delay, and a possible attachment disorder, though these diagnoses were often incorrect, based on temporary behaviors that stemmed from the unsettled circumstances that had brought the child to the adoption process. The child's personality and needs were always clearer after the first year in the new home, once routine had been established and life was secure.

Fine, I thought and quickly revised my vision of my child—I would have a little boy. *A little boy. A little boy.*

Matty was born in Podolsk, an industrial city not far from Moscow, and had been in the system for two years. There was no information on his life before the orphanage in the paperwork I'd received.

"What happened to his mother?" I asked Vera over the phone one evening. I'd called several times already with questions—so many that she had given me her cell phone number. "Is she still living?" I asked. "Why couldn't she keep him?"

"I'm sorry," Vera said, simply. "There's nothing. He was left at a church. That's all."

I crossed the globe on the fifteenth of March.

Children's House Number 57 was a large, square, white building on the outskirts of Moscow. It was raining when I arrived, and I dashed up the concrete walk and stood on the stoop under an overhanging roof, rang the bell, and spoke into an intercom. There was some confusion at first, and I repeated, "Привет!" loudly into the receiver several times, as if volume were the issue, while from inside a woman's voice answered me, incomprehensible but clearly frustrated; in a moment a second voice beamed through the speaker, telling me in English to wait.

I was shown to a playroom at the back of the house—a large, open room, stocked with a few child-sized tables and chairs. There were bins of toys on the floor. Some children sat cross-legged on a blue carpet in one corner playing board games, and another girl drew alone at a table. The walls were hung with the children's finger paintings and schoolwork, but the room smelled of disinfectant and stale food, and I was reminded that this was an institution—that just upstairs there was a long corridorlike room lined with identical, white-sheeted beds and a lavatory with a trough-sink and a row of stalls. "Hello," I tried with the little girl at the table. "Привет." She looked up from her paper, registered my smile, and turned away.

A different woman—an attendant, it seemed, as she was dressed in cotton pants and a loose shirt with a swipe of what looked like finger paint across one shoulder—appeared at the doorway, her fingers gripping the wrist of a small boy: Matty. I recognized him with a physical pang, a stinging charge in my chest that almost made me gasp, it was so unexpected. *Joy*, I thought, and, I admitted to myself, relief. He was really here. He was coming home with me. Finally.

The attendant urged the boy forward, and he shuffled in my direction but did not meet my eyes.

"Hello," I said.

He was smaller than I expected, both shorter and thinner, and he looked younger than my vision of a preschool-aged child. I tried not to jump to assumptions about his health. He'd been well fed and well looked after, had had all of the routine physicals and had passed them with a clean bill of health; I'd been assured of all of this a number of times. Still, I had a package of M&M's in my purse that I'd offer him the moment we left the house.

He was dressed in a blue sweatshirt with a picture of Donald Duck on the chest, a pair of canvas shorts, and brown oxford shoes, scuffed

across the toes. His legs were skinny, his knees knobby. There was a
bruise on his left shin and a Band-Aid on that knee; the woman in
the T-shirt said he had slipped while playing. He looked at the social
worker and touched the knee. He had sandy hair and large eyes, and
his skin was so thin that the blue veins laced beneath it were visible on
the surface of his forehead. "Isn't it a little cold for shorts?" I asked. I
had a pair of sweats for him in my luggage, in case of an accident on
the plane, but nothing there with me at the house.

"He insists. This is what he likes," the woman said with a shrug.

I wasn't sure if I should shake his hand or hug him. I put out both
arms, offering the hug. "I'm Nina," I said. This was in line with Vera's
advice: "Don't expect him to call you 'mother' right away. He may remember his birth mother. He may need time to warm to you."

He stepped back. The woman tsked, leaning over and whispering
to him, but he wouldn't be moved.

"He'll warm up," I said.

"The children are often shy at first," the social worker assured me.

"It's fine," I said. "I know."

Matvei was holding a dust-colored shoebox, the lid taped down.

"What's in the box?" I asked.

"He will leave that here," the woman said.

He looked at her and pulled the box closer, tucking it under one
arm. At this, the social worker told him something, and he narrowed
his eyes, said a single, hard word. "No. Not on the plane," the social
worker said in English, for my benefit.

"He can keep what's in it," I said. "Tell him he can keep what's in
it." I unzipped my purse. "Here, he can put it in here." I stepped forward and got down on my knees. "Can I have this?" I asked him. He
let me slide the box from his grasp and raise the lid. Inside: a pink-
flecked rock, an empty film canister, a plastic spider ring. I dropped
the rock and canister in my purse and slid the spider ring on his finger. "For safekeeping," I said.

When we stepped outside, the midwinter sky was the color of

cooked oatmeal, the ground frozen, the lawn patchy and drained of color. The icy puddles beneath the swings in the play area reflected white flashes of sky between the mounds of stiff mud that rose from the water's surface. I had paid my taxi driver to wait in the drive.

We had time to kill in the airport. I scheduled an overnight flight thinking he could sleep, but it was all too much, and he wouldn't close his eyes. He ate the last of the bag of M&M's and then his bag of airline pretzels and mine. He wolfed down the in-flight dinner. A flight attendant brought him a cup of ginger ale and he licked his lips after every sip. Finally full, he reclined his seat and occupied himself with pushing the radio buttons on the seat's armrest.

There was nothing but black on the other side of the window. Black, black sky. Black, black sea below. Ocean indistinguishable from sky. Now and then the light at the tip of the plane's wing caught a swift of cloud and illuminated it blue-green and ghostly, floating in the midst of the deep darkness. "See the clouds?" I said to Matty. His eyes had begun to look glassy with fatigue. "They're nothing but water, you know," I said. "Well, ice, really, this high up. Billions of ice crystals and particulate matter. Dust and salt and things like that. Chemicals that have risen into the air." As I spoke, he kept his eyes on the window, and I chose to see this as some level of interest in what I was telling him, or just an attention to the sound of my voice—a start, at least, to communicating. I had read that when a baby is born, he emerges recognizing his mother's voice. The plane's wing caught another fibrous thread of cloud. "Beautiful, right?" I said, and smiled. He turned his face to mine and studied me, then let out the smallest of sighs, leaned his head against the tiny airplane pillow, and closed his eyes. In five minutes he was asleep. I requested a blanket and unfolded it over his legs—my first go at tucking him in for the night.

It could have been a dream, the plane ride. Time was as hard to measure from my seat beside him as it is when one drifts in and out of sleep, though I didn't doze; I was wide awake, more awake than I'd ever been, I thought. I had the sensation of time stilled and polished, the minutes like beads of air suspended in glass, lovely and impossible accidents. The only sound was the low humming of the plane's engine and the quiet rushing of air from the circular vent above my head. Silvered droplets of condensation formed between the panels of window glass and vibrated, and for a moment it was as if the whole plane had gone underwater and we were submerged far below the surface of the ocean, the darkness outside pressing at the sides of the plane with the full weight of seawater and not the airless compression of high altitude atmosphere. *I am happy*, I told myself. *We two are going to be fine.*

Beside me, Matvei slept with his mouth open, his breath stale when I put my face close to his. He had tiny freckles on his cheeks. His eyelashes were red-brown. I watched him for what must have been an hour, two, and when he seemed well into a deep sleep, I put my hand on his knee, just gently. He jerked awake, his eyes wide and immediately on mine, his stare terrified. It was the look he'd give a stranger. "I'm sorry," I said, and he curled away from me. In a moment he was asleep again, his breath steady once more.

Near dawn the sky went lavender and then blue, and then, like a basin draining, empty white. I craned over Matvei to see outside. The flight attendant brought me a cup of coffee. Just as the light outside yellowed with sunrise, the brown rim of the continent I was bringing him home to appeared, far away and small below us.

Once Matty falls asleep, I shut off the radio and climb onto a chair to replace the curtain rod in its fixture. The room is quiet. This, again, reminds me of snow, of waking too early to an unnatural silence. The smell of smoke, like burned newspapers, is fingering in below the fine crack between the window and the sash, and there is a white film of fire dust, too fine to call ash, along the ledge outside. There's nothing to be done, though, so I settle the rod in the brace and let the curtains fall before tottering off the chair and scooping Matty from the floor into my arms. This is the only time he'll allow himself to be held, when he is sleeping. I carry him down the hall to his bedroom and sit on the edge of his bed, rocking him, smelling his good sleepy smell. I put my nose to his hair, which smells like the tear-free baby soap I still use in his baths, and then ease him onto his pillow and pull the quilt up over his knees.

It is too late to go back to sleep myself, so I shower and make coffee and sit in front of the TV. The news is fixed on the fire. The governor has declared a state of emergency. Nearly six thousand acres of the national forest just north of the city have burned now, the winds speeding the fire's growth. A still "before" image flashes onto the screen: a pristine hillside, green with sugar pines and bay laurel and chaparral. "Now," the reporter says, his voice stiffly sober as he meets the camera's eye, "all that's gone. The grand houses that once graced the ridges of these foothills are all just foundations in the wake of this devastating blaze." I put the TV on mute. Video shot yesterday runs, and the reporter's dialogue appears in white lettering at the bottom of my screen. People lug suitcases and duffel bags to their cars, strap boxes of hastily packed photo albums and treasured family keepsakes onto the roofs of their SUVs. Now the Santa Anas have picked up, and there is concern about keeping the fire from spreading deeper into the hills and canyons. Volunteers have dug a ten-foot-wide trench around the perimeter of the old mission. A video feed shows a crew of uniformed men using garden hoses to wet the landscaping on the UC campus. I recognize the entrance of the library, a corner of the grounds where, when I'm working, I often take my lunch.

I must doze off, because it is nearly nine when I look up again. A ticker is scrolling across the bottom of the screen: extremely dangerous air quality, evacuations mandatory for the neighborhoods east of the city center now. I consider leaving. Not evacuating with Matty might elicit another home visit, might jeopardize things. He's not officially a citizen yet, and this first year is a sort of probation. I imagine Vera calling, apology in her voice. But this is irrational, I know, and, beyond that, it seems impossible that the fire will cross the city. Impossible. How long has the mission stood? And if I left, where would I go? I have no retired parents in Tahoe or San Diego ready to welcome me and my son and his "possible attachment disorder" into their home for who knows how long; no best friend just down the highway. No, we'll stay. The disruption of leaving would unsettle Matty anyhow.

I shut off the TV and listen for him upstairs. Some days he wakes happy, pleasant, trudges down the stairs carrying his blanket, his hair still mussed from his sleep and his eyes somehow even wider than usual as he rubs them awake. But other mornings are a fight from the start, and today he will be tired and so prone to a poor temper. Upstairs a bedroom door closes. The toilet in the bathroom flushes. I wait, wondering what in the world he could be doing, but then, just as I'm about to head up to find him, he is at the foot of the stairs.

"Breakfast?" I ask. I try to hold a bright and cheerful note in my voice, smile at him, and motion toward the kitchen. "Let's see," I say. The therapist has also recommended speaking my thoughts aloud. Not all of them, of course. Certainly not all of them. I'm to narrate, rather. *Here I go, making the toast. Isn't toast lovely? Doesn't everyone feel better with a piece of toast for breakfast? Yum! Toast!*—that sort of thing. It's a way to surround Matty with language, the hope being that he will absorb words the way a sponge absorbs water. As I pour cereal and talk about pouring cereal, I try to imagine a lake swelling somewhere in him, the sound of my voice burbling up from its depths and sending rings out across the surface of Matty's consciousness. "Today is Tuesday," I say. "What do we do on Tuesdays?" I think. I hand him his bowl and spoon. "Swimming, yes? Today is swimming day, Matty. Did you remember that?"

I let him have a cartoon and eat at the coffee table. He still holds his spoon with an apelike grip. He eats in fits and starts, shoveling it in during commercials, then sitting completely still, his mouth ajar, when Curious George reappears on the screen. I am relieved when he gets up after the show ends and follows me upstairs without hesitating, when he lets me help him into his swim trunks and T-shirt without trying to wrench his body away from me. Outside a few minutes later, he gets into the car without fussing as well, and as a reward I play a CD of nursery rhymes as we drive, though I'm not entirely sure he understands this as a reward, nor that he cares for the CD; he's never exactly shown pleasure when listening to it, but neither has he complained. I glance at him every few seconds in the rearview mirror. "Should we sing along?" I ask—the song is "Twinkle, Twinkle, Little Star"—but he is straight-faced, his eyes on the window, his hands in fists on his lap.

The sky is the color of milky coffee, a dirty, orange aura over the downtown buildings in the direction of the fires, and the wind is hot and fiercer than usual and smells not like seawater but crisp and violent, like burned fur, perhaps, or hair. The lot at the YMCA is empty, and for the first time it occurs to me that I should have called about lessons. But we're here now, so I get Matty out of his seat. My hair whips about my face and lashes me in the eyes. "Hold your breath," I say to Matty, putting my own hand over my mouth and nose to show him. Matty grins, finally, and I laugh. "Do I look funny?" I puff out my cheeks with a held breath, shake my head in the wind. "Does my hair look crazy now?" He reaches up as if he could grab a leash of wind like the string on a kite and quicksteps toward the door. A gush of reassuring calm wells up in my center at this show of emotion from him. It's the fire, the strangeness of the day, cracking everything open. Overhead, the fringed tops of the palm trees that line the Y's lot toss and rustle, and the flag on the pole near the gym's entrance snaps and billows, snaps and billows.

When we reach the glass front door, though, it is locked. I shake the handle. The lights are on inside, a woman in a red polo shirt sitting at the reception desk. The woman looks up, shakes her head and wags a pen in our direction.

"No," I say. "Oh no. We came all the way down here." I rattle the handle again and the woman gets up, a look of clear irritation on her face, and comes to the door.

"Ma'am, we're closed today," she says when she unlocks and opens the door. "No lessons, due to the evacuation."

Matty tugs my hand, flails around, impatient. "Stop, please, Matt," I say to him. "We're near the parking lot. Be still, please." I hold his hand firm. He's ready to slip away, dart into the lot and then the street.

"Sorry," the woman says. But just then, behind her, Matty's swim teacher walks into the lobby.

"But he's here," I say, pointing to the teacher.

The man, a boy himself, really—Ben—looks up. He's lanky, baby faced. He has an irksome habit of showing up ten or fifteen minutes late for class and then letting the kids spend more time blowing bubbles than actually learning to dog paddle, but here he is, and he waves at Matty. "Hey, little guy," he says.

"There are no lessons today?" I ask him over the woman's head. "Please," I say. "You're here already, Ben. Can't he just go in for ten minutes?"

The woman at the door rolls her eyes, looks back to Ben. They seem to be negotiating something, but Ben shrugs. "Sure," he says. "There's no lifeguard on duty today though."

"I can lifeguard," I say as I release Matty, who slips beneath the woman's arm and gallops into the lobby. "Thank you, thank you," I say. "I promise I'll jump in if I have to, clothes and all."

The woman steps aside. "Ten minutes," she says, giving me a look, and she locks the door again at our backs.

Inside, the natatorium is calm without the other children, the water lapping rhythmically at the tile walls of the pool and the light coming in through the frosted glass ceiling creamy, the air soft with it and with the mist of chlorine fizzing off the water's aqua surface. I keep Matty on the bleachers while we wait for Ben to emerge from the locker room. Usually the children all sit lined up along the lip of the pool, but I know better than to trust Matty there. Three weeks ago he suddenly swung out an arm and hit the boy next to him, then dove forward into the pool so unexpectedly that the lifeguard actually did jump into the water. He had Matty in his arms within seconds, no catastrophe, but it was awful all the same. "I'm so sorry," I said afterward, when he handed Matty out to me sputtering. "I'm so sorry." I had done nothing though; I had not jumped in after my son. I had merely stood from my seat on the third bleacher and watched the whole spectacle unfold. "He knows better," I said to the lifeguard, to the others at the pool, and heard myself blaming Matty. I could feel the other mothers' stares on my back. In the pool, their children had all stopped swimming and looked on, suspended in the water, clutching their foam boards. "He's still adjusting to everything. Sometimes it's a little difficult." I wrapped Matty in a towel and carried him out. He was screaming then, wanting to get back into the water, not sure why he couldn't swim as usual. I put him into the car seat wet, wanting only to get out of the lot as quickly as possible. Later, I contemplated forgetting about swimming lessons altogether, never mind the tuition I'd already paid. I imagined the other parents' relief if we dropped out. But Matty needed the lessons. That was the bottom line. Matty needed to be around their children, if only for half an hour once a week.

"Hey, guy!" Ben hollers now from the center of the pool as I find a foam buoy belt from a pile on the floor, knot the belt's narrow rope around Matty's middle, and lead him to the water's edge. "Come on in!" Ben has tossed out a bucketful of plastic bath toys—rubber duckies in green and yellow, a blue boat and a green octopus—for Matty to paddle toward, but Matty sits on the tiled lip of the pool.

"You only have ten minutes, Matty," I say, though even as I say it I know ten minutes might just as well be an hour or a year to Matty, the concept of time, like so much else, still too slippery and vague for him to grasp.

"Come get this duck, Matty," Ben calls, squeaking the duck in Matty's direction. Eventually Matty lowers himself into the pool, but instead of swimming to Ben he turns his back and motors himself around in small circles, singing something under his breath.

"What's he saying?" Ben asks.

"A song," I say. "I don't know it."

Across the water, Ben starts singing the words to "Twinkle, Twinkle, Little Star." Matty stops his own song and watches him.

"Go on, Matty," I say again.

"It's okay. He'll come."

I throw Ben a grateful look. He continues squeaking the toys and put-puttering the plastic boat back and forth with emphatic motoring, clowning and splashing to get Matty's attention. Still Matty putters in the shallow end, looking at his fingers below the water's surface, tilting forward and backward to wet his face and then his hair. I strain to register the expression on his face. Is it curiosity or timidity or ambivalence? I ought to be able to read him by now.

After twenty minutes, I stand. "Thank you," I say to Ben. "I guess he isn't going to really swim today."

"Hey. No big deal. I was here anyway." Ben ducks beneath the water and swims in a fast crawl toward the wall where he hoists himself out.

"Really, I'm sorry," I say as he shakes his head. "You went to extra trouble for him. I appreciate that."

"It's fine." Ben ruffles the water from his hair. There's a tattoo of the red cross and the word *Lifeguard* in script across his bicep that somehow makes him seem even more adolescent than his young face. At the start of the swim class he reported that he had just graduated from the university in December. In another world, he could be my son. I'm old enough.

"I should get changed," Ben says. "They're closing shop for real here by noon." He holds the locker room door for us, and I coax Matty from the pool, then unlace the knots binding his buoy to his waist. He fidgets and fusses as I work and quiets only at the promise of a soda from the hallway vending machine.

"See ya, Matt," Ben says as we leave, and Matty doesn't even raise his head.

In the lobby, I stuff change into the vending machine and hand Matty a can of grape soda. "Wait," I say, and grip his wrist. "Don't shake it." He is still wet, shuffling in a pair of flip-flop sandals and leaving puddles behind on the tile floor. The woman at the counter huffs her irritation as I tug Matty past the reception desk and push open the front door again.

"Have a lovely day!" I say to her pointedly as we go, and I let the door slam shut behind me.

When I get in the car I let the engine idle, the inane song about a yodeling ostrich running loudly on the CD player and Matty sucking at the mouth of the soda can in the back seat. I hear again my own voice telling the therapist that I'm a bundle of nerves these days. But it is less nervousness than uncertainty, I think now, or maybe anger. *Yes*, I wanted to say to the woman at the reception desk as we passed her, *this is actually the best I can do.*

I turn around to look at Matty. "Did you have fun?" His mouth is stained purple from the soda and his eyes meet mine briefly before he looks away.

At home, we eat peanut butter and honey sandwiches at the coffee table together, both of us on our knees, Matty hunched forward over his glass of milk, blowing a foam of white bubbles into his cup. The TV is on again, and there are more images of the fires, the field reporter's voice backed by the cellophane static of the burning. The city is evacuating the hospital, the university, a number of residential districts, all of them downtown now. Several familiar neighborhood names scroll along the bottom of the screen in a red box. I stand and clear the plates and shut off the TV.

"You need a bath," I say to Matty. "That pool is full of chlorine; your skin will itch."

Upstairs, I wait outside the bathroom door while he uses the toilet—a privacy he insists on and I respect, though he seems too young to be left alone in the bathroom. I picture him eating the toothpaste, climbing onto the counter and pulling from the medicine chest the Bic razor I use on my legs, clogging the toilet with an entire unspooled roll of toilet paper. None of these things has actually happened, but I find it easier and easier to envision disaster. "Are you okay?" I ask, my hand on the doorknob, my ear close to the door. The toilet flushes; water runs in the sink. When I open the door he is drying his hands and everything is in order; he scowls up at me.

I pull back the shower curtain, start the water, and am bent over the tub testing the temperature when the phone rings. "Come on," I say to Matty, and turn off the water, then shepherd him down the hallway to the bedroom. I catch it on the last ring; it's my office secretary calling from campus.

"I'm not interrupting you, am I? How's that baby of yours?"

"Hello, Martha," I say. "Was there a reason you called?"

"They're evacuating campus, you know, but I'm still here for a little while if you want to come by for your things. Whatever you want to be sure is spared, that is."

I picture first my own office—a blank square of a space with a standard issue desk and a potted cactus probably long since browned on the windowsill—and then that of Martha, the stout, bob-haired office secretary, a woman in her late sixties, whose own desk is a clutter of paperwork and trinkets and framed five-by-seven photographs that must be decades old.

"You heard they're evacuating us, didn't you?" Martha says.

"I saw that. It's too bad." At my side, Matty has flung off the towel and is spinning circles, his arms wide and his head tipped up toward the ceiling. He laughs as he spins.

"I just wanted you to hear, in case you missed it. I know you're supposed to be on leave this term, but you might have things in the office you'd want to come get, in case—you know."

"I'm right in the middle of something here. I don't think I'll make it in, but I'm sure nothing will happen."

"You're sure? I think you ought to come."

Matty stops midspin and stumbles forward, falls. He sprawls on the floor, his body a star, his eyes closed and the Russian words of another song familiar only to him playing on his lips. "Martha, it's thoughtful of you to call, but it's Matty's nap time, and I try to adhere to that."

"Oh, yes. How important that nap is!" she laughs. "You know, though, I could stop by later. If you tell me what you want, I could bring it to you so you don't have to interrupt his schedule." She pauses.

"Fine," I say. "I'll try to get there."

"Super. I'll wait then. And I have something for your little one."

"Shit," I say as I hang up, and then: "You didn't hear that, Matty." I get him dressed again. "We'll do the bath later," I tell him when he begins to fight. I raise my voice a cheerful octave and grin widely to stir him toward cooperation. "It's backwards day! How fun is that?" I load him into the car with a juice box and his blanket, and he goes silent as the car begins to move, his eyes on the window as he takes greedy gulps of the apple juice.

We drive the side streets, meandering. I will him to drift off, figuring it will mean he'll be drowsy when I stop at the office, and so less likely to run wild. Downtown, the shops and restaurants have closed and the sidewalks are bare. The reflection in the black glass of the bank building's mirrored windows is oddly still, and the grocery store parking lot all but empty.

"Isn't this strange?" I say to Matty. His eyes haven't drifted from the window and he seems to be listening.

On the next block, in front of a row of white stucco apartment buildings, a little girl not much older than Matty stands on her front stoop watching the spray of an opened fire hydrant across the street, the water frothing white from the spigot and flooding an oily pool across the pavement. "Look, Matty," I say, and he shifts his gaze. The girl watches us pass, raising her hand in a slow wave as I drive away.

Above, the sky is low and mottled with the smoke and soot. A few flakes of white ash as fine as snow flutter against the windshield. I turn one corner and the next and then am as far west as I can go: the beach. I move the car down the wide avenue along the waterfront and find the flat span of the Pacific gray-blue as always, though the sand is weirdly deserted. "Matty," I say, and arch to look at him over my shoulder, to point out the white lifeguard towers he likes, but he has fallen asleep, his head lolling against one shoulder, his mouth open and his cheeks flushed with the heat of the car, the juice box tipped in his lap and spilling a dark stain on the leg of his shorts.

I pull over and park facing the water, pick up the juice, and turn on the air conditioner. He can sleep. We won't make it to campus, but it doesn't matter.

Ahead, the waves of the tide roll in even intervals. When we first moved to California, my ex-husband and I used to like to drive down and sit looking out at the water here when a storm was coming in from the Pacific, visible from miles off, a dark gray swath of sky moving steadily toward the coast, a veil that was really rain hanging between the crest of the sky and the lip of the horizon. Now and then, there might be a flash of lightning, a bright ribbon reaching from cloud to sea, but at such a distance even that was drained of any threat and seemed merely beautiful.

Today, though, I can see nothing but smoke, smoke for miles out over the water, as if a lid has been lowered above the sea.

Ash collects on the windshield as I sit, the flakes papery and lacking any of the fine detail of snowflakes. Eventually I turn on the wipers and they whisk across the glass in rhythmic sweeps, scattering a little out of view.

There's a car in the drive when I pull back up to the house, and it isn't until I'm parked and opening the door that I recognize Martha sitting on the front step.

She stands as I unbuckle Matty. He is sweaty with sleeping, his shorts wet with the juice mess, and he fusses when I lift him from his seat, then blinks and wipes his eyes and fights to be released as I carry him to the step.

"This must be your boy," Martha says. She reaches out as if to hug him and I stop her.

"He's just been sleeping," I say. "He doesn't wake in a good mood."

"Well, who does, right, honey?" She bends, crouching forward to meet him at eye level. "I have a present for you." She reaches into her purse and holds out a lollipop. "Can he have it, Mom? I had knitted you a baby cap when I thought you would come to us a tiny thing, but that wouldn't do for a big boy like you, would it? A sucker is a better treat."

I take the candy and unwrap it, give it to him. "Say thank you, Matt," I say, but the lollipop is already in his mouth, and he says nothing. "His English," I apologize.

Martha nods. She seems oblivious to my embarrassment, to Matty's whining, and clucks at him just as she would an infant, telling me that he has beautiful eyes, telling him that he's lucky to have freckles. "They mean good luck, you know," she says. She turns to me. "I was just sitting here in your driveway thinking, 'How long should I wait for her?' And then here you were. I'm so glad I caught you."

At the end of my arm, Matty pulls to be let free of her. His mouth and chin are shiny with the green sheen of the lollipop's sugar.

Martha nudges a white box at her feet. "I brought what I thought you'd want, if you were me."

I unlock the front door, and Matty slips into the house. "Shoes, Matty!" I call, but he's gone. I drop my purse just inside the door.

The breeze has picked up, and my eyes burn with the smoke it carries. The sound of it rustling the blanched tufts of ornamental grass in the garden is like insect chatter. From above, there is the dry, sifting sound of the flat eucalyptus leaves shifting against one another and against the texture of the breeze. The air is sooty and clouded with the particulate dust of the fires. Looking through it is not unlike opening one's eyes underwater and trying to see clearly through the diaphanous haze.

"It was unnecessary of you to go out of your way like this," I say.

"I know," Martha says. She has soft eyes and graying hair. She smiles. "You never brought the little boy by to see us, you know. We were all so hoping you would."

I apologize. "I will," I say.

"You're both doing well though?"

"To be honest, I really can't—I just haven't been able to do anything extra." My face warms.

"Oh, honey," Martha says. "I do remember how that feels. I had three children, all of them little at once, barely a year between each of them. Like stair steps, I had them. Two boys and a girl. And they've given me six grandchildren. My daughter's working in Texas now. They lived with me for a few months last year, she and her three girls—maybe you remember. I brought the girls by a few times." She waits for a sign of my recognition and I nod, though I don't remember any children coming by. "But my daughter found a job."

"Good for her," I say. "I'm sure you're enjoying a quiet house again." I pick up the box and balance it against my hip.

"I never minded the children's noise," she says. "I was happy for having them around. To tell you the truth, I think they'd have been better off staying with me."

I shift the box. "I'm sure your daughter appreciated having someone to help her out."

"Yes, well." She shakes her head. "It never is easy, is it?"

A gust chatters against the door and the wind chimes clang on the back porch.

"I've taken enough of your time," Martha says. "You have packing to do, I'm sure."

"We're staying, actually. It'd be too much to try to evacuate now, with Matty. And, really, where would I go? Who would want us?" I laugh as if this is a joke. "We'll wait it out. We'll be fine." I open the door again, hold the knob in my hand.

"Well, consider it," Martha says. She leans forward and kisses my cheek. "It's important to think of someplace you can take that sweet boy for safekeeping if things get worse."

I watch through the window as she leaves.

The sky has turned a burnished copper and the clouds of smoke over the hills roil, veined now in the near dusk with bright threads—streams of dust still burning as they rise. There is the distant ticking of helicopters, and now and then one appears through the smoke, a tiny red-and-black spot in the sky, trailing a red plume of fire retardant. The words of the childhood nursery rhyme from Matty's CD play in my head: "*Ladybug, ladybug, fly away home. Your house is on fire, and your children will burn.*"

I set down the box and lock the front door. "Matty?" I call. It is strangely quiet. "Matty? I'm sorry that took so long. Where are you?"

I climb the stairs and move through the upstairs of the house, calling his name. "Come on now, Matt. Come out." In his room, I lift the bedspread and crouch down to look in the space below the bed. I open the closet doors, lift the lid on the laundry hamper. "Peekaboo," I say. "Matty?" No answer. "This isn't funny anymore, Matt. Come out now."

Remembering suddenly the full bathtub, I rush down the hallway. But behind the bathroom door the tub is undisturbed, the water silvered and still.

I take the stairs two at a time now. He is not in the kitchen. Not behind the couch in the living room. Not beneath the table. "Matt!" I call. Not tucked into the coat closet or curled behind a cupboard door. "Matty!" I scream his name. He turned the TV on before disappearing, apparently, and the calliope music of a cartoon tinkles quietly from the set.

This is it, I say to myself. My disaster, the loose end I've been waiting for. This is what I knew would happen. He's done something impetuous and I've lost him. I imagine him down the street or over the fence and already submerged beneath the surface of the neighbors' pool. My heart bangs against my ribs.

But in that second I spot him: a flash of movement beyond the back window. He is there—impossibly—past the child lock and out the bolted French doors, standing precariously on top of the patio table, his face turned skyward.

I rush to him. "You scared me!" I say as I grab him and pull him toward me. I can feel the rise and fall of his chest against mine, my own panicked heartbeat tripping wildly, and his, startled, doing the same. But this is not an accident—not even nearly an accident. Nothing has gone wrong. The patio is enclosed and completely safe. There is just the wind and the smoke, the motes of ash floating around us and the quiet gulp-and-swallow of water against the mouth of the pool filter next door. "You scared me," I say again. "I love you and I'm so angry with you right now, Matt. Can you understand that? Can you understand me, Matty?"

He says nothing. I pull him in again, hug him, and perhaps because I have frightened him, he doesn't push me away.

"Moon?" he asks when I let go, his inflection perfect this time, a clear question. He points at the sky—not an apology for slipping out of the house, but maybe an explanation. The layer of cloud is as opaque and monochrome as the ocean during a storm, and there, in a break between rafts, is the sun, a clot of thick yellow color just above the ridgeline of the mountains, bright and perfectly round—a yolk with a fuzzy aureole of paler, pinkened light circling it.

Looking so directly at the sun, I have the disorienting feeling of waking up after a long nap and finding the day gone and evening already advancing across the sky, like time has collapsed on itself or moved too quickly and then stopped. I think again of those Nebraska winters, the unsettled, lonely light coming through the folds of the blinds in the bedroom windows, so that it might have been either dawn or dusk. I think of getting up and going to the window, raising the shade, and finding the yard and the neighborhood blanketed, changed, both familiar and not.

"No," I say to Matty. "Not the moon." I look up, raising my hand unnecessarily to my forehead so that a triangle of darkness shades my vision. In this instant I make a decision: we will leave. We have to. Even if I can't think now where to go, I need to protect him. I touch his hair. "Not the moon," I say again, "the sun."

TIDES

It starts at dinner one night. She's been home with the children all day (because it is summer; and because they decided early on that this year camp was out of the question, given the expense; and because it is easier for her to work from home, or so he argued and she agreed, though she knew even then how the children can get to squalling and bickering and vying for her attention at every turn—as all small children will do).

It starts at dinner on an evening that is strangely, unseasonably warm for Seattle in July—so warm that by the time she sets a plate of cold sandwiches and a bowl of cold pickled onions (the evening's "vegetable") on the table, she is tired and sweating into her underwire and worrying at least a little bit in the back of her mind about climate change and the incredible, stubborn ignorance of the American government on this issue, and she is simply not in a temper receptive to even benign criticism when he sits down and says, "Sandwiches for dinner?"

Jesus fucking Christ, she thinks but does not say, because they long ago agreed to try not to swear in front of the children. Instead, she says, "I forgot drinks," and she gets up and goes to the kitchen and stands for a long minute with her body wedged between the opened French doors of the refrigerator, letting the draft of mechanically chilled air nook into the damp places beneath her T-shirt while she looks at the paper milk carton and the neat row of juice boxes and finally locates at the very back of the fridge two long-necked bottles of beer lying like downed troops on their sides.

Two hours later, the children have been bathed and brushed and bored into sleep by the long passage she's read to them from *The Hobbit*, and she climbs into the shower herself and has only just begun to suds up her hair when his face appears around the curtain. "No," she says simply. She doesn't even mean to, but she also raises her hand while she says it—an involuntary gesture exactly like the one she makes when telling the dog to *sit* and *stay*.

So that's how it continues, their fight, though *fight* is too active a word for what they're doing, which is more like declining to get along.

He drops the shower curtain, and for a few minutes she hears him at the sink, brushing his teeth and doing whatever that thing is that he does with the floss and his tongue. She hears him pee and flush and open and close the medicine cabinet's mirrored door two or three times, and when he goes, he shuts off the bathroom light so that she has to holler "Hey?" And then the light is back on, without comment or apology.

"The fuck," she says to herself, under her breath, but only because the shower is running and the children are presumably asleep, and there is no one to hear her.

In bed a while later, they lie back to back as always, and he says, "Night," and she says, "Night," and within seconds—truly, seconds— he is breathing the deep sighs of sleep. She thinks it's this she most resents, actually—this easy ability he has (and has always had) to sleep no matter what has just transpired between them. He has the body-brain divide, she thinks. She's recently discussed this with a woman friend—the body-brain divide that, the friend has posited, must be one of the male-specific genes carried only by the Y chromosome. *Yes,* she thinks now, and she considers that one of the trials of her day was that, while cleaning the bathroom, she discovered that her son—a nine-year-old, who has otherwise shown signs of being very intelligent and, according to a standardized test administered by the school district, even measurably "gifted"—has been periodically peeing into the waste bin next to the toilet. "Why?" she had questioned the boy when she discovered the reek and then opened the bin's lid to see a visible puddle of urine collected in a pool at the bottom of the plastic liner. "Why would you do this?" And the boy had just shrugged, an expression of not exactly remorse but (at least) embarrassment on his face. "I didn't think, I guess," he'd said.

"Uh huh," she now says aloud in bed, and her husband rolls toward her and makes a sound of semiconsciousness, and she pats his shoulder the way she used to pat their sleeping babies, and she rolls to her other side so that she doesn't have to be face-to-face with him, breathing in his expired air. Goodnight, love.

It's the next day, or maybe a couple of days later, when she meets a different woman friend at the park, and they sit together on a blanket underneath a maple tree on a hill crowded with other mothers on other blankets, all of them watching their children run screaming between the metal bodies of several brightly colored Dr. Seussian structures that either spout or gush or dump great quantities of chlorinated water. The day is once again unfathomably warm, and she and her friend repeat laments they've made before about the heat and about potentially carcinogenic sunscreen and about the irresponsibility of parents who let their kids bring water guns fashioned like assault weapons to the playground. As they do this, they open their soft-shell coolers and unload snacks—plastic containers filled with washed and cut baby carrots and sliced strawberries and snap peas

and chickpeas and snow peas. Waxed paper baggies filled with rice
crackers and puffed rice and little organic cookies shaped like farm
animals. They eat while they unpack, and soon enough the conversation comes around to a place where she can mention the sandwich
comment from dinner. "He didn't mean anything by it," she says, not
certain why she's excusing him other than that she doesn't want him
to look like a tyrant—he's not a tyrant. He's not cruel. And, more-
over, she's not the sort of woman who would let herself be roped into
a marriage to a cruel tyrant.

The friend sighs, says, "Look, they don't think about what it took
to get those sandwiches on the table."

She thinks about this. "Don't they, though?" she asks. And then,
hesitating, adds, "I mean, also, did it take that much, really, for me to
make sandwiches? Wasn't the point of sandwiches that they don't require very much effort, and is that so bad after a long day? Am I supposed to be up to coq au vin every night?"

"Oh, god," the friend says. "Don't start questioning yourself."

"This is why those blog women love their Crock-Pots," she says.

The friend shakes her head. "Don't get me started on the fucking
Crock-Pots," she agrees.

For a moment they both pause and scan the riot on the playground for their children's particular wet heads among the chaos of
other children's wet heads. Check and check. Everyone accounted for
and upright.

"I just think," she begins again, "I don't know how we got to this
place, you know? In our marriage."

"Inertia," the friend says.

"Right. But still. I thought it'd be easier."

"Everyone thinks that."

"I thought we were a postdomestic partnership."

"Everyone thinks that."

"This isn't even the fight I really want to have."

"Right," the friend says.

From the playground, a shrill chorus of screams. The big bucket has filled and it is tipping, tipping. There's a break in the voices as the water crashes down on the little heads, a splat as it hits the pavement, and then the children scatter, yawping, hooting. She spots her own daughter—dark ponytail, round little bottom in a pink frilled suit—who is galloping, clapping, soaked to the bone. This is the girl who is afraid of a full bathtub; who the last time they all stayed overnight at a hotel insisted on wearing her life vest even in the shallow end of the hotel pool, for fear she'd sink. And yet she loves this mock drowning on the playground, her girl.

"You know," the friend says, "there are all kinds of marriages. I met a woman at the co-op playgroup a while back who told me in confidence she was doing boudoir photos for her husband."

"Those are still a thing?"

"Apparently."

She groans. "Why?"

"He likes them. It was his birthday. Who knows."

"I don't see that. I don't see the appeal."

The friend lifts her eyebrows. "I took a burlesque class once at the rec center when I was getting tired of yoga."

She shakes her head. "Again, I just don't see the appeal."

The friend laughs—one loud *ha!* "You're prudish, though. You have all these principles that make you prudish."

This stings a bit, but it would be worse to deny it. Instead she repeats what they've already agreed on: "There are all kinds of marriages."

The friend nods. She's wearing large sunglasses that obscure not just her eyes but most of the upper half of her face. "Right. Maybe yours is just more traditional than you thought."

The word's such a sinker—*traditional.*

"Don't take that the wrong way," the friend says, laying a hand on her arm. "Mine's traditional, too. But that's just me. And you. Maybe some people have worked this all out."

Down below, on the playground, the bucket is nearly full again, and a crowd of children—hers included—stand below it, shoulder to shoulder, hands clasped, like tiny political protesters, waiting to be doused.

Later, at home again, she makes the children strip to naked in the laundry room, throws their wet suits directly into the wash, and sends them off to separate bathrooms for showers. The laundry room has acquired its summer smell—the mildewy funk of wet towels and sweaty socks. The tile floor is skimmed in a layer of beach sand and playground dirt and backyard grass. She'll do the laundry later. She'll mop later, she thinks. She'll do the whole house. She'll move the couch, too, and get whatever's underneath it—a colony of dust mites and lost LEGO blocks and great clouds of dog hair, no doubt. She should have done this already. Why is it so hard to keep ahead of all this mess? *Domestic entropy*, she thinks. *But no—more like a dust ball at rest stays at rest.*

She stalks into the living room and gets down on her hands and knees in front of the couch, her face to the nub of the area rug, to look beneath it and confirm, and yes—there it is, all of the detritus she's predicted. When she stands, she sees dust on the bookshelves, too. Scuffs along the baseboards. And that place in the corner— where it took her husband five tries to get the Christmas tree wired to the wall securely the first year they were childproofing—it's still un- repaired. There they are: five dark dots of the nail holes, never filled. *The stigmata of our marriage*, she thinks. But, no, that's not funny. It's too much. It crosses a line. Is she saying she's a martyr to something? Or they both are? What is she really saying? She doesn't know, but shit, she's spinning, and why? And for what?

When her mother said *traditional*, she meant safe. And who doesn't want to be safe? Especially right now, when the world is draining into the sea, and smart women have started actually paying to be photographed in their thong underwear. Isn't she supposed to want to be safe? Isn't everybody?

And it's at just this moment when the front door opens—he's home from work. "It's too hot out," he says instead of *hello* or *how was your day*, and he sets the clatter of his keys on the console near the door, empties his pockets onto the console—loose change and a wadded-up parking stub from the downtown garage and a knot of lint that nearly pushes her over the edge. But before she can assemble an argument against any of it, he says, "I was thinking we should take the kids down to the beach tonight."

It's only once a summer or so that they manage it—a weeknight beach dinner. She wrestles the kids back into their damp suits, which they'd normally protest, but the prospect of the beach at sunset—the thrill of bucking the evening routine—has sedated them, shushed them, and they are all compliance and cherubic pink flesh and sweet co-conut smell of sunscreen as she swats their bottoms and sends them, suited again, to fetch their sandals. The cooler is still damp too, but she fills it with more juice boxes, beers. She can hear him changing into his own swimming suit in the bedroom, whistling. Yes—he's the kind of man who whistles. He once told her he learned to whistle at summer camp. That was the kind of childhood he had—campouts and summers in the woods and whistling contests with other boys—and there's still something of that innocence left in him. It's here, in fact, in his happiness at something as simple as taking the children to the beach for an evening. How can it take so little to make a person truly happy? This trait is charming, she thinks. It makes up for so much, his affinity for contentment.

They pile into the car, stop for take-out burgers and fries, then navigate the long route down to the beach, following the one-lane road that threads the hillside overlooking the water. She prefers this route, but rarely takes it because of its impracticality—because of the twenty miles per hour posted speed and the series of slow S curves. It's beautiful, though. The road is lined on both sides by trees—maples and cottonwoods and alders—and tonight the evening light is like Karo syrup coming through their green canopy, slow and gold-white. Liquid seduction of summer. Beside her in the passenger seat, he is still whistling—a tune she doesn't recognize now—and in the back, the kids are under the spell of the road's bends and the swifting-forward of the car and the sound of their father's song and the magic of a broken routine.

She remembers when the oldest one was an infant and they used to drive him around in the dark of late night to induce sleep. This was poor parenting, she'd say now. Naive parenting. She recalls the trouble they had later getting him to sleep in his crib, he'd become so accustomed to drifting off only with the motion of the car. But in those early days of their parenthood they were so tired and so desperate. She remembers the three of them—their tiny family—together, buckled safely into the bubble of their car. *We are all here*, she remembers thinking then. It was a complicated thought. It spoke both her joy and her fear. They were together. They were together. If anything terrible was going to happen, they were together.

Now, she looks over her shoulder at the two children in the back seat, both of them grown lanky. Both of them all skinned knees and sun-crisped hair and sweet stink of kid sweat. The sunlight coming through the car windows flecks their freckled cheeks, spots their bare shoulders. The shadows of the trees flicker across their sleepy faces. Oh, how she loves them. Them and their father, too. Oh, how broken she is with love for them.

She reaches for her husband's hand, and he pauses his whistling to say, "You okay?"

"Yes," she says. "Fine."

A few moments later, at the beach, he takes one end of the blanket and she takes the other. They shake it smooth against the sand and sit. Nearby, the children run at the incoming waves, the tide pulling up, imperceptibly but steadily, each wave a fraction of an inch closer to the wrack line—a fraction of an inch closer to the blanket, to high tide, to deep night. The children don't notice this, though; they just keep leaping, scissoring their bare legs over the froth, shrieking when they stand still and feel the safe suck of the land slipping out from beneath their feet.

She used to play this very game herself as a child—trying to pin the water to the sand with her toes over and over again. Over and over again. Her heels sinking deeper and deeper into the cool muck of the shoreline with each wave's retreat. What did she love about it then, this game she was guaranteed never to win? What do her children love about it now?

They holler to her and to their father from the shoreline. "Mom! Dad! Look at this! Look what I can do!"

"It's dinner time," she calls back. "Come eat your dinner before it gets too late!"

But they don't come.

"We can let them play," her husband says. "They're so happy." The sun is flush on his face, and he smiles at her, handsome, loving. Loved. And for a single, spinning moment—one of those mad, disembodied moments of clarity that come now and then in the course of family life—she thinks: *It's this! It's this!* What she means by *this*, she doesn't know exactly, but it is a kind of answer, and it's the best she's got.

"Yes," she agrees. "We'll let them play. It's why we're here."

She sits back on her elbows beside him. They'll stay to watch the sun sink. They still have quite a while before the tide really starts coming in.

WHERE HAVE THE
VANISHED GIRLS GONE?

but my lips are stricken to silence, underneath my skin the tenuous flame suffuses;
nothing shows in front of my eyes, my ears
muted in thunder.

And the sweat breaks running upon me, fever
Shakes my body, paler I turn than grass is;
I can feel that I have been changed

Sappho, translated by Richmond Lattimore

The doctor examines me because I am still here.

Impossibly, I think, *I am still here.*

I climb onto the examination table. Paper crinkles under the bare
backs of my thighs. I am aware of my naked feet. I am aware of the

opening at the back of my cotton gown where my spine is revealed, exposed V of my skin. I shiver.

"Lie back," Dr. G says. I have been told to call him "Dr. G." His actual surname is long and full of hard consonants. He has a pompadour of black hair on top of his squarish head, gold-rimmed spectacles, a brown mole between his lip and nostril. His stethoscope is like a cube of ice when it touches my chest through the gown.

I have asked Ms. Bloom to wait in the lobby while I am examined, but I can feel her hovering outside the examination room door, her spirit trembling there, shimmering with worry. A specter following me and listening in.

Dr. G touches his fingers to the soles of my feet, the palms of my hands. "I see nothing unusual," he says. "But you say you sense a tingling? Can you explain this to me?" He frowns.

I want to say: *I am changed. I am girl-going-electricity. Girl-going-static-charge. Can't you feel that zap when you touch me? I'm not bones and flesh anymore—not just. I'm heat. I'm light. I'm whatever exists right before flames.*

I want to say: *Soon my skin will peel away and I'll be nothing but a vibration of space.*

Instead, I shrug. My cheeks burn. I let my hair fall over my face so that he cannot see me flushing. "Sometimes," I say, "it's like my entire body has fallen asleep."

"Hmmm," he hums. He drums his fingers on the examination table, visible gesture of thinking. Like a cartoon doctor.

I want to laugh, but I bite my lips. Overhead, the fluorescent light goes on, making its background buzz.

Dr. G turns away from me to type his notes into the wall-mounted computer. "I'm requesting a return visit," he says over his shoulder. "Six weeks. I'll see you again in six weeks." He flashes me a professional smile, excuses himself, and leaves the room.

I slide off the exam table and pull on my uniform skirt and blouse once more. The waistband sits lower on my hips than it did half an hour ago. There is less of me every minute.

The first girl disappeared in November. Her name was Eleni.

We don't use full names at school, so I never knew her as more than that. Here we are simply "the girls," and to be fair, there are certain universal traits among us. We are, to a girl, bright and mannered and hungry and bored. We come from good families who thought it best to send us away. We're worth more here, where they can't see us, than we would be at home or out in the world at regular schools, where we'd surely just get in the way. "Adolescence is like a blister waiting to be popped," our science teacher once said in a burst of frustration with the class, and I suppose our parents feel that way too.

What I remember about Eleni is insufficient to conjure a full picture now. She was a fourth year, seventeen and just months from leaving us. She intended on becoming a court stenographer. This always struck me as the most vanilla of ambitions. I often passed her in the hallways between classes, standing in a group with her tall and beautiful friends. They exuded a perfumed smell. Walking near them was like walking near a grove of cherry trees in April. When they smiled at me, courteous and disinterested, it was impossible not to notice the pink glow of their clean faces.

How she disappeared is equally difficult for me to pin down. Before all of this—the vanishings—began, I would have said that to disappear, by definition, was to wholly and instantaneously cease to exist. To disappear, an object that was one moment visible, real, and empirically concrete must the next moment be gone—absolutely. I know better now.

In early November, Eleni began to complain of headaches. One afternoon during her literature seminar, she famously vomited on her desktop and ran from the classroom in tears. The entire school knew within the hour.

The next day, she was at lunch, her head down on the cafeteria table, her friends clustered around her, their hands rubbing soft circles on her back, their coos of calm noted by every girl in the room.

The day after that, she was spotted leaning against her locker looking thinner, paler, weak.

How could you lose that much weight in two days? People wondered. How could your cheeks go hollow after just forty-eight hours? Even her hair seemed to have lost its color, people said.

"The fuck is up with her?" someone remarked the next hour in the gym locker room as we changed for phys ed. I turned to look over my shoulder: Cassandra. Fourteen. Resident ruffian of my own class. Green eyes like shards of a broken bottle. Legs like a wrestler's. She slammed the metal door of her gym locker shut, stood facing the rest of us in nothing but her white underwear. "Who knows what's really going on? One of you does. Give. She pregnant? She on something?"

"I bet it's Dilaudid or Oxy," another girl said. "My friend back home took that to lose weight. It worked right away. That stuff's the shit, but it's nasty if you don't know what you're doing with it."

Cassandra smirked, nodded. "I thought it was something like that."

"Come on, Cass. That's enough, right? Eleni's just sick. Drop it," said a slight girl at Cassandra's side.

"Ms. Bloom said it was flu," another girl chimed in. This was Damara. Tiny thing. Hair like the fluff left after a dandelion loses its flower. Puffy face the color of scalded milk.

Cassandra shook her head, bent to tug on her gym shorts, her bare breasts swinging forward toward her face as she tipped. "Whatever. If it's the flu, all you bitches should be worried."

For a moment the room was silent. I swiveled my glance from Cassandra and accidentally met the eyes of another girl—Petra. I'd seen her sitting in the front row of our homeroom class. Long brown ponytail and sturdy figure. Now a thought, shared and swift, flew between us like a sparrow: *Curious.* Again, heat at my cheeks and in my chest. How odd to be so certain of a shared and simultaneous thought. It had never happened to me before. I looked down at my body just to be sure I had changed and wasn't standing there nude. When I raised my head again, Petra had turned away.

The shrill vibrato of the bell broke against the concrete walls of the room, and we scattered, some girls spilling out the door to the gymnasium, some stooping to knot the laces of their shoes, some closing themselves behind the narrow doors of the toilet stalls to pee before class.

I faced my locker. An unnameable transformation had already begun. I felt it—a vibration, or a shift in a vibration. A thread of energy lacing one world to another was slipping loose under our feet.

We learned in basic first-year science that the world is made up of matter, and matter is nothing but atoms. Protons and neutrons clinging to one another in a cluster, encircled by an orbiting cage of electrons. Our bodies are little more than clouds of this nanoscopic stuff—a gathering of atomic grains in constant, invisible motion. And so is that chair, that desk, that philodendron in the corner growing leggy. So is the sky and the body of the ocean and the trench of mud that runs the perimeter of the softball field behind the school. All of it—all of it—is nothing but a brume of atoms, thrumming at a frequency beyond our hearing, busy being.

What, I wondered as I faced the postcard-sized mirror affixed to the inside of my gym locker's door, *was to stop one collection of atoms from becoming another?* Wasn't that exactly what we'd all already done in materializing, slowly, in our mother's wombs? Wasn't it exactly what we'd all one day do in death? *From dust were you made, and from dust you will return.* One kind of quickening exchanged for another.

The thought made my gut go liquid. I shut the locker and crossed the room, shoved out the door into the high, bracing light and noise of the gym.

Within a week Eleni was gone.

Her roommate woke the dorm hall screaming. It was six a.m., the mid-November sky beyond the dorm windows soot gray and wet with rain. We all emerged from our rooms groggy, rubbing our eyes, blinking.

The roommate was hysterical. She'd found the bed unmade, the shape of Eleni's body still present in the form of an impression on the white sheets. Nothing was missing from Eleni's dresser drawers or closet. Her journal was still closed around a pen on her night table beside the bed. The locket she wore around her neck every day was lying in a loop on her desktop. But the girl herself was gone.

Ms. Bloom was summoned. The rest of us were sent to showers, to breakfast, to class. We moved through that day as if the air had turned to syrup.

In French class I could not conjugate, my head all swimmy and my face hot, and so I was sent to the nurse, Ms. Lyon. She declared my temperature normal and told me to lie on the cot in her office for the rest of the hour. The room smelled medicinal, like vitamins and rubbing alcohol. My stomach flattened itself toward my spine as I reclined, and I felt hollow but not hungry. I felt agitated, but still.

I closed my eyes and thought about Eleni. It made the most logical sense to assume she had run away. Maybe she *was* on drugs. Maybe she *was* pregnant. Maybe shame and fear had swallowed her.

When I was small, long before my parents sent me to boarding school, I'd had a room in their house, and in that room a girl-sized single bed with a pink canopy and a ruffled duvet. At night, sometimes, when I was very tired, the bed became to me a boat on waves. I felt it rock beneath me. I felt it tip and sway, and I was terrified. I called out for my parents, and they both came to the door, their faces backlit by the lamp in the hallway. I could never find the words to explain, though, when they asked why I was crying. How could I say, *This looks like a bed, but it's a boat! I look like I'm on land, but I'm at sea!* How could they understand something they could not see? Instead, I only ever said, "Hold my hand?" And my mother would sigh and cross the room and kneel down beside the bed, clasp my hand in hers. Even at five, six, seven I knew this had to be enough.

Maybe because of this memory it did not seem strange to me to believe—as I did immediately—that Eleni had not run away. That she was neither an addict nor pregnant, nor even sick. She had just vanished, the same way my bed had become a boat.

This thought was interrupted by another girl being shown into the nurse's room, and the nurse repeating with her the same process I'd just been through myself. "No temp, no nausea, no rash," Ms. Lyon said. "Just lie here and see if it passes. There's something going around, I think." Soft padding of shoes on the linoleum, a click of the door.

"What's your name?" the other girl said to me, her voice quiet.

I sat up. It was her—Petra—on the cot opposite mine. She stared at me. Her eyes were the color of milky tea.

"Are you sick?" I asked.

She shook her head. "Ditching. Are you sick?"

"I don't know."

She rolled onto her back, folded her hands behind her head. "I saw you the other day. I saw you staring at me."

"I don't know what you're talking about," I said. I didn't know why I'd said it, except that I had learned—as we girls all had—that it was most polite not to be seen or heard, and I didn't like the suggestion that I'd been obvious and rude.

"Yes you do. I know you do."

On the other side of the infirmary door, the nurse's phone rang. We quieted while she spoke, but it was impossible to discern what she was saying or to whom.

"There's something going on," Petra said.

"Why would you say that?"

"Don't play dumb."

I considered my response. I could lie and dismiss her, but she didn't seem to be judging me. She didn't seem bullying, just certain. This certainty surprised me, charmed me, and I decided right then that I liked this girl.

"Okay," I said. "I don't believe Eleni ran away."

Petra grinned. "Me either," she said, and then, with a tone of game curiosity, she added: "What do you think?"

"I think—" I hesitated and lowered my voice. "I think she vanished. I think she stopped existing. Somehow." My face throbbed with its own heat. "You can tell me I'm ridiculous, but that's what I think."

Before she could say anything in return, Ms. Lyon stepped into the office, told me to lift my tongue once more for the thermometer. "Go on back to class," she said after she'd read my temperature aloud— "Ninety-seven point eight"—and she excused me as measurably normal, visibly well.

After that, it was as if Petra's willingness to speculate with me was a seed, and it sprouted from the top of my skull and grew. Everywhere I saw proof of my theory that we were experiencing an odd epidemic, a viral vanishing. As I stood in the line for the toilets one afternoon at the fifth-period break, I watched a third year concentrating on her mirror image over the sinks. Her lips had gone blanched, colorless. The girl gaped at herself and looked around as if mortified. Quickly, she slid a red lip liner pencil from her satchel pocket and drew herself a mouth where one no longer existed.

Another day, as I passed from my dorm room to the bathroom to brush my teeth before bed, I witnessed an older girl slip through what seemed to me an incredibly narrow crack between her doorway and its frame. Was she disappearing right before my eyes? Had she gone filmy and passed *through* rather than between?

A few days later still, on a Saturday morning in early December, the sky thickened. By noon fat, heavy snowflakes began to fall. We girls all rushed outside. It snowed so rarely in our coastal town, and when it did the snow always felt like magic. That Saturday the flakes drifted feathery and melted on our hands and hair and eyelashes. We tipped our faces skyward and laughed. We ran in circles. We galloped like horses. In the midst of the revelry, I happened to stop, however, and to catch sight of Aggie—a girl with whom I'd been partnered for biology labs and rhetoric assignments because our names were alphabetically consecutive—standing alone beneath the madrone at the edge of the school lawn. She held her gloved hands out in front of her, the fingers splayed like the points of stars. Only, one point was missing from each hand—the pinky fingers, both left and right, gone. I thought at first this sight was a trick of my distance. I started walking forward in her direction. "Aggie!" I called. "Aggie, are you okay?" I expected her to look up when I called her name, but instead she turned her face away, plunged her hands into her coat pockets, and ran back to the school building without ever meeting my eyes.

In the dinner line that evening, I passed Petra a note folded into the shape of a swan. *Meet me in the library at four o'clock tomorrow*, it said.

The next day I positioned myself in a library window seat nook and waited. I held a book open over my knees—a title I'd pulled at random from the nearest shelf, something about avian biology. Between the rough pages of text were glossy pages of colored images. A wren in profile, worm threaded through its beak. A pileated woodpecker with a red wedge-shaped head. A snowy owl. I slid my fingertips over the slick pages, distracting myself from the worry that Petra hadn't read my note, or that she'd read it but didn't want to come. Or that she'd read it and let everyone else in our class read it as well, making me the butt of a terrible joke. I'd never had a trustworthy friend.

"I'm here," she said, though, and I looked up. Her round face was bright, eager. "What's happened?" She climbed into the nook with me, folded her legs beneath her.

"You've been outside," I said. She looked puzzled at this, but I was right—she smelled like wind, like that nickel tang the air had when it rushed up the hill to the school from the sea.

"I do cross-country," she said. "We run on Sundays. I didn't have time to shower yet."

I liked this about her too—that she ran. She was strong, sure-footed, and probably fast. All things I wished I could have said about myself.

I told her about Aggie, what I'd seen. And once I'd done that, it was as if a dam had been opened in me, and I couldn't stop myself talking. I told her about my bed becoming a boat, and my question about matter, and my theory that a girl might—like a star—burn herself out and become dust. The more I spoke, the less I worried about speaking. I could hear my own blood moving through the vessels of my ears, my voice distant, as if below water. I was floating. I was weightless. It was thrilling.

When I'd finished, I sat back, touched my palms to my cheeks to cool them. "I can't help this," I said. I gestured to my pinked face. "It just happens to me. I don't know why."

"I get hiccups," she shrugged. "Bodies are weird."

I laughed. She laughed. I was relieved. Ms. Reins, the librarian, issued a shush from her desk.

"Listen," Petra whispered. "Let's say I take notes and you take notes, and then we meet again and see what we've got. Like detectives." She lifted her eyebrows—a question—and I nodded my consent. "Good," she said. "I have to go now. I've got to shower before dinner." She started to get up.

"Wait," I stopped her. "You don't think this is crazy, then? What I'm telling you? You don't think I'm wrong?"

"You might be wrong, but I don't think you're crazy." Her ponytail whipped her cheek as she turned and left.

I took to looking for signs. I carried a steno pad and a pen. But nothing more happened. I had been frightened, but now I was frustrated.

Had I been imagining it all from the start? Had Eleni simply gone home, sick, in the middle of the night, as some girls said? I had nothing to say to Petra, and so I didn't meet her. When I passed her in the hallways, I nodded my hello and kept walking. I wished I hadn't confessed so much to her so quickly. I'd humiliated myself. Surely she'd never stay my friend now. When I thought about what I'd told her, I wanted to evaporate, to crumble. I wanted my theory to be true if only to kill me and save me from my own embarrassment.

Two weeks later, though, a flock of girls lost their voices just before the annual Christmas concert. The entire choir, all at once. Word was that the silence happened during a practice, midnote. Like the volume had been shut off. One moment a chorus of beautiful young female voices blending in harmony, and the next nothing. Or so I heard. Everyone was talking about it.

Ms. Bloom took to the podium at the head of the cafeteria over lunch that day and announced an outbreak of laryngitis. "Girls, I urge you to look after your own health as we near the end of our term and the worst of the winter virus season." She gripped the microphone and furrowed her pinched face in a look of serious worry. "Get your rest. Eat those three squares a day. And, for goodness sake, wash your hands!" She made a jerk of her head—a curt nod—and stepped down from the podium, returning the cafeteria to its china-toned lunch chatter and hum of voices.

I looked across the room for Petra and found her two tables away, sitting with the other girls from the cross-country team. She met my eye, and for a split second I thought she meant to stand and walk over to my table, to sit beside me. But without even an acknowledgment, she looked away again, rejoining her team and their conversation.

We all left school for the winter holidays and returned the first week of February. I was glad to be back. My parents, who had work to do, had enrolled me in a ski program in the mountains, and I'd spent most of the holiday in a different dorm, with a different set of girls, waiting for the break to end so I could return to Petra.

When I did get back to school, I found it changed. What was altered I could not specifically point out. Were there more empty beds in the dorms? Were there more empty seats at the lunch tables? Who might be missing? I murmured names under my breath to myself like secrets: *Cynthia? Lyra? Meg?* I met Petra and told her my suspicions. She must have talked to her teammates, who must have talked to other girls, because soon everyone was speculating. Girls were passing notes under the cover of desks during classes. It was odd; at the same time I was worrying about disappearance, I also felt myself becoming—for the first time in memory—part of the whole.

"But forget how one vanishes," I interrupted the conversation of a large group of girls gathered outside the cafeteria one day to ask, "where does one vanish to?"

The others looked at me as if they'd just noticed my presence.

"Good question," a lanky redheaded girl said.

Someone in the group suggested kidnapping. Out of the ether of gossip, a figure materialized, someone strong and swift and able to slip in and out of the school at night with the bodies of girls slung over his shoulders like laundry bags.

Someone else used the words *human trafficking*. I'd never heard the term. I pictured a highway, but instead of cars, it was crowded with the bodies of girls, all of them dirty and bumping against one another with their sharp elbows and knees as they walked forward, en masse, headed into the fog that marked the edge of my imagination.

When I told this to Petra in our spot at the library one afternoon, a look of unmistakable disbelief crossed her face. She seemed on the verge of laughter. "It means sex slave," she said in a hushed voice. "How can you know so much about chemistry and physics and—I don't know—birds and not know stuff like this?" She sighed. "Trafficking. *Trafficking.*" She lifted her eyebrows meaningfully, and I shook my head. "It means girls get kidnapped and sold for sex. What you said doesn't even make any sense."

I flushed at my own ignorance. *But buying a girl does make sense?*

I wanted to ask. I said nothing and left the library, claiming a sudden headache.

A few days later another theory emerged. A girl remembered a gruesome true crime story she'd read. It featured a young woman only a couple of years older than us living in Los Angeles early in the last century. She'd disappeared without a trace, and weeks later a child found just her legs in an empty field. *Just her legs.*

This led to new questions: Was it possible to vanish only partially? Could a person's body go missing only in pieces, and—if so—what life would be left in the bits that remained?

In the following weeks, the tension spread. We were hungry for answers, ready to speak aloud the worries and terrors we'd each been silently harboring since it had all begun. Around every corner, behind every closed door, girls stood in twos and threes, heads together. Girls tucked themselves between the stacks at the library, met in pairs inside the closed stalls of the bathrooms, walked loops around the blacktop track at lunchtime with their arms linked and their heads tipped in unison against the last of winter's cold. The sound of our school was the sound of standing at the edge of the sea, along the line where shore meets wave: *Hush. Hush. Hush.* The sound of the sand being sucked from beneath your feet right where you stand.

It wasn't uncommon anymore to wake to the high, terrifying sound of a girl's wail. Nightmares were an epidemic. The screams paralyzed me. I could never bring myself to get up and investigate. I lay in my bed, rigid beneath the sheets, sweating, my heart flapping under my ribs like a hummingbird in the bell of a bowl.

Petra, however, believed in seeing the monster. She confessed to me that she'd taken to sleeping with the branch of a maple tree she'd found fallen on the lawn. When looking for the source of a scream, she carried it like a club and stalked the dark hallways of the dormitory, brave and determined.

Eventually, however, she gave it all up—her bravery, her hunting, her belief. "This whole thing has gotten out of hand. I'm tired of pretending," she said, irritation in her voice. "No one's prowling around. There's no kidnapper. No shadow man. My coach says it's hysteria, that's all. I'm bored of it. We're all bored of it."

This caught me off guard. "What are you saying?" I asked.

She stopped and turned to face me. "You know, some of my teammates know you're the one who started this. They say you're crazy. That you're just trying to get everyone's attention." She leaned in. "I didn't want to tell you this, but people have started asking me if you're as weird as you seem."

"Me? I started it?" My voice came out louder than I'd intended and broke on the last word.

Petra looked around. A group of third-year girls nearby had stopped to stare. "Are you about to cry?" Petra said. She let out one high, clipped laugh. "Are you for real about to cry?" It was a slap, a whip's long tail slashing my cheek.

"I need to go," I said. "I have work to do."

Thinking back now, it is this moment I'd pinpoint as the real onset of my own vanishing, though all I felt then was a tingling. A cold, white burn.

In my steno pad I wrote this:

Have you ever woken in the middle of the night to find that someone has left an arm beside you in your bed? It's shocking. *An arm!* you think. You move to recoil in terror, to pull away from the grotesque thing and draw up your sheets. But you can't. You can't move! And then you realize: the grotesque thing is you. It is your own arm beside you, dead to the world, absent all feeling and sense. You take your living arm and lift the other, move it, flap it up and down the way you would a flag on a stick at a parade. *Wake up! Wake up, dumb thing!* you think, and slowly it does, with the pain of a million fire ants biting, a million points of a million needles poking.

That was my change coming on—first numbness, then the sizzling burn of forcing myself back into existence. That day, walking away from Petra, I felt it in my toes. It was like walking on blocks of ice. The next day, it was my right hand, "asleep" during math class. The following day, embarrassingly, it was one buttock. *My circulation is off,* I thought. It took me a few days to realize what was happening: my body was testing it out—disappearing—one part at a time.

Then one day I woke to my scalp tingling. I reached up and touched my head on my pillow, certain I'd find nothing there. My fingers slid through the curls of my hair, tapped the curve of my forehead, the soft tissue of my eyelids. I rolled from the bed and stumbled across the room to the mirror that hung on the back of the closet door. There I was, head to toe, present. I lifted my nightgown to be sure nothing beneath it had gone, and I found myself intact. I was slimmer, maybe, and paler. The bones of my ribcage and hipbones stuck out like the balsa wood bones of the model dinosaurs we'd made in science class back in the fall. Thinking of this, I raised my hands like a T. Rex's tiny arms, turned them to claws, and leaned into the mirror to scare myself. If a girl could disappear, could she also shape-shift? Could she turn bat or boat or velociraptor? Could she will her skin to feathers, hollow her own bones, and fly away?

I went to my desk to get the steno pad and pen. I would write it down, leave a record. Eleni hadn't put it together before she was gone, but I understood. And Petra would understand. She'd find my notes and know I'd been right. I wrote: *It's like pixelating under your own skin. It's like becoming a hive.*

Behind me, my roommate stirred in her bed, waking, and I startled, dropped the steno pad into the drawer, and leaped across the room into my bed again. Under my breast, my heart thundered like the earth cracking open and the ground turning to ash.

Without Petra's help, I kept up my careful observations alone, recording my study of my own body's slow transformation from one state to the next. I made more notes in my steno pad—for after I was gone.

In March we were all called to an assembly at which Ms. Bloom, Ms. Lyon, and a man introduced to us as a health educator from our local hospital spoke to us about personal hygiene and adolescent development. There was a movie. The overhead lights went out, plunging the gym into darkness. We saw a flicker, heard the purr of a projector. Across the gym, the far wall burned blue-green and a video stuttered to life. Here was a female body, large as a house, illuminated in Technicolor brightness. This screen woman had no skin, though. She had no muscle or bone. She was like a machine, each piece of her color coded and well defined. Lungs like pink sails fanned open. The red lump of her heart with its antennae of rubber-tube aorta and superior vena cava, both spurting raindrops of cartoon blood on the diagram. Here was her spleen and her stomach and the green jelly bean of her gallbladder. She had a long, looped, pulpy-looking intestine, radiant as a blood orange; and a little pink crab-shaped uterus, fallopian tubes and ovaries poised above it like raised pincers, ready to snap.

The hospital's health educator spoke from the dark floor, only the bald back of his head haloed by the projector's cone of light.

Why had they sent a man to teach us this? some of the girls hissed to each other in the bleachers.

The health educator used a laser pointer to direct our attention to the various parts of the body cavity. "This is a normal human woman," he said. Then he corrected himself: "Or a girl. A normal human girl."

Someone behind me giggled.

He directed us to put our hands on our own midsections. "Below the ribs, you'll find your stomach. Below your navel, your intestinal region. Ovaries to the left and right, just inside the hipbones."

I pressed my thumbs into the soft pillow of my abdomen. They sank in deep. Beneath them, I could not feel anything definite—no clear, firm masses of my organs. All I could feel was the thrumming, the whirring of me becoming cloud.

When the man spoke again, we all saw him turn his face to us, white moon in the black room. "There you have it," he said, tone of ambivalent praise in his voice. "Good job, young ladies. Good job."

The whole show was to prove to us our own substance, I supposed. The hospital man had verified our existence, and therefore we existed.

I was light-headed. The heat had risen in my cheeks again. I must have looked sickly.

Next to me, alphabetically seated Aggie frowned. "Are you okay?" she said. I looked at her. She was sitting on her hands.

"It's wrong," I whispered.

She rolled her eyes, smiled. "I know, right? Why are we even here?"

"I don't know," I said. "I don't know."

I felt dizzy, seasick. The room sloshed from side to side. I scanned the row of seated first-year girls for Petra and found her staring forward at the screen, her profile glowing faintly green in the light of the projector.

At the end of the assembly, the lights blazed on again, and we all blinked and groaned. Ms. Bloom took once more to the microphone, waited for us to quiet. "You are reasonable, sensible young women," she said. "I hope you will make good choices for your mental and physical health." She paused, and when none of us clapped, she started it herself. We joined her in a minute of awkward, spotty applause, then rose from our seats and filed out, back to class.

That was Friday, March 15. On Monday, Petra was gone.

I looked for her at breakfast but assumed she'd overslept. When she didn't arrive in class the next hour, though, I worried. Several times during the first period I looked over my shoulder at her empty chair, her desktop blank and gleaming with the glare of the frail sun falling in through the classroom windows. It was unlike her to miss class.

She didn't show up for lunch, for phys ed, for the meeting I'd written to ask her for in the library at five o'clock. I waited. I sat in our nook with my spine pressed against the wall, the same book of avian biology opened over my legs. Outside the library window, the school grounds were still. I'd been too distracted lately to notice that it was nearly spring. The trees weren't skeletal with winter anymore but spotted with the pink or green or neon yellow dots of leaf buds. The grass had erupted from the ground again, long and thick and bright green.

I skipped dinner that night. I felt too shaky to eat. I climbed into my bed and wound my blankets around me, buried my head. A new fear was uncoiling in my gut like a worm: I didn't want to stop existing, but I also didn't want to be left alone.

The next two days were indistinct. Petra didn't return. Time felt slow and sloppy, walking through the hours like walking through slush after a thaw. I was sent to the nurse three more times, made to lie on her uncomfortable cot and have my temperature taken. I was tired and enraged. Why had no one mentioned Petra's absence? Why was no one but me concerned? I had horrible, violent thoughts. What if I opened Petra's gym locker and found her legs standing there in place of her gym shorts? What if I woke one morning and found only part of myself vanished—my hands, say, or my face? What if everyone but me vanished, and I was left entirely on my own in the empty school?

I wanted to pull my own hair, slap the heat from my cheeks, rip the thermometer from beneath my tongue and smash its glass under my heel. It would be satisfying to hear the crack, to watch the silver beads of mercury scatter, uncontrolled and loose.

It wasn't until the Friday after Petra's disappearance that I was called to Ms. Bloom's office. She stood when I opened the door, gestured to the seat in front of her desk, and waited for me to sit.

"How are you?" she asked. She folded her long hands one over the other on her desktop and looked at me. When I didn't respond, she went on. "Ms. Lyon says you've spent quite a lot of time in her office in the last week. Are you unwell?"

I shrugged. Beneath my uniform blouse, my armpits tingled and sweated.

Ms. Bloom frowned. "I hope you know that you could share anything with us—with Ms. Lyon and with me. We—" She paused, let her eyes travel the space above my head for a moment, and then finished her thought: "We care for you. We care for all of you girls, you know."

"Where is Petra?" I asked. It was as if the words were bile and I could not stop them bubbling up.

Ms. Bloom unclasped her hands, laid them flat against the desktop. "Petra who?" Her voice was calm, patient. She spoke to me the way adults speak to toddlers.

"Petra," I said. "Petra." I paused. I didn't know Petra's last name.

Ms. Bloom looked at me with worry, opened a desk drawer, and handed me a business card. "Ms. Lyon often recommends this person to students in need of a little more emotional support than we are able to offer here at school."

"What?" I asked.

Ms. Bloom nodded at the card. "There's nothing wrong with getting help to sort out complex emotions. Adolescence is a challenging period in everyone's life. It can help to feel heard." A patient smile.

I narrowed my eyes to force the card's text into focus. *Leda Floros, Clinical Psychologist (specializing in adolescent development).* Block letters, each of them raised just a bit from the surface of the card, like distorted Braille. I ran the pad of my thumb over their welts.

"We're vanishing," I said. "You know it's happening." It took all of my will to say it without screaming. Inside my skin, the last of me was splintering. There was a crack like lightning ripping a tear in the sky. I was sure Ms. Bloom had to have heard it. It came from inside my own chest. *Crack*, and I saw behind my eyes a shimmering, like a handful of glitter thrown. "Why doesn't anyone ever believe a girl when she tells them the truth?"

"Anastasia," Ms. Bloom said. My name sounded like a razor blade in her mouth.

I stood up with a jerk, shoved the chair back so hard it hit the metal filing cabinet behind me, then I vomited on the floor.

"Oh, god!" Ms. Bloom said.

.●.

Now here we are, Ms. Bloom and I. She ushers me out of Dr. G's office and into the parking lot. She tells me to keep hold of the plastic bag between my hands, just in case. "Just in case," she says, cheerful, her jaw clenched around her grin. She puts her hand to my shoulder, pats me.

Overhead, wind. Wind brisk enough to push the clouds across the sky with visible speed. I stop moving and look up, watch the white cloud bottoms cruising the thin blue like skiffs on a turbulent sea.

"Are you okay?" Ms. Bloom asks.

"The air smells like salt water," I say.

She casts me a troubled expression.

We drive the length of road back to school, passing strip malls, houses, the stretch of dark pine trees that fence the edge of the school's wide property line.

It wouldn't be hard to run away, I think. Petra could have run. Eleni could have run.

I picture them both, together, hand-in-hand. They are not girls anymore, but wind. Their bodies are light. They are energy moving. They gust through the school's open front door and out onto the green, green lawn. The grass blades bow beneath them. In what were once their chests there is a billowing, an expansion of something like breath, but bigger. Their bodies swell, invisible, enormous, full of the power of the wind rushing down the schoolyard hill and through the fringed boughs of the pines.

Where will they go?

Out. Out across the rooftops of the houses downtown. Over the rough plane of the road. Over the breakwater at the beach and out— out to the sea.

Ms. Bloom turns her face to me, says, "How're you feeling?"

"Better," I say.

"That's right," she says, relief audible in her voice. A sigh. "You just needed someone to reassure you, to help you get back on track. You just needed a reminder to get your thoughts clear."

I want to speak to her, to answer, but my lips have finally burned away. Behind them, my tongue has become a tongue of flame.

I press the button on the car door that opens the window. The wind gusts in around us both, tousles Ms. Bloom's hair, lashes my face with its invisible tassels.

I know that when I open my mouth next, I will speak like this—in gusts, with force. I will sound like fire moving through a forest, like thunder rolling under the breasts of the clouds. Like a girl finally broken open.

VICISSITUDE

All those years ago, it was she who drove Sam the nearly two hundred miles to sixth-grade sleepaway camp, though she'd planned on the whole family making the trip. Back in April, when she'd registered Sam for camp, she had also booked a double room at a Holiday Inn in Eatonville and had planned on leaving a day early. They'd take their time on the way down to Mount Rainier, stopping as the whim caught them, staying the night at the motel, eating out, and then arriving at camp the next morning. It was exciting, a miniexploration. The drive wouldn't take more than half the day, she told her husband, Max, and the motel had a pool. It would be good for the family to reconnect. When was the last time they'd all been away together? Years ago, it seemed. Before their lives became a strict routine of piano and ballet and ice-skating lessons, of soccer games and karate tournaments, of teenage social events. She wrote the weekend on the calendar. She ignored her teenage daughter Lucy's complaints about missing her skating lesson and told Max not to make other plans.

On Friday night, however, when she reminded him about the camp drop-off, Max said he'd forgotten and had already agreed to lead a weekend seminar for visiting graduate students at the university. It was fine, wasn't it? he said. This way Lucy wouldn't have to miss her lesson. He could take her to the skating rink before he had to be on campus. And wouldn't this be a good mother-son bonding opportunity? Hadn't she been saying all year that Sam was growing up too fast?

There was a fight, but in the end Iris packed herself an overnight bag and dug out the old AAA map. What else could be done?

When she woke the morning of the camp drive, Max and Lucy had already left, and Sam was at the kitchen table, scowling at the bowl of cereal in front of him. "I thought we were all going," he said. The edge of bitterness in his voice suggested he was accusing her of having ruined the plans. As if their solo drive were her fault. As if a weekend alone with her were something to dread.

"Your father had a thing on campus that he couldn't get out of," she told him. She stooped to kiss the crown of his head, but he ducked away from her.

On the countertop, there was a torn sheet of notebook paper beside the empty coffee pot in Max's sprawling hand: *Enjoy the drive to camp. You and Sam will have fun. Take your time coming home Sunday if you want.*

"Take your time," Iris repeated. As if he were granting his permission. As if she needed it. She balled up the note and threw it away.

"If we're not all going, I want Dad to take me," Sam complained again.

"I told you," she said, "he has an obligation." Iris dumped yesterday's coffee grounds on top of Max's note in the trash. "You get to go to camp. You'll just have to make do with me."

By ten o'clock she had resigned to make the best of it, and she and Sam were on the road. Most of the drive—south through the deep green stretch of the Skagit River valley and into Seattle—was pretty enough. She treated him to lunch at a burger place in the city, and they took a refreshment break at a convenience mart outside Tacoma. By the time the day had begun to seem endless they were nearly there, and at four they checked into the motel. "You can swim before we find dinner if you like," she told Sam as she set her bag on the fold-out luggage rack in the closet and unzipped it, looking for her toiletries case. The road had given her a headache, and the room was smaller than she'd hoped, laced with the vague, noxious fug of old cigarette smoke and the last guest's stale body odor. "I asked for nonsmoking," she said to herself as she puttered. "Doesn't anyone listen anymore?"

Sam had his swimming suit in his hands. "How do you know they didn't listen?" he said. "Maybe they just call it nonsmoking if you're not going to smoke in it."

"Aren't you Mr. Cute? You know that's not how it works." She turned to ruffle his hair, but he was already headed into the bathroom to change.

The motel pool was indoors, a thirty by fifteen rectangle with a deep end too shallow for diving. They had the place to themselves. Iris took a seat in one of the plastic chairs on the deck and opened the magazine she'd bought at the convenience store. Paging through it, she wasn't sure why she'd wasted her money; it was all pictures of food she had no desire to spend time cooking and glossy features on home renovations and crafty projects she would never attempt. She'd once subscribed to this magazine and remembered now why she'd let the subscription lapse: the vision of domesticity it presented always left her feeling disconnected from her own life, though she couldn't quite name how.

In the pool, Sam swam a few laps and practiced his handstand. She watched him disappear, his submerged body a streak of color. A moment later, his feet materialized again, toes pointed like a dancer's, legs wobbling as he worked to find his balance. Silver bubbles emerged from his mouth and broke on the pool's rippling skin. When he resurfaced, he came up spluttering, wiping water from his eyes. He tipped his head side to side, thumping first one ear and then the other.

"I didn't know you could do handstands," she said.

He sidestepped this compliment. "It's no big trick, Mom."

Everything he said lately came with a cut. As a little boy, he'd been generous, affectionate. He'd liked to sit in her lap and put his chubby palm against the flat space just above her breast where he could feel her heartbeat. "Wub-dub," he'd say. "Wub-dub, Mama." He'd put his ear to her chest, and she'd stroke his hair, which back then had been fine and blond, his head always gilded with the sweet, doughy scent of babydom.

Remembering this, she felt a wash of forgiveness: it wasn't his fault adolescence had left him with all the charm of a paring knife. She put down the magazine. "I think I'll slip on my suit and join you."

"Why?" he said.

"Because we can swim together. That'd be nice, right? I used to be able to do that handstand move. I'll show you."

He looked dubious.

"Just get out a minute while I change."

He dunked his head beneath the water, popped up again, and shook his hair like a dog. "I don't need to get out. I'm swimming."

"You can't be in the pool without an adult here."

"Mom, I'm not going to drown."

"It's just the rules," Iris said. She pointed to the sign screwed into the wall. The last aura of her headache was still circling her vision. "The rules," she said again.

In the pool, Sam lagged, trying another handstand and taking another sloppy lap while she waited.

"Come on," she called, her patience thinning. "Out. Now."

When he finally pulled himself over the lip of the pool's edge, she pointed him to a deck chair. "Sit here and don't move," she said. He was shivering. She tossed him a towel and picked up the magazine, dropped it in his lap. "Something to read while I'm gone." Water fell from his hair to the paper cover and bled dark blots onto the smiling face of the cover model and the pristine icing of her cake.

Back in their room, she dug around for her swimsuit, thinking briefly that she'd forgotten it. It turned out to be buried under the bottle of wine she'd brought, though, and as she pulled the suit free, she considered opening that bottle now, having a quick glass to smooth out her temper, to relax her a bit. She shuffled the clothes in her bag, looking for a corkscrew in each of the pockets before realizing she hadn't brought one. "Shit," she said to herself as she tucked away the wine again. She'd taken a women's studies class at the university in the spring—just a lark, free to her as a professor's wife— and had been shocked and then intrigued by how easily the twenty-something students said *shit* as if it were simply another word. *That shit assignment.* Or *I don't give a shit.* She wondered if she'd been missing something all along and resolved to pepper it into her own speech more freely, if only when her children were out of earshot. Her favorite usage was the compound curse word, such as *shithead*— such as, *My husband is such a shithead for sticking me with this trip.*

In the bathroom, she wiggled herself into her suit. It was blue—a dreaded "practical" cut, with a high tank line and a flippy little skirt that immediately declared to any other swimmers how embarrassing she found her middle-aged backside. She'd bought it several years back for one summer excursion or another and hadn't worn it but once or twice. Now it felt tight at the leg openings, fit close at the belly. She turned this way and that in front of the mirror, half naked. Her thighs swelled from the suit, thick and dimpled and as white as the bellies of bottom-dwelling fish. She'd also neglected to shave, and no matter how she tugged, the suit's crotch wouldn't fully cover the few wiry hairs that poked out around her bikini line. "Bikini line," she said aloud. "Right. Never again."

It was when she leaned forward to shift herself into the bra's cups, though, that she felt it. She stopped and stood straight, faced herself in the mirror. Something there. She let the suit's bodice hang like a flap of loose skin at her waist as she stared at her bare chest. Her breasts looked only as they always did—pale, a little elongated and triangular, silver-zippered in stretch marks—the scars of pregnancy and nursing. They were, in other words, unremarkable. She felt the left one: normal. She felt the right one, and yes—there it was again— a pebble, a lump, just beneath the pink round of her nipple. Size of a pencil eraser. Two centimeters, maybe two and a half. That's how she'd been trained to size such lumps, back when she was working as an internist's nurse: pea, pencil eraser, fingertip. She lifted her arm and thumbed the hollow of her armpit, the phantom face of Debra Winger floating up from the depths of her mind. Shit. *Peach pit, BB, marble. Ping-Pong ball, blueberry. Bomb.* But no—nothing under her arm. There was just the one lump. Just the one. Just one. Probably nothing.

She pulled up the suit.

When she got back to the pool, Sam was already in the water. She didn't bother to reprimand him. She'd been gone longer than she'd promised, and he would soon be doing whatever he liked at camp anyway. That, and she was suddenly exhausted. She sat back down on the chair at the far end of the pool, picked up the magazine, which was now warped and waved with the wet prints of Sam's fingers, and paged aimlessly through it.

"I thought you were swimming," Sam said. His voice echoed around the tiled room in rings of muffled sound.

"Maybe in a bit."

"God! Why'd I have to get out and wait for you then?" He slipped, seal-like, below the water before she could say anything about his mouth.

The room felt sweatier than it had been before, even though she was wearing less. The glass of the skylights and the windows was chalky white with chlorinated residue, and the sunlight came into the room subdued, only half as bright as it had been outside. Iris felt like she, too, was underwater. She hugged herself and covertly pinched the exposed fat of her upper arms, wishing she'd brought a robe. In the corner a silk palm lolled to one side in a wicker basket. How could silk plants wilt? Beside this, a stack of bleached white towels sat on a rack, probably mildewing in the damp.

For over an hour she flipped through the magazine without reading, letting Sam swim until he finally tired of it and climbed out. His feet slapped wet across the deck to her, and he held up his hands for her to examine. "I stayed in too long," he said. "My fingers pruned." Sure enough, every fingertip was a white raisin. Iris remembered that they'd looked like this exactly when he was first born—that, in fact, all of his skin had been pruney at birth. He'd been a week past his due date and had emerged looking waterlogged, the top layer of flesh peeling from his tiny feet and palms and lips. She told him this as they pushed through the pool doors and into the cool of the hallway.

He grimaced as he wrapped his towel around his waist. "Gross, Mom."

"Why gross? I still thought you were beautiful. Amniotic water does that to all babies."

"Gross. Please don't say *amniotic*."

She tried to put her arm around him, but he rolled his eyes and stalked ahead of her down the hallway, dripping a trail of wet splots on the carpeting.

It struck her that beyond her driver's license and her credit card, he didn't need anything from her on this trip. The pool rules had required adult supervision, but if a real accident had happened, what could she have done about it? Her maternal urge to protect him had become more or less irrelevant. What was her use to him now? If he'd hit his head on the pool floor trying another handstand, or had swallowed a lungful of water and sunk to the bottom like a rock, she could not have saved him. He'd grown lanky over the summer, all arms and legs, and he easily weighed almost as much as her. She could never get him to the surface in time, and that was what mattered in life-and-death situations, she knew—not wasting any time.

She rounded the corner and saw him waiting for her outside their room, the towel around his shoulders now and his lips faintly blue with the chill of the air-conditioning on his wet skin. "I'm freezing," he said when she reached him, and as she put the key in the lock, he leaned against her. The gesture surprised her, and she stopped and put both arms around his shoulders, held onto him for a moment, his wet head against her chest.

"I'm sorry about this morning," he said. "The attitude, I mean."

"I know." She kissed the top of his head and opened the door. "Get right into a warm shower. I'll take care of finding dinner."

As he disappeared into the bathroom, she caught sight of herself in the mirror over the hotel bureau—her red hair frizzed from the steam of the pool, a dark blotch on the breast of her suit where Sam had hugged her. She turned away, pulling off the suit and getting back into her clothes quickly, not wanting to be seen in the nude.

That night, after Sam fell asleep, she used the motel room phone to call home. Max was up, as she knew he would be. Lucy, he told her when he answered, was still up too. She'd had a bad practice at the rink and was rethinking her dream of professional skating.

"Well god bless us everyone," Iris said. "I'm sick of these early morning rink times. She was never going to be *shitting* Oksana Baiul, anyway. Don't tell her I said that."

"Oksana's not her girl," Max said. "I asked her in the car. She says Oksana sounds like the Cold War. She likes Nancy Kerrigan."

"What does that even mean? How does she know about the Cold War?"

"Wait—can we step back a minute?" Max asked. "Did you use *shitting* as an adjective just now?"

"If you're on to making fun of my grammar, I'm going to assume we're done fighting."

"I was never fighting with you. I just had to work, and you got angry."

She let out a breath. Sam had turned on the air conditioner while she was in the shower, and it was still running, the whir of its motor drowning out the sounds of people passing in the hallway and talking in the room next door. It felt like winter in the room. She looked over at him in the other bed, his long body uncovered, goosebumps pimpling his arms. In sleep, he still looked young, a little boy. She thought again of the weight of his head against her chest when he hugged her. "Hold on," she said to Max, then stood, set down the phone, and rounded the foot of the bed to tuck the blanket snug around Sam's shoulders.

"Okay," she said when she sat back on her own bed, "I need to tell you something. I found a lump in my breast today. When I was putting on my bathing suit. A couple centimeters. Size of a pencil eraser." She clarified: "Not the cap kind—the kind that comes attached to the pencil."

"Okay," Max said. "So, small."

"You say that as if small makes a tumor okay."

"You don't know if it's a tumor."

"I know it's not an eraser."

Max laughed.

"My grandmother had breast cancer. I remembered that today. She didn't die from it, but she had it. She would have been about my age when she was diagnosed."

"See then? You don't need to worry."

"She lost her breast."

"They're better at treating it now."

"Why aren't you worrying?" Iris said.

"I am. I am worrying. I don't want to scare you, though."

"I am scared."

"I know."

Iris frowned. With her free hand, she reached beneath her pajama top and cupped her right breast, imagining its absence, the rough crosshatch of a scar above her ribs where the breast itself was full and heavy now. Her grandmother had worn a prosthetic, a flesh-colored piece of foam that she kept on the bureau in her bedroom at night, beside the blue plastic case that held her dentures. She'd called it her *mammy*—a word that had embarrassed Iris as a girl. There was something coarse and dismissive about the term that just didn't align with her German grandmother's usual insistence on being "ladylike" and modest; and during the summers of her childhood, when she'd stayed with her grandmother for weeks at a time, she'd hated the sight of the pink thing lying there on the bureau top, its appearance made more repellant by the word that flooded her mind whenever she saw it: *mammy, mammy, mammy.*

To Max, she said only, "I wish I'd found the lump at home. I don't want to be alone right now. I want to see your face." She began to cry.

There was a pause, and she couldn't gather what Max was thinking on the other end of the line—couldn't tell whether his silence was concern or apology or irritation at her breaking down like this.

"Hey, now," he said finally. "Hey." And then, a mistimed joke: "You don't want to see my face. I didn't shave today. My face is bristly."

She shook her head, wiped the back of her hand beneath her nose. "No," she said, giving in. "I guess I don't want to see that. I didn't shave either. I was an embarrassment to our son at the pool."

"Let's not start worrying yet. You'll be okay."

"Will I, though?"

"You're always okay."

"Right," she said, though she felt his words like a stone sinking through her.

When they hung up, she went to the bathroom and stood naked from the waist up before the mirror. She pinched both nipples, but there was no ache, no twinge, nothing. If she had cancer, wouldn't there be another sign? No. She'd been a nurse before the children were born. She'd seen infants die at birth, young people lose their lives in car wrecks and accidental shootings, older people in perfect health suddenly fall ill. There were no guarantees. Too many things in life happened quickly, before you were ready for a change; why would this be different?

The next morning, she and Sam drove for what felt like hundreds of miles along a two-lane road, making one hairpin turn after the next. Old-growth pines and cedars lined the left shoulder, and a steep drop cut away into a ravine on the right. Turn and turn and turn until, around a final corner, the landscape opened up on a lake so big Iris couldn't see its far side. The water was creamed green, the color of a jade stone, and here and there a tree stump rose out of it, dark and water-warped, like the half-hidden body of a diver, spiked feet point-ing to the sky.

"Wow," she said, but Sam's face was impassive. "It's so eerie, isn't it?"

"It's a lake. I've seen lakes before."

"But look at the tree stumps in the water."

He turned away, and she gave up, regretting all that had changed between them. When he was small, Sam would have been fascinated by the stumps and by the lake's color. He was all energy then, as rest-less and fidgety as a little animal. The lake would have excited him. They would have spun a story about it together as they drove. They would have pulled to the roadside and got out and tramped around, Sam running ahead of her until she called to him to stop. They would have wondered together at its strangeness. What had happened to that boy? Maybe he still had some of that intensity, but he'd already gated it in himself, as adults must do, and being on the outside of that gate felt like loss to Iris.

A few miles beyond this, they passed through the town at which the camp was based—nothing but a post office, a tavern, and a market. "I feel like I've gone back in time," Iris said. "This place reminds me of the town where my grandma lived. You never went there, but I used to spend summers with her. I loved it."

Sam looked out his window. "It would suck to live here."

Iris shook her head but said nothing.

The camp was not much farther up the road, a circle of squat wooden buildings at the end of a dirt lane shadowed by pines. Iris helped Sam unload his things, and they stood waiting with a group of other campers and parents outside the main office until a tall man in a polo shirt and cargo shorts opened the door and beamed at them—the director. The counselors would take campers to their cabins, he announced. Goodbyes should be said here.

Iris looked around at the other families. Most were in mom-and-dad pairs, and again she wished that Max had come with them on this trip. The other parents likely assumed she was a single mother, divorced. The thought bothered her—her whole life so easily erasable—and she felt self-consciously aware of herself as a woman standing alone as she leaned forward to hug Sam.

"Have fun," she said as she squeezed his shoulders. "You want help with the bag?"

"He said we do it ourselves." He looked at her, his face stiff. "Doesn't anybody listen anymore?"

A sting like he'd slapped her spread across Iris's cheek, and then she realized—he was parroting something she'd said at the motel. It was a joke—poorly framed, but still a joke. She smiled. "Ha ha, funny guy," she said. "Apparently you do."

He grinned. This was the closest thing she'd get to a show of affection from him.

"Hey. I'll miss you," she said. "Have fun."

"You already said that, Mom." He hefted his duffel and turned away, started off down the road behind another group of campers.

"Goodbye!" she called. She waved, but he didn't look back again.

The car was empty without him, vacant, bereft. In town, Iris stopped at the market and called Max from the payphone. The camp drop-off had been fine, she wanted to say. It had all gone fine, and she was coming straight home. She missed home. She wanted to let go of her worry like he'd suggested she do last night, but she really wasn't sure she'd be okay. How could she be sure she was okay? She felt like—what?—like she was on the very edge of falling apart. Could he understand that? Like she could crack in two at any second and turn to dust.

She wanted to say all of this, but the phone rang and rang, and when the answering machine picked up, Iris set down the receiver. Maybe Max had taken Lucy out to lunch. Maybe to a movie. Maybe they were both just gone, doing whatever each of them felt like doing with the day. She touched her breast through her shirt, felt for the lump, and thought: *If I had died when the children were small, life would have been hard for him, but they are not small anymore.* It was a terrible thought, followed by one even worse: *If he died now, we would all be wrecks.* When had she become so dependent? She remembered thinking at their wedding that she loved him—oh, how she loved him!—but he still loved her more. Or, at least, he required her more than she did him. Now she saw that somewhere along the way—probably when they had the children—the balance had tipped against her. Shit.

She got back in the car. The light had changed in the hour since she'd driven into town, and now it cut through the trees overhead in hard shapes, flattened the leaves to a stock green, the color of construction paper, and spliced the shadowed spaces between them in a rigid geometry: diamond, rectangle, triangle, diamond. Snip, snip, snip, snip. She turned on the radio and searched for a station, but out here, away from the city, it was all static.

Then, just as before, the lake came into view out of nowhere around a bend, green and strange, its ghoul-stumps still lumbering out of the water toward the road. Iris's heart leaped in her chest. She slowed, edged onto the gravel shoulder. There was a breeze, and the smell of lake water carried toward her on it—clean, but also earthy, like a body in sweat. She got out to stretch her legs.

Bees hovered over the thicket of blackberry bramble that separated the road from the shore, and in the vines she spotted a sign—a scenic overlook marker. *Rich Lake Reservoir*, it read. *Constructed 1939 by the Civilian Conservation Corps.* There was a dam at the south end that couldn't be seen from the road, and when the dam was built, they'd flooded the town of Rich, which was still there, ruined, under the water. On the sign's right margin, a black-and-white photographic inset pictured the town as it had been before the flood—a main street of wooden storefronts, a neat row of narrow houses, a grid of dirt roads. On the left margin, two smaller photographs showed objects people had more recently found along the lake's shore, relics of that past—a rusted door hinge in one and a lady's hair comb in the other.

Iris stood and looked out at the lake. It was bigger than she'd been able to tell from the road. Its color was as bright as a spill of schoolroom tempera paint, and its texture was too thick to be believably liquid, as if it had not only drowned but hardened around the town it had swallowed. The thought unsettled her, and suddenly she wanted to see the whole of it, to make a full round of its shore if she could. She got back in the car once more.

As she drove, she wondered what Max would say about this—about the lake and about her detour. Before the children were born, they took long road trips every summer, never making any plans, but always stopping where and when the impulse struck them. That had become an unreasonable way to travel with infants, however, and now that the children were old enough to be good passengers, Max rarely had much time free from the pressures of his research, his writing, his students. If he'd come with her on this trip, they wouldn't stop at the lake. He'd have schoolwork pulling him back and no time to dawdle. He would say, *Didn't you want to get home quickly? Weren't you the one who wanted to get home and phone a doctor?* He'd remind her of the very worry he'd downplayed the night before, and it would irk her, because he would be right—she had wanted to get home.

It wasn't until she reached the far western side of the lake that the large log house and A-frame outbuilding appeared on a stretch of open grass between the road and the water. What was it? A home? A park building? She eased off the road. *Rich Lake Resort.* White letters on a small wooden sign. *Welcome! Vacancy.* Iris paused for just a moment, considering. It was out of character for her to stop. It was unplanned and possibly foolish. Who knew what she would find there? She was a woman traveling alone. She heard Max's voice again, telling her she was always okay. In her head, however, it wasn't a reassurance; it was a challenge. She turned down the drive.

The woman who ran the resort was thick faced, her blue eyes just a touch too close together and her nose sharp at the bridge, as if the flesh had been pinched to a peak there. She had a fine, visible dander on her cheeks under a layer of pink powder blush, and she wore a cotton sundress short enough to show her muscled calves. Iris tried to gauge her age and couldn't quite. Maybe sixty? Sixty-five? Maybe fifty? She met Iris at the door.

"I don't need a room," Iris said. "I just pulled over to see the lake from this angle."

"No trouble," the woman told her, brusque but cheerful. "I have guidebooks, if you're interested. And some pictures of the town. Sometimes people like to stop on their way up to the mountain and have a look around, and I always offer the books. I think the history enriches the experience. You want to come on in and have a pop while I get them? Free of charge, of course. I'm offering—you didn't ask."

The house was as dark as Iris had expected it to be—even the kitchen, which looked out on the lake. "It's quiet," she said. "You must like the quiet out here."

"The logs are so solid, nothing gets through. Original. This used to be the boardinghouse, before they put in the lake. You're on the outskirts of town right now. The old town, that is." She handed Iris a glass and a can of Coke. "Let's find those books."

The house had two floors. On the first, a sitting room, a reading room, and a dining room. "When the place went up," the woman explained, "most of the customers were long-term stays—gyppo loggers, that sort. Boys who couldn't find a place at the camp where the full-timers worked. Upstairs is the bedrooms. I'd show you, but I try to keep them nice. For guests. No footsteps on the carpets. You understand."

"Of course," Iris said.

The books turned out to be in the reading room—"Go figure," the woman said and laughed at herself. She opened an old photo album first. The photographs Iris had seen on the roadside marker were there, pinned to the page by black paper corners. There were photographs of loggers in suspendered trousers and white shirts, one of a trio of women standing before a church, and another of a woman with a child on her hip. Everyone wore the same dour expression. "It's because of the cameras they had then." The woman stubbed her thumb against the photograph, tapped. "They had long exposure times."

"But these can't all be that old," Iris said. "Look at their clothes." She pointed. "And there's a car in the background here."

The woman leaned in to see, frowning, then closed the album. "I don't know. People get used to things, don't they? Someone tells you to hold still for the camera, and you hold still your whole life."

"Yes," Iris said. The phrase sent a ripple of déjà vu up her spine. Her grandmother had always said that before a photo: *Hold still. Hold still, you wild girl.* There was pride in it, though—in that phrase, *wild girl.* There was an echo of something Iris hadn't understood as a child, but which she saw now must have been recognition, empathy, the complicated acknowledgment of having passed along this particular inheritance to a granddaughter. She looked at the woman, who had risen to slide the album back into its spot on the bookshelf, and said aloud again, "Yes. That's it exactly."

The woman smiled over her shoulder. From another shelf, she pulled a box. "No one ever asks to see these, but since you seem so interested, and I do like to take them out." She set the box on the coffee table. "They give you a real picture of someone's home life, don't you think?" One at a time, she took out the handle of a china cup, a button, a doorknob, the hinge and the comb from the road sign picture. She arrayed these before Iris. "That's all I've got. I look for more, though, every time I'm at the lake."

Iris picked up each object, turning the knob as if opening an invisible door, squinting at the button's four pinholes of light. It was nothing, really—a scrap. How many buttons had she lost in her lifetime, off the cuffs of sleeves and the pockets of coats? And more than that—single earrings, the loss unnoticed until she went to remove the mate at night; socks, disappeared between washer and dryer; handfuls of cereal rounds and crumbs of biscuits when the children were teething, slipped under the rolling wheels of the stroller or into the crevasse between the cushions of the sofa. So much, so much. She thought once more of her grandmother's bureau, always crowded with the accoutrements of her femininity—long hat pins, a brooch she wore to church, a tiny pot of rouge, the mammy. What had happened to these things when her grandmother died? When the house was sold? Who knew? Iris had been away at college by then and hadn't thought to ask for anything. Her grandmother's belongings had disappeared along with her grandmother. The daily flotsam of one domestic life was nothing, really. None of it held any value past the moment of its loss. Not to most people.

"Don't you have to wonder," Iris said.

"Wonder what?"

"Oh, I mean—what would the people who owned these make of us sitting here with all this now? It's all so ordinary, isn't it, if you really think about it? Wouldn't they laugh to see us?"

The woman stood and took the button from Iris's fingers, began to pack the objects away again.

"I'm sorry," Iris said.

"Yes, well, it's not your people. You have no connection."

Iris heard the accusation again in her mind. The words were soft, porous—the echo of a thought she herself had been tucking down and down for days, for months, bubbling back up. She didn't have any connection, did she? Not really. Here she was, traveling alone, not on her own terms—not because she'd chosen to be alone—but because this was the great catch of motherhood: to care for your family so well that the labor of your love might be invisible. So that your bond to your children might be self-dissolving, like a good stitch in a deep wound. It was too plain a grief to say aloud without seeming petty. *Oh now*, Max would say if she tried to explain it to him. *We need you, don't we, kids? We still need you.* But there would be a dismissal in the reassurance, just as there had been over the phone last night. "You'll be okay," he had said. "You're always okay."

How had she prepared them all for the world without remembering to prepare herself? Iris was suddenly furious, and the fury surprised her. She wasn't lonely; she was angry—at Max and the children, but also at herself.

She squinted out the window at the lake's placid green shine. She could imagine herself sliding under that brightness, pulling herself forward with broad strokes, carrying herself from one shore to the other, her own breath buoying her up to the surface again.

She stood. "Do people swim in this water?"

"They do."

"I'd like to swim from your beach, then," Iris said. "I have a suit in my car. I could be ready in a minute."

The woman gave her a startled look. "It's a private beach. For guests."

"But you have no guests right now."

The woman puffed at this. "I might have, though. I might have guests just coming, for all you know."

"Who would I be bothering? Please."

It took only a little more convincing. Iris went to the car and got her suit, and then, stumbling across it still buried there in her overnight bag, also the bottle of wine. Inside again, she held up the bottle for the woman to see. "I don't have a towel, but I do have this. It's the good stuff. Twenty dollars. If you have a corkscrew, I'll trade you a drink for a towel."

The woman pursed her lips. "I don't usually drink before supper, but I suppose this once is fine. Since you've already brought it inside." She took the bottle of wine and left saying she'd find a corkscrew.

By the time Iris had pulled on her suit in the bathroom, the woman was back and waiting for her at the front door, a striped beach towel wrapped around her thick waist and a yellow plastic bathing cap over her hair. In her hands, she held the opened wine bottle and two glasses. "You have a towel by the door," she said. She looked older with her hair covered and the wrinkled skin of her arms and chest exposed, and smaller.

"You're swimming with me?"

"There's no lifeguard. I can't let you drown off my property."

"I used to be a good swimmer. I won't drown."

"Good," the woman said.

"I just realized I don't know your name."

"Doris," the woman said. "Yours?" When Iris told her, the woman repeated it. "*Iris*. Family name?"

"Yes. My mother's family. My grandmother. Her name was also Iris."

"It's an old-fashioned name."

"I've never thought of that," Iris said. "But yes. I suppose it is."

"You say *Iris*, I picture a ninety-year-old." The woman smiled.

"I'm only forty-three."

The woman clucked. "Forty-three. Still very young, in my book."

"I feel young," Iris said, hearing the truth of this as she said it. "No matter what people want to tell you about forty, I still do feel young."

They crossed the long, summer-blanched stretch of grass between the house and the shore. There was a light breeze and again that scent of the lake like a body, and Iris thought of blood, of sweat, of bodies she knew. The stripe of sweat that always appeared down the back of Max's T-shirt after he'd been running. The curls at Sam's temples when he woke hot from a nightmare. The sweet-dank girl smell of Lucy's leotards lying like pale pink skins she'd shed on the laundry room floor. *Oh*.

At the water's edge, the woman walked in up to her knees, melting forward, suddenly elegant, her whole body submerged in an instant and just her yellow bathing-capped head left visible as she swam forward in a crisp breaststroke.

Iris stood with the water lapping at her ankles, then her knees, then her hips. It was disconcerting not to be able to see her feet beneath her. She envisioned the lake bottom. It felt like nothing but the usual lake mud between her toes, but she pictured the whole drowned town down there: china cups from kitchens long lost, baby doll heads and the black-bead eyes of stuffed bears, the missing mate to the lady's comb that sat in the box in the house. How exactly had the water come? Had it poured in slowly, nothing but a trickle for days, so slow it was hard to see the rising? Or in a wild gush, everything there one second and gone the next? A single, disastrous wave? She pushed her toes into the soft lake bottom and saw herself walking over the seams of quilts, the fibrous cushions of someone's couch.

The daveno, she heard her grandmother saying in her head. An echo. *No feet on the daveno if we want to keep it nice.* Iris leaned forward and the water washed over her stomach, her breasts, the top of her head. It filled her ears as she swam forward.

In the end, as Max predicted, the mass she'd found had turned out to be nothing more than a calcification. A little bit of nothing. A "mineral deposit," her doctor said. Quite common among women her age. Something to watch, but nothing to worry about. Summer ran its course, and she sent Max to collect Sam from camp. Lucy abandoned skating. School began again. All that season and afterward Iris didn't mention the lake to Max. She didn't say anything about the woman, or the swim, or the drowned town under the water, though for a long time she felt the strangeness of that day surrounding her still, as if she'd absorbed some measure of the lake and it was sloshing around in her, filling the soft parts of her, the fleshy thighs, the wrinkled paunch, the loose and floppy breasts. Or maybe it was just her memory floating in there—the memory of how weightless she had felt in that water on that day, and how reassuring it had been to hear so loudly the sound of her own blood moving behind her eardrums, steady and even and in sync with the beat of her heart in her chest as she swam, but feral too. A force. It was the sound, she'd decided later, of her life going on, as it would. As it did.

As life does, she thinks now, looking back and looking forward, too. As life always does go on.

ACKNOWLEDGMENTS

This collection was created and assembled with the time and support of residencies at the MacDowell Colony and the Mineral School; a commission from the 2013 Hugo House Lit Series; faculty support grants from Purchase College, SUNY; and a fellowship from the 2016 Jack Straw Writers Program. I also owe a debt of gratitude to the journals that first published some of these stories: "Endlings" was published by *Ploughshares Solos* (issue 6.3); "Tides" appeared in the summer 2017 issue of *Joyland*; "Dear Mistress" was published in the journal *Willow Springs* (issue 78, summer 2016); "Wheeling" was published by *The Pinch* (fall 2013); "Matter" was published by *Freight Stories* (issue 8, fall 2012); "The Remainder Salvaged" was published in *Willow Springs* (issue 68, fall 2011) and later longlisted as a distinguished story in the 2012 *Best American Short Stories* anthology; "Where Have the Vanished Girls Gone?" first appeared in *North American Review*.

Thank you to Lee K. Abbott and the panel of judges who selected this book for the Flannery O'Connor Award for Short Fiction, and also to the University of Georgia Press for their continued support of the short story form. My gratitude to you is endless.

This book would not exist without the encouragement, brilliant critiques, and friendship of my writing group—Judith Alexander-McGovern, Deepa Bhandaru, Michael Boudreaux, and Arzoo Osanloo. I would most certainly have stopped writing long ago if Jacqueline Kolosov had not been a friend and workshopping partner. Sam Ligon offered editorial support that made "Dear Mistress" and "The Remainder Salvaged" much stronger stories, and I'm ever thankful for his sharp eye. Jane Hodges is an inspiration and a superhero(ine). Gail Hochman is a source of endless encouragement and understanding, and I'm immensely thankful for the privilege of working with her. I will always feel only gratitude for Pam Houston. The Hugo House is a beaming light in the already bright Seattle literary community, and their support of my writing and teaching has been essential.

Additionally, I am incredibly lucky to have the emotional consolation and readerly insights of an exaltation (can I use that collective noun here?) of brilliant women: Tamara Scott, Erika Wright, Shannon Brugh, Christina Miller-Larsen, Jess Burnquist, Joanna Penn Cooper, Lauren Gordon, Ginny Robinson, Jessica Mesman Griffith, Kristen Millares Young, Karen Finneyfrock, Wendy Call, Janine Kovac, Jane Wong, and Catie Bull. Their words and motivation sustained me when the writing felt impossible, and I thank them.

Thank you a million times to everyone at The Attic Learning Community for the care you daily shower on my family, for your support of my dual teacher-writer life, and for the inspiration to keep growing. I am also in great debt to the students who have learned alongside me over the near decade it has taken me to write this book (I love you all).

Finally, and with deepest gratitude, I want to thank my family. Thanks to Steve, Laura, and the whole Lunstrum clan, for taking me in from the start (as well as for the hours of childcare you've given me so that I could write). Thank you, Britt and Rob, for always bringing laughter and the best desserts. Thank you, Paul and Dorinda Sundberg, for *everything* (but especially for that Sundberg-Lunstrum Writer-in-Residence year). You are (and always have been) love itself. Thank you, Finn and Virginia—my beloveds, my heart. Your lives have made the world brighter and my stories better. And last, thank you to Nathan, who is still (always) my favorite human, my pulse, my partner in it all.

The Flannery O'Connor Award for Short Fiction